ALSO BY KAY BRATT

Silent Tears; A Journey of Hope in a Chinese Orphanage
Mei Li and the Wise Laoshi
The Bridge
A Thread Unbroken

CHASING CHINA

A DAUGHTER'S QUEST FOR TRUTH

KAY BRATT

Printed in the United States of America

First Printing, 2011

ISBN-13: 978-1466478572

ISBN-10: 1466478578

www.KayBratt.com

Copy Edited by Misti Wolanski @ Red Adept Editing

Formatting by Streetlight Graphics

To my amazing husband, Benjamin.
With you by my side, I see glimpses
of the woman I strive to be.

At the center of your being you have the answer:
You know who you are and you know what you want.
— Lao Tzu.

PROLOGUE

"LET her chase her dreams—remember, they almost always come home," he murmurs as she leans her head on his shoulder, tears streaming down her face.

I hear my father as I move through the security line at the airport, my boarding pass in my hand—final destination: Shanghai, China. His words aren't spoken to me—they are whispered to my mother and somehow float over the heads of nameless strangers to land unintended upon my ears. They can't see my own tears; there is definitely dissent in the ranks, but I refuse to let the little traitors free. I won't let my parents see me falter; they need to believe I am determined and strong and will be fine without their protection.

I don't want to break her heart—and I *will* come home. But is home the land I'm leaving, or is it the land that sits waiting patiently for me to discover? In time I hope they'll understand that I need to know who I was, to be able to go forward and be who I am meant to be.

Finally processed through the line and eliminated as a possible terrorist, I put my shoes and belt on. I throw my bag over one shoulder, my guitar case over the other, and give one last look behind me. I straighten my shoulders and head for gate 41.

It's time—time to unravel the mystery of my birth, time to find the truth.

CHAPTER ONE

Suzhou, China 2011

MIA used the towel to dry her face, and then leaned in to study her reflection more closely. Here she was on the other side of the world, in the country of her birth, surrounded by hundreds of people with her own heritage, yet she didn't look any different than she had on the opposite side of the ocean. Staring back at her were the same almond-shaped eyes, and the familiar wavy, dark hair framing her face—and there was the flat nose that she had despised through puberty and her mother insisted was the cutest thing on her.

She knew it was illogical to expect that just being here would make her look and feel different—more Chinese. But nope—she was still the same ol' Mia. She reached up and traced the almost invisible scar over her brow, earned from her famous fall from the big oak tree when she was twelve. She'd always considered it her badge of courage after proving her brothers wrong when they said she couldn't possibly climb as high as them. She moved her fingers down and, as she had done all her life, lifted the lids to make her eyes wider. She held them for a moment before dropping her hands away from her face.

Mia stretched, trying to ease her aching back and shoulders.

How do they stand these hard beds? She had even taken a blanket from the closet and used it underneath her for extra padding, but she was still sore. She yawned and looked at her watch. In just a few hours she would attend a life-changing event, one she had dreamed about for many years.

Doubt suddenly overwhelmed her, and she wished she were in her own bedroom, where any minute her mom would poke her head in and tell her to get her lazy butt ready so that they could make the most of her weekend away from school.

Anxiety and a swirl of questions crowded her jet-lagged brain. *I'm about to see the orphanage I lived in! What's it going to be like?* Would anyone recognize her, or had all her nannies moved on? Would they be able to tell her anything to help her trace her birth parents?

She quickly applied mascara and lip gloss and pulled her suitcase from her closet. After changing outfits several times, she settled on wearing what she'd wear on any given day to her university lectures: nice jeans and a simple shirt. She grabbed her bag and made her way down to the lobby to wait for her escort.

Much to her relief, Xiao Jo, the translator she had met online and hired to accompany her, was dressed similarly, putting her at ease about her choice as she climbed into the taxi.

Mia dropped her bag between them to keep a measure of personal space, something she had noticed a definite lack of in China. She clasped her hands together tightly in her lap, unfolded them and wrapped one around the door handle, then put both hands on her knees, casually using the denim to soak up the collected perspiration in her palms.

"Miss Mia, are you ready for this?" the young woman asked.

"You have no idea how ready I am. And please—just call me Mia." She could feel the woman's eyes on her as they rode through the city on their way to the orphanage. Mia began gnawing at her fingernails, imagining what she would find. Would walking on the grounds she once played on trigger buried memories? What would she learn about her early years in China?

The sudden flood of emotions was surprising, and it made her anxious to reach their destination and gather whatever remnants of information she could. She rapidly drummed her fingers on the armrest. The day she had fantasized about was finally here.

Xiao Jo patted her on her leg. "Don't worry. This will be an easy journey."

Easy for you, maybe; you've probably never lived in an orphanage. "Well, we'll see. I'm anxious to learn more about where I came from." She was sure the girl could hear her heart beating frantically and was embarrassed at being so flustered.

"Did you always know you were adopted?"

Mia burst out laughing, her nervousness making the simple question funnier than it probably was. When she finally got her laughing under control and had wiped the tears from her eyes, she answered, "Um, yes—because I'm Chinese, and my parents and brothers aren't. That was obvious from the start, even to my four-year-old self." She mentally flipped through family photographs—the almost perfect postcard images of a white, middle-class family protectively posed around a dark-haired girl with different eyes.

"You should feel honored; you were one of the first daughters of China to be a part of the international adoption program. But was it hard for you, to grow up knowing you were adopted?"

Mia usually didn't like to discuss her adoption feelings but decided it might calm her nerves to talk about it, and how much could it hurt to open up to a total stranger whom she'd never meet again? Maybe it would take her mind off the fact that she was literally only a few miles away from the orphanage she had lived in.

"I guess you could say I kept my feelings hidden for most of my childhood. My counselor in elementary school referred to me as an *issue-free* child once. She had no clue about the turmoil going on inside me—no one did." She realized now that she didn't even know that little girl who'd skated through life, living a lie. It was only when she went off to college and began living in an adult world that she realized her life up to that point had been nothing but a carefully constructed façade, built to keep everyone clueless about how much the mystery of her birthparents really bothered her.

"Why would you hide your feelings?" Xiao Jo pursed her lips in confusion.

"I don't know. I was always trying to prove to everyone—and myself—that being adopted didn't bother me. I never wanted to burden anyone with my problems." Talking wasn't helping ease the sick feeling in the pit of Mia's stomach, and she wished the girl would stop asking her questions.

"But your family, wouldn't they understand these feelings? What did your parents say when you told them you wanted to go to your homeland?" Xiao Jo squeezed Mia's leg, encouraging her to continue talking.

"It took me a few months to get up the courage, but when I told my parents my plan, they were supportive. Sort of." She cringed as she remembered her mother's expression at the time.

"That's good. Really good. Right?" Xiao Jo eagerly nodded her head.

"Okay, maybe *supportive* isn't the right word—my mom was hurt and even asked if she'd failed to be the mother I wanted. That broke my heart to think I had given her that impression. We went through a rough patch, but we talked it out, and she finally understood."

"You are very lucky you have understanding parents. In our culture, we would not do so much *talking*. Actually, our parents talk, and we mostly listen."

Not sure what the proper response to that cultural statement should be, Mia nodded and turned to look out the window. Actually, her parents had both wanted to accompany her on the journey to China. Mia convinced them it was hers alone to experience, but really she didn't want them hovering over her, protecting her, shielding her from hurt as they had always strived to do. They'd made one last attempt to dissuade her from going unaccompanied: They pleaded with her to go with a group of other adopted girls on a *Finding Your Roots* adventure, but to Mia, the journey was personal and not to be shared with anyone—she would go alone or not at all.

Xiao Jo pointed out the orphanage building and surrounding walls as the driver came to a stop.

"*Wu shi kuai,*" he asked for his fifty-yuan fare, and Xiao Jo paid him.

ℭℬ

So this is it; this is where it all began. Mia climbed out of the taxi and stood in front of the gated complex of buildings with Xiao Jo. *So far, nothing looks familiar.*

A ten-foot-high wall surrounded the entire area, topped with three rows of barbed wire. To Mia, it looked more like a prison than an orphanage. Perched high in a place of honor was an engraved sign that read *Jiangsu Social Welfare Institute* in English next to artistic Chinese characters. While Xiao Jo stopped to talk to the security guard, Mia hung a few feet back, watching as their conversation became increasingly more animated. She was relieved when he finally waved them through.

"Xiao Jo, where are the children? I don't hear them," Mia asked.

"We are too far away from them to hear." She pointed to a tall building opposite the guard shack. "We are going to the administration office over there to register as visitors."

Xiao Jo gestured past another few buildings to the other side of the compound, to another gate guarded by a short, skinny guard wearing a rumpled blue uniform at least a few sizes too large. "Through that gate and across the alley is the children's area. The children are kept separate from everyone else. See the building in the distance?"

Over the wall, Mia could see the top few floors of a tall, rundown building. Bars on the darkened windows gave it an ominous appearance, and the grim-faced guard standing at the gate was anything but welcoming. She followed behind Xiao Jo, anxious to get through the preliminaries and on to the tour.

In the main office, Mia and Xiao Jo were greeted by a secretary and shown to a seating area with hard but elegant teakwood chairs. The young woman brought them cups of hot water steeped with green tea leaves and set it before them. Xiao Jo sipped hers, but Mia wasn't sure how to drink it without getting leaf bits into her mouth.

Giving up after pulling a particularly large stem from between her front teeth, she leaned forward to set her cup on the coffee table. As she pulled away, her shaking hands caused the flimsy paper cup to topple over, spilling the contents.

"Oh crap! I'm sorry." Mia looked around frantically for paper towels, napkins, or anything to use to keep the liquid from moving across the table to the floor.

"*Mei guen xi, mei guen xi.*" The secretary rushed over, assuring Mia it was okay as she used a napkin to sop up the tea.

Mia stood, took a deep breath to calm her racing pulse, and stood in front of two large posters taped to the grimy walls. As she clasped her hands in front of her to hide the trembling, she wondered if one of the tiny faces displayed belonged to her. She examined the dates; the children were all recent residents. Most of them wore the same somber expression.

The sadness settling around her was interrupted at the sound of heels clicking loudly on the stone floor. Director Zhu, flanked by two women, bustled into the room.

Xiao Jo grabbed Mia's elbow to turn her around to greet the woman. The director was dressed to impress and had a no-nonsense attitude to match her severe, short hairstyle and the gray skirt and jacket she wore.

"*Ni hao,*" Director Zhu said, bowed, and held her hand out

to Mia.

Surprised at the woman's firm handshake, Mia returned a weak *"Ni hao."*

Using the translation skills of Xiao Jo, a flurry of introductions were made to introduce the rest of the staff. Mia watched the assistants bustle around the director, pens poised and hovering over their notebooks to wait for any instruction that Director Zhu might drop. They didn't speak unless spoken to, only nodding in agreement to every word that left the director's mouth as she spoke to Xiao Jo.

Despite the Mandarin lessons her mother had insisted on for years, Mia struggled to comprehend their foreign words. She briefly felt irritated as she thought what a waste all those hours of tutoring were, especially now that she really needed to understand. At least she could communicate in the Chinese airport and taxis, as long as no one tried to have an in-depth conversation with her.

At the prompting of Xiao Jo, Mia produced her passport for inspection and signed the visitor's log. Once the initial awkward moments passed, and Mia presented the director with the expected gifts of American collector stamps, lotions, and chocolates, they began their walk to the children's quarters.

She would finally see the rooms where she had lived her first four years of life. As they stepped out of the administration building and she was guided towards the other side of the grounds, Mia wasn't sure what she was feeling; she could only describe it as anxiety or possibly a silent panic. But she was determined not to give herself away—she wouldn't let them see anything but a confident, successful young woman.

Heavy sadness continued to stalk her now that the reality of her abandonment was no longer camouflaged by stories of fate and how it had put her where she belonged. The longing she had struggled to stifle for so many years, for information about her birth parents, broke wide open, and she allowed herself to silently grieve the life she might have had and the family she might have known.

Not that she wasn't thankful for her parents now, or the years of joy they had given her. She loved her family! But she wanted to know the circumstances about her birth mother and how she ended up an orphan—she *needed* to know all she could about the woman who had given her life.

As they approached the gate leading to the children's area, she still didn't feel any connection to the grounds, or any of the staff they passed along the way. She had really hoped to feel some sort of recognition, but it just wasn't there.

Now standing in the courtyard, Mia saw a few children through the window of what appeared to be a classroom with a piano perched in the corner. They were sitting at wooden desks, repeating the English alphabet after the teacher as she pointed to the board. The small group of students appeared happy to be there, giving all their attention to their young teacher.

"They attend school here at the orphanage?" Mia asked.

The director answered Xiao Jo using a local dialect, and Xiao Jo turned to Mia. "The children who are eight and older go to school in town. These are like kindergarten classes for the younger children, as well as other older children who are too disabled to attend public school. The musically gifted children also take piano lessons from a volunteer who visits once a week."

"They're so adorable—I didn't know children in China learn the English alphabet." Mia pulled her camera out of her bag; the director immediately waved at it and insisted she put it back. *No pictures allowed, I guess,* she thought as she quickly tucked it away again.

They passed the room and climbed a set of concrete stairs, still slippery from a recent mopping. In the hall on the second floor, Mia saw a tiny girl of about five years old, pushing along a small wooden chair as she struggled behind it to put one foot in front of the other. She didn't make a sound, just slowly shuffled forward with her head down, her shoulders slumped in defeat.

"What's she doing?" The girl's battle with the heavy chair concerned Mia.

"That is walking therapy." The director beckoned her to move along, waving the girl out of the way as if she were a pesky fly. "She has a spine disease and must learn to walk before she can be adopted. She has to push that chair across this long hall and then carry it up to the next floor and go across that hall. We have told her if she does not learn, no mother will come for her."

"How is she supposed to get it up the stairs? Why doesn't she use a real physical therapy walker instead of such a heavy chair?" The hall was stifling hot, and the girl's hair was already damp around her face. She lifted her tiny tear-streaked face just a little—enough to make a split moment of curious eye contact with Mia—then obediently continued her efforts.

"Because a walker is too light and she would fall behind it," the director answered, with a finality that indicated the subject was closed.

Mia's heart broke for the child, so alone in her challenge to learn what to some would be a simple exercise, but to her might have seemed like an impossible goal. At least the girl would have benefited from someone to cheer her along and praise her for her progress, instead of making her believe her disability was the cause of her being in the orphanage, Mia thought.

She dutifully followed along, intent on hiding her feelings. Finally arriving at the children's quarters, they entered a room, and an older *ayi* looked at her and smiled. The director told them the nanny had helped to care for Mia when she was a toddler.

Is she for real? How in the world would the woman know me by just one look at my face all these years later? Mia didn't want to question the director's story but couldn't ignore the doubts that lingered in her mind as they moved on.

Director Zhu introduced her to many of the nannies who were gathered around, whispering to each other. In their matching pink outfits, the young women reminded Mia of the candy stripers at the hospital when she had fallen from her horse and broken her leg. The practice of calling them *ayi* (auntie) was confusing and awkward to Mia, but as that was the custom, she would comply. Mia greeted them politely but anxiously wanted to get past the nannies and move closer to the children who curiously watched them.

Though she knew the children she had lived with were long gone, either to adoptive families or to life outside the orphanage, the children around her now were her sisters and brothers in a way no one but an orphan could understand. Even if these children were to know life within the protective walls of a family, as she was blessed to have experienced, Mia knew they would feel that same empty hole in their hearts when they grew up and thought of their birth parents.

As she looked at the many faces, she wondered why they were abandoned. Many of them were very cute babies—she couldn't imagine a mother walking away from them. Even knowing the Chinese cultural preference for boys and the problem of the one-child policy, Mia would never stop wondering if she wasn't pretty enough, or smart enough, or if she had been a bad infant in some way, or what possible reason her parents had to leave her in the middle of a busy train station, discarded to create a new destiny for herself.

The poor condition of the rooms and halls didn't surprise her—she had been well prepared by reading many blogs and articles written by others who had visited orphanages. She also knew that if she had visited in the wintertime, she would have been more taken aback by the unbearable cold the children were rumored to endure. But if so many families who adopted gave donations and continued to support the orphanages their children came from, then why weren't the children's living conditions improved? Where was that money going?

As they continued along, Mia noticed that many of the walls and ceilings were stained with water spots and grime. Most of the windows lacked screening, and the ones with screens showed too much wear to be of much defense against mosquitoes. All the furniture appeared outdated. Even the tiny toddler beds were old-fashioned, without any type of railing to protect the children from rolling off. Clothing was also noticeably shabby—the babies wore the traditional split pants over their diapers, and the older children wore mismatched outfits.

In what looked to be the nursery, Mia broke away from the director and Xiao Jo and moved closer to the children. One little girl caught her eye as she sat tangled in a twisted sheet in the corner of her crib, quietly playing with her tiny fingers. The lack of toys or anything colorful to stimulate the baby's senses made Mia feel sad for the poor girl. She couldn't have been even a year old, but she had such intense eyes, and Mia wondered what she had witnessed in her short life. The toddler was dressed in a soiled red shirt and ragged blue split pants, with her soggy diaper showing through the gap.

"What's her name?" Mia asked the director as she moved closer to the child.

"Xinxin. It means *heart to heart*; she was named this because she has a defective heart." The director gave the information mechanically, without emotion.

Mia moved around an *ayi* who was wiping down the bamboo crib mats with a sponge and bucket of strong solution. She went to the baby girl, holding her arms out to pick up the child, but Xinxin looked confused. Mia talked to her in a soft voice that made the small girl raise her eyebrows even higher, causing Mia to chuckle. The expression was adorable but also comical, as the eyebrows raised to heights that seemed impossible for such a tiny face. Mia picked her up, and in spite of the child's inability to mold to Mia's body as most babies would, she seemed content to be held.

The child gazed silently into Mia's eyes, and everything

around them faded away for a moment. All of these months leading up to this trip, Mia was sure she wouldn't get emotional—she prided herself on her ability to hide what she was feeling, even from her parents who watched her so closely for signs of discontent. But holding the baby girl close to her heart finally opened the door to the room in her mind where she stored all of her hurt feelings of being abandoned. She fought back tears as she rocked the baby back and forth in her arms.

This was me so many years ago! Why? Why didn't my mother want me? Mia turned her back to hide her face from the others as she struggled to bring her feelings under control. The director and her entourage were concerned, but Xiao Jo waved them away to give Mia a moment to compose herself.

How could this tragedy happen to so many children around the world? Mia was overwhelmed with the truth of the situation—that most of the children would go through life without knowing who gave them birth, if they had siblings, what their medical histories were, or even where their hometown was. *It just isn't fair—everyone should know who and where they came from!*

As the baby began to fidget, Mia swallowed the lump in her throat and straightened her shoulders. She pulled herself together and replaced her anguish with a stoic expression, just in time to face the director as she beckoned for her to join them in the hall.

Mia kissed the infant on her sweaty forehead and whispered to her, "*I'm* a witness to your life, and you *will* be loved one day. Don't lose hope, baby girl." She lowered the child to her bed and walked away, leaving her with her fascination of her own fingers, the only comfort that couldn't be taken away.

CHAPTER TWO

THE rest of the tour was a blur to Mia, who couldn't imagine living in such an environment. She mentally compared the surroundings to her own modest but cheerful home. *How do the children stand it here? Why can't they at least brighten the rooms with paint or wall hangings?* It was so depressing that she couldn't help but form a negative opinion about those who controlled the funds for the institution.

They passed another few rooms, and in each one Mia glimpsed at least one sad case: a boy staring longingly out the window; a girl holding a pair of soiled underpants, her face crumpled in defeat; a nanny yelling at a group of children to be quiet. Feeling overwhelmed, Mia did her best to block out the faces of children clustered together in the next rooms. She followed behind the director, nodded when expected, and answered the many questions about her own life in the States. The director was very interested in what Mia's parents thought about her return to China, as well as other details of her day-to-day routine as an American.

"Were your parents angry that you wanted to return to China? Did they pay for your trip here? Do you have American brothers and sisters? Do you have a driver and an *ayi* to clean your home?" The questions were endless and a bit intrusive, but Mia did her best to answer each one as honestly as possible.

When the subject shifted to college life, the director obviously considered Mia very lucky to attend an American university. Mia wanted to tell her about the several years of intense focus and the tedious challenges of applying for every scholarship she could unearth, but she felt her commitment to studying wouldn't be acknowledged, and she was probably expected to verbally credit China's government for allowing her to be adopted. Perhaps Mia was being sensitive, but the director's smug attitude when she talked about the China Center for Adoption Affairs matching her with her parents was starting to grate on her nerves.

"Xiao Jo, how much more are we going to see today?" Lightheaded, Mia tugged on the girl's sleeve before she stopped on the stairs to steady herself.

"Not much more," Xiao Jo whispered. She backed down a step and took Mia's arm to help her climb to the landing.

On the next floor, the director led Mia down the hall. As Mia passed a set of windows, she peeked in to see about a dozen or so children sitting quietly, barely even moving. One small boy of about seven years old sat rocking back and forth in his chair, his eyes vacant. Mia couldn't see anything at all in the room to entertain the children or break up the monotony of their days, only the scattered and mismatched wooden chairs they sat on.

Behind them stood a row of tall lockers used as a room divider; on the other side were rows of single beds with bamboo mats rolled tightly at the feet and placed atop tiny squares of blankets. An eerie silence surrounded the gloomy atmosphere.

"What about those children? Why are they in that room?" she asked the director.

"Those children have severe disabilities and cannot go to school or roam the institute. That is where they live," the director answered, walking briskly past the depressing room.

"What kind of disabilities would exile a child to a room like this?" Mia leaned closer to the window, peering in at the children. Where were the books, games, or even a television? The little boy may have been autistic, but even so, shouldn't he have some sort of color or diversion in his gray surroundings? Maybe he wasn't autistic but simply retreating into a protective shell of self-preservation from depressing reality.

"Mia, we must talk about this later," Xiao Jo whispered as she gestured for her to hurry along behind the director.

Mia refrained from pushing the issue. She reminded herself that she was only seeing a small part of a big institution and should not judge based only on one quick tour.

Mia asked Xiao Jo to find out when they could sit down and talk about her history. Seeing the rooms she had toddled around in was interesting, but she wanted some clues about her birth family. She hoped the director could tell her more about the day she was abandoned: what she wore, if they were sure there wasn't a note, and possibly even who had found her.

The director replied that they would first eat an early lunch and began guiding them back to the administrative office—all the while continuing to talk about the many grown children who were doing well in other countries after their adoptions, because of the affluent parents who took them in. Mia wondered if the director thought she was also rich. She'd surely be surprised to know Mia's mom was a coupon clipper and didn't spend her days lounging around with a maid fulfilling her household duties.

"A United States senator has adopted two of our children, so I'm sure they will become important people in politics one day. They are very lucky children."

"Hmm, that's great," Mia replied, mustering up only a smidgen of enthusiasm. She had not prepared herself for that line of conversation, and she struggled to show the amount of appreciation she felt the director was looking for. It wasn't that she wasn't grateful—she felt like she was just as thankful as other girls her age—she just didn't usually give credit to China for her status in life. For so many years, her parents had strived to avoid making her feel different, and now the words Xiao Jo was translating implied that she should have been full of gratitude for her mom and dad making the trip to China to *save* her. Mia didn't know whether to be discouraged or angry—and at whom? Her parents for making her feel normal? The director for pointing out that without China's adoption program, she wouldn't be living such a lucky life?

Lucky—if she had to hear the word one more time, she would scream. Mia tried to keep her mind on the goal: to get information about her birth family. She would have time later to deal with the emotional toil of the groveling she had to do to get further along in her quest.

Before they reached the administrative area, they passed a group of teenage girls sitting in a circle under the shade of a towering tallow tree, enjoying the cool spring weather. Two of the girls played a card game while the other girls took turns braiding each other's hair. Mia was relieved that they were allowed to keep their hair long instead of having the usual institutional-chopped style.

Physically, the girls didn't look much younger than Mia, but they were obviously much less mature. They stopped what they were doing to stare, and time seemed to stand still as Mia considered that one of them could have been her, if not for a special set of circumstances that had landed her in a different life. Mia even had difficulty with how much she looked like them, because only in the last few years had she begun to embrace her Chinese heritage. For most of her preteen years, she had tried to pretend she was just like the rest of her family. She had avoided doing anything that would make someone compare her to the Chinese stereotype and had even refused to go to more Chinese cultural camps. Her mother had finally stopped pleading with her to learn more about China's culture, and they had compromised on the language. If Mia would continue her Mandarin classes, she wouldn't have to go to camp.

Once her mother stopped trying to push her to befriend other Chinese-American girls, she realized that something made her gravitate towards them anyway. Perhaps subconsciously she wanted to grab onto some small part of China, even when she vehemently insisted she wanted nothing to do with it.

When Jenny came to her school as a foreign exchange student from Beijing, she and Mia became close, and she had learned more from Jenny than from any cultural class or camp she'd ever attended. Most of all, looking at Jenny each day had made Mia realize she was pretty *because of* and not *in spite of* her

Asian features. It took a long time, but these days she appreciated the face she saw in the mirror.

The orphanage girls reminded Mia how childish she had been when she refused to accept her parent's attempts to keep her connected to her birth country. Now she could easily see that they were only trying to do what her heart would eventually need to heal. She now wished she could erase her past efforts to look anything but Asian—the crazy red streaks in her hair, the time she didn't speak to her father for a month because he refused to allow her to have surgery to make her eyes appear bigger. It embarrassed her to think about it, now.

Even in their humble surroundings, the girls seemed perfectly at ease in their own skins. A twinge of envy ran through Mia as she hurried along behind the director and wondered why the girls weren't in school.

In front of the main building, a small gathering of people competed to get a look at Mia. The director stopped in front of an elderly woman standing at the center of the crowd.

"This is Lao Ling. She was your foster mother when you were a little girl," the director explained first in English, and then Chinese for the old woman's benefit.

Lao Ling grinned from ear to ear, rocking back and forth on her heels while she clasped her hands around her rounded belly. Her clothing was a drab gray, but over it she wore a neon green apron with pockets around her thick middle. The pockets bulged with items, most invisible except for the shapes protruding through the material. Mia was amused to see a smoking pipe and a candy cane poking out of one pouch. *Where in the world do they find candy canes in China?*

"What do you mean, foster mother? I was never in foster care." Mia was sure this was a mistake. *She must be thinking of another girl.*

"Yes, you were in foster care for your last year in China. This woman took very good care of you and has never forgotten you." The director emphatically nodded as she watched the foster mother shyly take Mia's hands in hers.

"Um, okay. Hello," Mia said. She wasn't convinced of this revelation and was completely clueless about what to say to her. *Thank you? That would be weird—best just to keep quiet.* She didn't understand why she didn't remember this woman. Throughout her childhood, she had dreamed about a woman singing her a lullaby, but Mia was sure this wasn't the face she had seen glimpses of in her sleep.

"*Ni feichang piao liang de haizi le.*" The woman giggled, showing a few gaps in her toothy smile. Xiao Jo translated to Mia that the foster mother said she was a very beautiful child.

Hmm… That's what Mom's told me, but doesn't everyone say their child was beautiful? That didn't prove anything. Mia kept in mind that if she had been in foster care, her parents would have known it. However, she was relieved to see that Lao Ling was at least friendly, a nice thought if she was still fostering children from the orphanage—and, come to think of it, could probably help her out with some details.

"Can I ask Ms. Lao Ling a few questions?"

Xiao Jo translated the question to the director and was immediately rebuffed. "She says not now, maybe after lunch."

The director asked Lao Ling—*my supposed foster mother*—to come with them to share the meal being prepared in the main dining room. As she led the way past the various buildings, Mia hoped she would get the opportunity to ask Lao Ling if she had any information that could lead her to her birth parents, or at least any photos of her from that time.

"Xiao Jo, who are those women walking back there?" She gestured to the threesome straggling behind them.

"No worries. They are probably only local women curious about you, because you once lived here but are now an American."

Mia silently wondered if perhaps they had known her or her birth family and had heard about her return. They appeared overly interested in her, and she was slightly uncomfortable to hear them whispering to one another as they stared. When they moved further along the hall, the women disappeared from sight, and Mia wished she could ask more questions about them, but thoughts of the upcoming selection of Chinese dishes diverted her attention.

They came upon a neat modern area, in which the director pointed out a building with five floors. It was quite different from the structure that housed the children, impressive with its shiny windows and ornate entrance of stone-carved crouching lions. Even the area around the front walk was artistically designed, with a pagoda in the center of a fishpond, and trees and flowers abundantly placed to create a peaceful resting place. Elderly people sat about, some in wheelchairs and others strolling along, chattering to one another. The line of old men in wheelchairs watched their every move as they walked by, their gnarled hands gripping the sides of their chairs.

"This is our retirement facility," the director boasted. "It has a cafeteria, an exercise room, and even an activity center for the elderly to participate in events. We had our grand opening only two years ago."

Now Mia understood where many of the overseas donations were probably going—and it appeared it wasn't to the children. She wondered if the many parents who donated their hard-earned money knew or would approve of the way it was being used to ease the lives of the elderly, rather than improving the quality of life for the orphans in the rundown buildings. The children's side of the compound was a stark contrast to the retirement side, and though Mia didn't want to begrudge older residents their comforts, she felt the wealth could be distributed more evenly.

As a group, they walked across the courtyard to another building and up some stairs. The director, her two assistants, Xiao Jo, Mia, and Lao Ling entered a small room that held a large round table set with glasses, bowls, platters, and chopsticks. A wooden turntable was set in the middle of the table and already covered with dishes of various relishes and cold foods.

After guiding Mia to the honored seat furthest from the door, the director sat down beside her and began to use her limited English skills. The others all quickly found their seats and sat down.

"You can use chopsticks, yes? These are for you." The director handed her a box. Mia opened it to find the most exquisite chopsticks she'd ever seen—carved from stone, embossed with a winding vine and held together with a delicate chain at the top. They all looked at her expectantly, as if being born Chinese made her automatically skillful at using the utensils.

"Thank you!" Mia exclaimed as she examined the intricate detail work. "These are so beautiful."

To be honest, Mia had practiced at home, but only with the cheap Chinese takeout wooden chopsticks, which were much easier to use than the fancy-but-slippery chopsticks placed before her now.

"I can use chopsticks, but I'm very slow." She grasped the chopsticks in her right hand, adjusting the sticks several times to find the least awkward position. She wished she had taken more than a few weeks to practice and again marveled at the fact that her mother tried to tell her this would happen.

The two young assistants covered their mouths to muffle their giggles at the awkwardness of the foreign Chinese girl, as Mia prayed she could get through the meal without embarrassing herself.

The director reached under the table and pulled up a bottle of Sprite. She filled one of her glasses before passing it to Xiao Jo on her right.

A young girl wearing a uniform quietly moved around to fill the other cups with water, furtively peeking at Mia every few seconds. She was obviously very interested in their guest, and Mia wondered if she was an orphan or simply a paid worker. She didn't feel it would be polite to ask questions about her, so she kept her curiosity to herself. She was quickly learning that in China, everyone had a place or status in life, and the lines were clearly drawn. Despite her curiosity about the girl, she did not want to bring her any trouble.

A wave of homesickness flowed over her as Mia thought

about the informal way of life she had grown up with, where starting a conversation with a waitress was perfectly acceptable. However, she was old enough to understand that each country has its own customs and she had to respect the differences.

The table took up almost the entire room, and Mia was flattered that the staff went to so much trouble to present a welcoming luncheon for her. The director was very inquisitive about her life and the level of luxury in which her family lived, but Mia knew she didn't intend to be rude. She remembered reading somewhere that in China, it was common for people to talk about income and approach subjects that were somewhat more guarded at home.

"Is your house very big? Do you live in a high rise in the city? How much is your university tuition? Were you in New York when the planes crashed? Did you vote for the first black president?"

Mia thought the questions would never end, but she tried her best to answer each one as more dishes began arriving. Cold dishes first—her mom had told her to expect that, and she was right, because the director rotated the turntable so the long, green cucumber-like creations pointed right at her. Embarrassingly, Mia dropped the vegetable on the first two attempts to move one to her plate. She tentatively took a bite and was pleasantly surprised at the somewhat sweet but tangy taste.

After Mia's first bite, the others joined in, and chopsticks were clicking and clacking quite rapidly around her. Good thing, because the food would take a bit of the focus off Mia to allow her to mentally line up her next questions, and for Mia to also get a handle on which technique of using the chopsticks would cause her the least embarrassment.

Lao Ling particularly ate with gusto, stealing glances at Mia every few bites. She giggled often, and each time she let out a laugh, she'd try to cover her toothless grin with her hand. Her swollen belly pushed up against the table, making Mia wonder what she ate to stay so plump, for so far everything she'd eaten in China appeared very healthy. After Mia clumsily dropped another slippery cucumber, Lao Ling reached under the table into her apron, and her hand reappeared armed with a sturdy set of tongs that she tried to pass to Mia. The director waved her hands frantically until the old woman slipped the tongs back in one of her apron's many pockets. Mia wondered what other treasures Lao Ling had stashed away.

While Mia pretended great interest in her food, the director barked an order at the waitress, making her scurry out of the room. The girl returned less than a minute later with a large platter of food. She came around and set the dish directly in front of Mia.

Director Zhu waved her arm dramatically across the table, "This is *Sung Shu Huang Yu*, or you may call it Squirrel-Shaped Mandarin Fish. Very famous in Suzhou. No bones and very soft meat."

The head of the fish, its mouth wide open, pointed away from Mia, the tail bent upward to give it the look of a squirrel. The fish body was artistically carved into spikes to resemble fur. The chef had pulled out all the stops, finishing it with shrimp, dried bamboo shoots, and what looked like a sweet-and-sour sauce.

"This is the best dish, and it is placed in front of you because you are the guest of honor. You must start first," Xiao Jo explained.

Mia successfully picked up a small portion for herself, and then turned the platform in the direction of the director. She was not usually a fish eater, but in this circumstance, she felt she couldn't say no. She gingerly took a bite and immediately felt a rush of flavor tease her taste buds.

"Director Zhu, this is delicious! How do I say so in Chinese?" Mia asked.

"*Hen hao chi,*" the director answered, beaming with pride.

Lao Ling pulled out an entire bottle of green spicy sauce and generously dumped some on her plate before offering it around and then tucking it back into her apron. The director rolled her eyes as the girls around the old woman laughed at her eccentric ways—and Director Zhu shooed Ling's hand away when she tried to pass them wet wipes. Obviously, the nice linen napkins on the table didn't meet Lao Ling's expectations.

Could this woman really have cared for me, fed me, and kept me in her home? That unexpected bit of information still didn't seem real. Mia couldn't wait to call Mom and tell her. *She's going to be so shocked.*

"*Qing wen,*" Mia interrupted, excusing herself. "Can you ask Lao Ling how old I was when I came to live with her?"

Xiao Jo translated the question and received a stern look from the director.

"Eat first. Talk later."

Director Zhu's made her authority obvious, Mia mused as Xiao Jo blushed and lowered her eyes to concentrate on her plate.

More heaping dishes arrived, and despite her bloating stomach, Mia searched each one for the famous Chinese dumplings she knew she was sure to enjoy. The story of how the *jiaozi* were invented was one of the few tales she remembered from Chinese cultural camp. A famous doctor went to his hometown to save the locals from dying of typhoid fever by mixing medicine with tasty concoctions and rolling it up in thin dough pieces to resemble ears. In addition to their illnesses, the people were starving and were suffering from frostbite from the bitter cold. With the doctor's recipe, the people began to heal, and a new delicacy was born and spread all over China.

Every Chinese New Year, Mia's mom presented the family with dumplings in a tasty sauce—and each year she improved upon her technique, until last year's dumplings were close to perfection. Mia couldn't wait to see how the real thing compared to Mom's creations and hoped she could even snap a picture.

After the jellied bean curd—a dish Mia didn't care for at all—another dish piled high with shaved potatoes and green peppers arrived, making her thankful to see something she could finally recognize. She twirled the turntable until the dish was directly in front of her and raked a heaping portion onto her plate with her chopsticks. It looked like such an easy recipe yet was a welcome burst of unique flavor—different from any she had ever experienced from simple potatoes. She was excited to try all the dishes in front of her and hoped Xiao Jo would write down some of the names so she could order them elsewhere in Suzhou.

Mia hurried to eat as much as the tasty potatoes as possible before the next dish was placed in front of her. The director suddenly stood to make a toast, and Mia jumped to her feet, almost knocking her chopsticks off the table.

The waitress appeared with a bottle of *bai jiu* liquor in her hands, much to Mia's discomfort. *One small shot of it won't hurt me*, she thought as she beckoned the waitress to go ahead and pour the clear liquid into her miniature wine goblet. She didn't want to offend anyone by refusing to participate in an honored custom, and also didn't want to go through the cumbersome chore of explaining to the director that she wasn't quite old enough to drink. She figured it couldn't be much worse than the tequila shots she had taken at a frat party last year.

Like everyone else around the table, she stood up and held out her glass to wait for the signal to down the liquid. A minute of rapid-fire Mandarin, smiles all around, and then a translation from Xiao Jo made Mia understand the toast was in thanks for fate bringing a child of China back to the motherland.

"*Gambei*!" the director exclaimed and reached across the table to clink her glass with everyone else.

Mia lifted her glass to her lips and flinched at the overpowering smell of alcohol. She closed her eyes and swallowed it in one big gulp that immediately took her breath away. She felt like her throat was on fire, and she rubbed at the instant tears that sprang to her eyes.

The director and everyone else at the table laughed at her reaction. As Mia fought a fit of coughing, she put her hand over the top of her glass to block the waitress from refilling it. She insistently pointed at the bottle of Sprite. Custom or not, she wasn't drinking another drop of the lethal concoction. The waitress smiled shyly and filled her small glass with Sprite.

Lao Ling was next to give a toast, and she held her glass high and made a small speech. Mia didn't understand a word she said but began to smile and nod anyway—she was anxious to pour the Sprite over the fire in her belly left from the *bai jiu*. As she looked around, she was surprised to see the director and Xiao Jo not joining in. Instead they stood frozen in place, their glasses still poised in the air.

"What? What's wrong?" Mia asked Xiao Jo, searching the faces around her. *Have I committed some kind of faux paux? Are they upset because I'm using Sprite instead of the liquor? What are they staring at?*

The director put up her hand to stop Xiao Jo from translating. Lao Ling pulled a small fan from her apron pocket and waved it frantically in front of her face, hiding her flaming cheeks behind it.

"Tell me! What's going on?" Mia demanded. She knew Lao Ling had said something about her, and her ears burned with embarrassment for the unknown transgression.

Everyone else joined Lao Ling in sitting down as silence fell across the room. The director's assistants, Xiao Jo, and the chastised foster mother kept their eyes downcast and waited for the director to make the next move.

ᘓ

The walk back to the alley to find a cab was quiet. What had started as an exciting opportunity to find out more about her past had quickly turned into a dead end because of the unknown words from Mia's supposed foster mother. The director had rushed them through the rest of the meal, and the coveted dumplings came and went so fast that Mia barely had time to judge them against her mother's; but even so, she decided that her mom got first prize, hands down. However, she was intelligent enough to not let the others know that a foreigner could meet the skills of their chef.

Xiao Jo refused to explain to Mia what the old woman said to cause everything to turn sour, and Mia thought it ridiculous that she was the only one left wondering what the heck had happened. She wished she had not already paid most of the fee for the girl as a guide, or she'd be tempted to renege on their deal.

Just as she and Xiao Jo were getting into the taxi, she caught a glimpse of the same three women she had seen upon her arrival to the orphanage. Again, they were definitely following, but they were far enough back that they obviously thought they were hidden in the midst of the other pedestrians around them. Something about the trio caught Mia's eye, and she once again wondered why they were so interested in her. The hooded young woman in the middle held tightly to the arm of one of the older women, and together they watched Mia get in the car.

"Xiao Jo, are you sure you don't know who those women are?"

"Not all of them, but I think I saw the one in the middle working in the children's quarters," Xiao Jo disinterestedly answered.

Disappointed that she had not been able to ask any more

questions about her birth family or her finding details, Mia tried to remain focused on the positive: that the director had said Mia could return the next day with Xiao Jo for another visit. *Hopefully, an opportunity to find out some useful information.* At least that night, she would have time to digest all she had seen and prepare the questions she would definitely ask tomorrow. She was determined to get some answers before leaving China.

Xiao Jo sat on the far side of the backseat with her head leaning on the window, her eyes closed. They made the ride back to the hotel in silence, and Mia wasn't surprised that Xiao Jo didn't ask her to meet for dinner as she had the night before. Instead Xiao Jo told her to be ready the next day at noon, and they would once again make the trek to the older side of the city, to the orphanage. Mia hoped she would be more successful at pulling information out of the director on the second go-around.

"*Zai jian*!" she called out good-bye as she climbed out and shut the car door. Mia was relieved to have the whole evening alone to explore the area around the hotel. She'd take a small nap, and then she'd hit the town to find supper and souvenirs for her family. She didn't know where she'd go, but it would be exciting to see where her feet took her. Mia couldn't wait to experience more of her adventure.

CHAPTER THREE

HER long black hair moved gently back and forth to the sway of the swing. Mia wished the lady would turn towards the window so she could see her face—the singing was mesmerizing, the song familiar but not quite known. Mia had never been able to understand more than a word or two at time. She strained to hear, pressing her face against the window until the glass shattered into a million tiny shards.

Mia was awakened by a clatter of dishes and drunken laughter in the hall outside her hotel room. She sat up in bed, disoriented for a moment, and then remembered having the dream again, the one she'd had at least a hundred times since she was young. The first time, she hadn't been so sure it *was* a dream, and a part of her still believed it had really happened.

In the wee hours on her eleventh birthday, she had awakened to the sound of singing below her bedroom window. When she crawled out of bed and stumbled to the window, she saw a dark-haired woman swaying back and forth on the tire swing tied from a branch of the big oak tree. The woman's head was thrown back as she softly sang strange words. The moonlight had cast an eerie glow, emphasizing two or three butterflies fluttering around her.

Mia had rubbed her eyes and looked again, to find nothing there. *It's just a dream*—or at least that was what she thought until she woke up a month or so later, hearing the song again. She never saw her again, only dreamed of the woman's singing, but she still watched the swing whenever she got the chance in case she returned. Once in a while, she could swear the same butterflies rested on the swing, also waiting for the woman. She had kept the dream to herself, her one little secret from the rest of her family.

When she was younger, she thought that telling someone about the woman would keep her from returning. When she grew up, she realized that describing her encounter would land her an immediate appointment in the chair of a local psychiatrist.

Now she was as far from home as she could get, and the dream still followed her. Mia stretched and looked at the bedside clock, then jumped out of the bed to peek through the heavy curtains. The lack of traffic and pedestrians below made her look at her watch again and wince. *Oh, great. Jet lag kicked my butt, and I slept right through the afternoon and evening. Mom and Dad are going to be worried that I didn't make my Skype call.* And now her sleeping routine was turned upside-down, and it was going to be a long day.

She only vaguely remembered waking up a few hours after crawling onto the hotel bed to take a short catnap. Every muscle in her body felt heavy, and try as she might, when the alarm began beeping to wake her, she couldn't get up for even a moment. She had just rolled over and given in to the familiar dream; the soft voice and the comfort the song always brought her had lulled her straight back to sleep.

Now wide awake and hungry, Mia wondered what to do. She pulled a pack of Ramen noodles out of her suitcase, and once again thanked her lucky stars that her mom had put together a care package of snacks and instant foods. She filled and plugged in the water kettle and waited to hear the bubbling. In the meantime, she popped the top of a can of Coke and grimaced at the super-sweet taste of China-made cola. Remembering the lecture her mom gave her about avoiding dehydration, she also opened a bottle of water and drank the entire contents in one long chug. After devouring her noodles and a dessert of Oreo cookies, she took a steamy shower and dressed in the long comfortable skirt she had snagged for a bargain from her favorite vintage consignment store. She topped it off with a loose but feminine blouse, slipped on comfortable sandals and then took another five minutes to apply her daily dose of mascara and lip gloss.

Fully dressed but knowing it wasn't a safe time to venture out alone, Mia wandered to the window and looked out at the sleeping city. Her imagination took a few minutes to construct what it would have been like to live here as a child. She wasn't a city girl and couldn't imagine living where she couldn't see grass, trees, and blue skies at all times. Visiting bustling cities was fun, but she always enjoyed returning home to a quiet, calm pace of life. She didn't think she'd make a very good city girl.

She picked up her guitar and began to slowly strum the tune that had been relentlessly reverberating in her head for the entire flight over to China. A melody came to her. She reached for her tattered notebook and rushed to scribble the notes on a scrap of paper before they disappeared from her head again.

Words to match the melody were so far only sporadic and not coming together, but this was one of those songs that, until she was able to put it together, it wasn't going to leave her alone. Her brothers thought it amusing that she sacrificed one of only two allowed pieces of luggage to bring her guitar with her to China, but for Mia, it wasn't even a question. Clothes really weren't such a big deal to her, but the guitar was her constant companion and over the years had helped her to express the hurt of abandonment without actually talking about it. It was much easier to let out her grief in melody and lyrics than it was for her to speak the words that might hurt the parents who had given her the gift of family.

Mia put down the guitar, made the bed, and picked up all of her clothes haphazardly thrown about. She picked George off the floor where he had fallen in the night and perched him in the center between her pillows. *Nope, I don't care if the maid laughs about me sleeping with a stuffed monkey.* In the bathroom, she put the cap back on her toothpaste and wiped out the sink. She didn't care if they thought she was childish, but she sure didn't want housekeeping to think she was a slob.

She had used up a few hours, but it was still too dark to go out. Using her iPad, she logged on to the Internet and e-mailed her parents at work. She told them she was fine but had fallen asleep early. She really wanted to tell them about meeting her foster mother, but she decided to wait to do it on Skype. Instead, she briefly described the orphanage and the precious baby girl with the heart trouble. She ended the e-mail by reminding them how much she loved them and missed them, just in case they were worried that she was becoming too attached to her motherland.

She smirked as she saw another five messages in her inbox from Collin, her rat of a boyfriend—*or who used to be my boyfriend before I dumped his arrogant butt.* She wasn't going to ruin her day by reading what he had to say, doubtless more pleas for forgiveness and lame excuses for his scumbag behavior.

Now fresh-faced with a full belly of noodles and bored with unsuccessfully trying to log on to Facebook, Mia closed her iPad, picked up her bag and decided it was time to do some exploring. She could hear doors opening and suitcases being rolled down the hall, so she decided it was safe to go out. She debated whether she should try to figure out the instructions to use the safe for her passport or not, but she was antsy to get out of the room and didn't want to take the extra time.

After confirming her passport was safely tucked in the interior pocket of her bag and zipping it closed for safety, she slung the bag and guitar over her shoulder, pulled the key card from the wall slot, and left the room.

ᘓ

As she waited for the slow elevator, Mia examined her face in the decorative mirror. Being in China let her feel what it would be like to blend in with a crowd, something she had never experienced in her own mostly Caucasian small town.

Sure, there were a few Asians and other minorities, but not enough to extinguish the ongoing curiosity about her ethnicity or to stop people from asking questions about why she looked different from her family. It was embarrassing to think about it now, but when she was younger, some of the intrusive remarks from strangers—as well as her own friends—had really hurt her.

"That's not your *real* mother" was one that she resented the most. She first heard it in the third grade when her mom accompanied the class on a field trip to the nature museum. Mia was chosen out of the group of kids to come forward as a volunteer. At first it was exciting when the guide draped a giant snake around her shoulders, but when the snake started to move its head toward her face, the first words out of her mouth were, "Mom, help!"

When the guide removed the snake and she once again joined her classmates in line, one of the popular girls made a big deal out of the fact that her mom wasn't Asian like her. Over the years she'd heard it a few more times, but mostly as whispers from people who thought they were sharing juicy gossip by announcing Mia was adopted. She'd love to say it no longer bothered her, but the truth was that more than anything she wished she looked like everyone else in her family so that she didn't draw attention to the question of her birth details.

Her thoughts about her family were interrupted when two businessmen walked up behind her.

"*Zao*." The tallest man acknowledged her with a nod of his head.

That was an easy one, and Mia nodded and returned his

greeting of good morning. She hoped conversation would stop at that so they didn't become curious at her lack of fluency in Mandarin. The two chattered to each other as they all stepped through the opening doors, and the elevator eased down to the lobby floor.

At the entrance to the hotel, two young doormen in pristine uniforms stood at attention as she walked through. Leaving behind the quiet elegance of the lobby immediately set her in an entirely new and noisy environment as Mia paused to decide which way to go. Waiting in front of the hotel was a line of taxi cars, with drivers waving to get her attention. She smiled and returned their banter with a friendly *"Bu yao, xie xie"* (no, thank you) and began walking to the pedestrian lane. Looking at her watch, Mia calculated that she had three hours until she needed to be back in front of the hotel for Xiao Jo to pick her up and take her back to the orphanage. *Three whole hours!*

Hopefully Mia could stay out of trouble for that long.

CHAPTER FOUR

MIA was surprised at the number of people out at such an early morning hour. At home, she would have been met with an almost empty street, but in China the people appeared to have been up for hours. Hordes of cars and bicycles lined the streets, and the sounds of horns blaring created a symphony of chaos as people competed to be the first to arrive at their destinations.

At the intersection, she waited for the walking signal, and when it blinked, she took a deep breath and practically ran across, barely making it before the light turned back to red. *What a rush of adrenaline!* She glanced back at the cars honking at her—at least she thought it was at her. *Would they really just run over me, or were they only threatening to bump my knees to get me out of the way faster?* As she looked around, she was amused at the way the pedestrians kept their expressions neutral, even with cars looming towards them.

Still looking around to take in the sights around her, Mia felt something hard brush her arm and stepped to the side just as an electric scooter whizzed by, almost knocking her off her feet. On it were three people; the small girl stood between the knees of her father with her feet planted securely on the bike base, and the young mother sat behind the man, holding him tightly around the waist as he wove the scooter in and out between other vehicles. Over the woman's shoulder hung a child's backpack, indicating they were probably going to drop the girl at school and then go to their own places of work.

Mia couldn't imagine herself growing up in the Chinese culture, dealing with such hardships. *They have only one scooter to provide the entire family with transportation? What do they do during the bitter cold months? Does their child have to battle the freezing temperatures all the way to school?*

She felt a bit guilty at the thought of her red Honda Civic sitting unused in the student parking section of her university, even if it was ten years old, sported a set of ratty bucket seats, and lacked a working radio. She also reminded herself that unlike most of the students in her dorm, she worked a part-time job at a local vintage music shop to pay for her own gasoline and insurance. The pay wasn't much, but it made her feel like Lola was really hers—squeaks, creaks, and all. It wasn't the best-looking car, but it was hers, and her dad always checked the oil and did an overall vehicle inspection to make sure it was safe to drive before she returned to school.

"Lola's ready to go!" Dad would say, slapping the car trunk when he finished his routine inspections. It was just one of the small ways he showed her how much she was loved.

She smiled as she remembered the time she returned to school and emptied her bag of freshly washed laundry to find an envelope tucked between her sweatshirts. Inside was a short note from Dad, telling her to never forget that he missed her each and every minute she was away. In it he'd slipped a gas card and certificate for her favorite restaurant. He was always doing stuff like that, finding sneaky ways to help her without her mother knowing.

With the added help of the gasoline card that month, Mia had enough of her paycheck left over to see her roommate perform in the theater drama of *Beauty and the Beast*, which brought back some sweet childhood memories. When she was little, she'd pretend she was Beauty and her dad was the Beast. When Beauty and the Beast would begin dancing across the television screen, if her dad was home he would pick her up and dance around the room, growling in her ear to make her giggle. For Storybook Week in the second grade, they had an exact replica of Beauty's yellow gown made, and Mia wore it to school, feeling like a princess all day.

Mia snapped out of her daydream to find herself in front of a small shop of everything Hello Kitty. Purses, shirts, hats, phone covers—you named it, and they had it. Not much of a Hello Kitty fan herself, Mia still found it amusing and snapped a photo with her cell phone. It would make for a good profile picture on her Facebook, so it was added to her growing collection. As she lingered outside the window, a young woman rushed out and beckoned her to come in and shop.

"*Guo lai, guo lai.*" The shopkeeper called out to her to come in.

Embarrassed at being caught taking photos, Mia moved on until she was once again a part of the rushing crowd.

She soon found herself blocked by a crowd of people gathered around a street vendor, vying for their turns to purchase breakfast. After peeking through to see what they were waiting for, she decided to try one of the delicious-looking pastries. She stood there watching to see how much money the other patrons were handing over so when she finally made her way to the front, she had her one yuan ready and waiting.

"*Zhe shi shenme*?" Mia asked the cook what he was making. She tried not to let the man's appearance put her off from her moment of culinary bravery. Dressed in a soiled white chef's jacket and matching cap, he stood behind a portable grill and a huge pot that had seen better days.

The chef gave her a skeptical look. "*Jidanbing guozi,*" he mumbled as he continued to pour batter on the steaming grill with one hand and held the other out for her to drop her coin into. He put down the bowl and along with her change, held out her order for her to grab.

At least he understood my question. Mia left him holding the change and immediately bit into the delicious concoction. *Wow—China has its own breakfast burrito.* She held it out to examine it closer and discovered what was basically a thin crepe-like pancake topped with cilantro, eggs, green onions, and a spicy sauce, then wrapped around a deep-fried cracker like a burrito. She walked along the crowded sidewalk, feeling truly Chinese, eating her street food and moving quickly with the mass of people.

Two city blocks and three right turns later, she discovered the walking street that Xiao Jo had told her about. One long line of shops, souvenir booths, and an ancient temple right in the middle, and Mia determined it had enough to keep her busy for the next two hours. She stopped to sit on a bench in front of the temple to observe the people for a while. Leaning on the guitar propped between her knees, she let herself be immersed yet invisible in the intriguing bustle of energy around her. Her senses on overload at the noise, smells and visual entertainment, she didn't even see the guy approach until he was already sitting beside her. *Wow, he also doesn't believe in personal space. He's cute but that's a little close for comfort.*

Mia scooted over a bit to put more distance between them and give her the opportunity to study his profile. She had never been attracted to Asian guys, but this one had an interesting face. It was hard to tell, but she guessed him around her age or maybe a few years older. He wore his hair in a short, layered cut, the bangs pushed up in front to create a spiky, stylish focal point over his chiseled face. His jeans looked like they could have been bought straight off the rack at Hollister or Gap, frayed hems and all. He leaned back against the metal back support of the bench like he had all the time in the world to sit and enjoy the cool spring morning.

As she tried to identify his sneakers, he looked her way, and they made direct eye contact. Mia felt herself blushing at being caught checking him out.

ଓ

"*Ni hao.*" He greeted her to break the awkward moment. He had actually noticed her sitting on the bench ten minutes before, but it had taken him a while to get up the nerve to come and sit down.

Watching her from afar, he had been struck by the confident way she held herself. Most of the girls her age he had met in China were different from what he was used to—awkward or childish for their ages—but the girl beside him had an independent air about her. She also wasn't dressed in the ever-popular frilly dress or jeans with a silly graphic tee shirt, usually set off with a pair of high heels. He loved the simple skirt and the flowery top she wore, and her long hair was a welcome sight in the midst of the bobbed hair most girls wore. He didn't even have to wonder if she could play the battered guitar she clung to—she and the instrument were obviously very attached to one another. He'd given himself an ultimatum: either go sit beside her or go away and stop acting like a stalker. So he sat.

"*Ni hao.*" She smiled, her nose crinkling in such an adorable way it made him forget the next part of the Mandarin greeting he normally had no trouble remembering.

"Um…" He stuttered a bit until it came to him: "*Ni mingzi shenme?*"

She looked at him blankly and spread her hands helplessly.

"Name?" he hesitantly asked, in English. She looked as unsure as he felt. He was determined to attempt a conversation, but unfortunately he couldn't be sure whether he had just asked her name or said something about good morning. *She's going to think I'm an idiot.*

"Oh! My name's Mia."

Whoa—that was some perfect pronunciation she just threw out there! "Oh, cool. You can speak English." He released a relieved sigh.

Her eyes widened as she answered, "Uh, yeah. Of course I

can—I'm American."

"Me too!" Both of them began to laugh at the irony of two Asians sitting outside a temple in China, struggling to speak Mandarin when they were both as all-American as apple pie.

"Where are you from?" The question came from both of them at the same time, causing another spontaneous burst of laughter.

He waved his hand toward her. "Ladies first."

"I'm from Lynden, Washington."

He raised his eyebrows. "That's amazing! I live about two hours from there in Seattle. Right now I'm doing a six-month internship at the Shiradan Hotel here in Suzhou. I was feeling homesick so I decided to come out here—I thought the diversion of the crowded streets would yank me out of my pity party. I can't believe I've found another American, and how ironic that we'd meet walking around in a city of several million people! That's really cool." He paused at her amused expression. "Now look at me—I can't shut up. Sorry. Your turn: What are you doing here in China? I'll let you talk."

"I don't mind, really. To tell the truth, it's nice to run into a native English speaker. This is my spring break, believe it or not. I've been planning this trip for over a year so I could come and learn more about my heritage. And if it makes you feel any better, I've only been here for three days and am a little homesick, too."

"Hmm…"

She looked embarrassed to admit the homesickness as she sat with her arms wrapped around her guitar, her eyes downcast. He could've sworn he saw the glimmer of tears threatening to spill over. She sure was homesick, and he should know—he'd been pushing through his own melancholy for weeks.

"I have an idea if you're up to it. Why don't we hang out today and I'll show you some of the sights around the city?—if you feel safe with me, that is. I promise I don't bite. You can even call my manager at the hotel if you need a character reference. Maybe later you can show me what you can do with that battered piece of wood you seem so attached to," he joked and then held his breath and hoped she would agree. He hadn't felt this happy in weeks and didn't want to let her go just yet.

He watched her consider her options and probably think about the strict warnings her parents most likely gave her about meeting strange men on this trip.

"Um, sorry. I can't. I have to be somewhere in a little while." She looked genuinely sad to turn him down.

"Oh. Okay. That's cool. I just thought you might want some company, since you probably don't know anyone here and all that. But whatever—it was nice meeting you. Good luck." Jax was seriously disappointed that he couldn't talk her into hanging out, but he didn't want her to know that.

Mia stood and threw her guitar strap over her shoulder. She gave a quick wave and began walking away from the bench.

☙

About twenty feet away, Mia looked back over her shoulder for one last peek only to see the guy staring out at the crowd, a pensive look on his face. Her pace slowed as she silently argued back and forth with herself—weighing her good sense with her longing for more interaction with an English-speaking human being. She knew she might not get another chance like this during her trip. But she also knew she shouldn't just agree to hang out with a complete stranger in a foreign country.

Screw it—I'm already taking a chance by even traveling to China all alone. I must be invincible or at the very least have a guardian angel looking out for me. She turned around and walked back to the bench, unseen by the guy until she tapped him on the shoulder and he looked up at her.

"Can we exchange names first? I feel a bit weird agreeing to spend time with someone who I don't even know. As you already heard, I'm Mia."

He jumped to his feet, stammering. "Oh hi—you came back! That's great! I'm so happy—I mean glad—I mean… oh, Mia? That's pretty. My name's kinda weird, so please don't laugh. I'm the ordinary, the mundane—Jaxson Hu." He took a deep and threw his arms out wide as an introduction. "It's actually Jax for short—and don't ask how they came up with it. It's a long story." He sat down again.

Mia thought it was an attempt to hide his very un-cool moment and she sat down beside him on the end of the bench.

His embarrassment was endearing, and Mia chuckled before answering. She was rewarded with a shy smile that produced a set of the cutest dimples she had ever seen on a guy. Why had she always thought Asian men were unattractive? That definitely wasn't the case with this one— and mundane was the furthest from the adjectives that immediately came to mind while she studied his face.

"I love your name and you're going to think this is hilarious—but our names rhyme."

He looked at her, raising his eyebrows skeptically. "Mia and Jax rhyme?"

"Yes!" She laughed. "You're Jaxson Hu and I'm Mia Su."

He laughed loudly. "Okay, you're right. That's funny. But I don't think we should tell anyone else that. It makes me sound like a geek."

"And it makes me sound like a sweet southern belle, which is why I don't use the whole name. Actually, the Su is spelled the Chinese way. My parents wanted to keep a part of the name I came to them with, but they also wanted to give me my grandmother's name. I inherited Mia from my maternal grandmother, and Su from my own birthright—but you can just call me Mia."

As soon as she said it, she realized she was already letting her secret out. At the confused expression on Jax's face, Mia decided it was going to be hard to spend time together and avoid the inevitable subject.

"I was adopted from China when I was four years old, and I don't know anything about my birth family. Actually, that's why I'm here—to see if I can learn more about them or at least find out why I was abandoned." Mia felt relieved to just put it out there instead of having to guard her words.

"Really? Wow—you're the first person I've met here with that story. I know it's not the same, but my best friend back home is adopted. Adam—that's his name—is Hispanic. He was taken from his mother when he was born because she was a drug addict. His adoptive family is white, but he doesn't seem to mind."

"Did he ever know his birth family?"

"Nah, but he jokes around and says one day he's going to go on one of those reality shows and raise the ratings by getting blindsided by a psycho mother. I think he only says stuff like that because he's holding back some resentment. That's a lot of baggage for a kid."

Mia and Jax rose at the same time and began to walk towards the short stone wall surrounding the temple. They watched the long line of people moving toward the black cylinders stationed in the center of the courtyard.

"They're burning *yuan bao*, otherwise known as ghost money." He pointed to the plumes of black smoke curling towards the sky.

"Ghost money?"

"It's fake money. Some call it ghost money, hell money, or even heaven money. Sometimes you'll see them burning paper clothes, televisions, and even paper cars! They're sending it up to their family members in the afterlife."

"They really believe that?" In her imagination, she saw dollar bills and jackets floating up to the clouds.

"Sure. They believe the ghost money is to repay the mystical debts their ancestors have racked up over their lifetime. In the afterlife, the deceased must find a way to obtain a body and fulfill a purpose to achieve peace."

Mia leaned over the wall, straining to get a closer look at the faces of the people.

"But they can't embark on their journey towards peace if they've got unpaid debts, so they depend on their descendants to pay it from earth. If their descendents don't burn paper money and clothes, the spirit will be humiliated in the afterlife because they must remain undressed." Jax laughed. "I wonder how many naked Chinese grandpops are running around up there, cussing their grandkids for ignoring the customs that will give them back their clothes."

"Hmm. I think I'll tell my parents about this tradition in case anything happens to me." She chuckled at the visual her imagination conjured up.

Talking about her parents made her remember the reason she was in China and she looked around the temple courtyard, focusing on the faces of those gathered in small groups. To even consider that her birth parents might do this mysterious ritual was intriguing. Perhaps her birth parents even burned incense on her behalf. Did they even know if she was alive or dead? *Maybe they are here right now!* Mia studied each female face gathered around the fire pits for familiarity, but she saw no one who shared her features enough to possibly be related.

She took a deep breath and told herself to snap out of it. She had plenty of time to find the answers she was searching for, and she should take some time to experience China. She looked at Jax and decided to live in the moment for once in her life.

CHAPTER FIVE

"SO, what were you going to do today?" Jax asked her, looking relieved that she had suddenly shifted from a somber expression back to her cheerful smile.

"Well, I'd really like to get some shopping done. My bartering skills aren't what I'd hope for, so I was trying to work up the courage to start. Maybe you can help me with that? I want to take souvenirs home to my parents and three brothers—if I can figure out what to buy them."

"That's easy. In China, you can find some cool stuff pretty cheap. Let's start with your mom. Does she like silk? Oh wait—that's a stupid question. Every woman loves silk. I've just the place to show you, and it's right around the corner. Did you know Suzhou's famous for silk? Here—let me carry your guitar."

She handed him the case and let him lead her down the street and through the gates to Silk Row.

In front of her, the three long buildings housed vendor after vendor selling silk in bolts, dresses, pajamas, fans, pieces of art, and other items to showcase the fabric their city was famous for. The inside of the buildings were laid out similar to indoor flea markets in the States: many booths separated only by tables, piled high with silk items of every type imaginable. The vendors stood before their tables, competing loudly to get each passing customer to stop and look at their wares.

Jax thumbed through a rack of silk ties as the shopkeeper watched him closely.

Beside him Mia stroked the slippery red silk of a robe embroidered with a gold dragon and knew her mother would love it. The Chinese-style robe would be the perfect gift to return home with. Jax whispered to her to stay silent so that the shopkeeper wouldn't know she was a foreigner, and they could get a local price.

"*Duo shao qian*?" he asked the shopkeeper, with a firm voice she hadn't heard him use. Mia grinned as she stayed in the background, nonchalantly admiring a silk dress displayed on a mannequin as she listened to the conversation between the woman and Jax. She was impressed that he sounded very Chinese.

"*San bai kuai*!"' the tiny woman replied that she wanted three hundred yuan. With her bobbed hair and sensible clothes, she looked like quite the businesswoman. It was clear to Mia that she wasn't going to be easy to talk into a bargain.

Jax immediately put the robe back and said, "*Tai gui le*." He grabbed Mia's arm to lead her away, and just as she was about to stubbornly remind him she wanted the robe, the shopkeeper beckoned them back with a promise to give it cheaper.

"*Liang bai kuai*." She came down by one hundred yuan, but Jax whispered it was still too much.

He looked at the woman and sternly said, "*Yi bai kuai*."

They once again started to walk away, but the shopkeeper nodded and exclaimed, "*Hao de, hao de*." She mumbled her agreement to the negotiated price of one hundred yuan and put the robe in a bag. They exchanged money, and Mia and Jax strolled out the door towards the next block of shops.

Mia called back to the lady, "*Xie xie ni*!" The least she could do since Jax did all the work was to thank the woman herself.

"That was interesting." Mia raised her eyebrows at Jax and burst out laughing. She knew that the Chinese were famous for bartering, but she was impressed that Jax had already learned the technique in the short amount of time he had lived here. *Maybe it's in the blood, after all,* she mused.

"Don't worry," he whispered. "That was a fair price, because last week I saw a local woman get the same robe for only fifty yuan. We gave her a foreigner's price."

Mia laughed. She was just happy to find something so beautiful for her mom, and she didn't mind paying a bit more than a local Chinese—she was technically a tourist, after all.

Their next goal was to find something for her father and brothers, so Jax guided her up the walking path.

"What does your dad like to do?"

"My dad is an outdoors kind of guy. He likes to fish and hike, and he plays a lot of golf. He and my brothers go at least twice a month. Dad thinks if he keeps working with them, he'll have the next Tiger Woods in our family."

Jax opened his mouth to speak, but a young boy shoved between them. In the blink of an eye, he had Mia's purse in his hands and was running down the street as fast as his feet would take him.

"My purse! It's got my passport!" Mia was paralyzed with shock at the implications of losing her money and passport.

Jax didn't say a word, just tossed her the guitar and sprinted off after the boy. Mia could only see glimpses of his yellow Nike shirt as he darted in and out of the crowd. She tried to follow, but people weren't moving out of her way fast enough and she soon lost sight of both of them. Not knowing what to do, she sat down on the curb and put her head in her hands. She was sure that Jax would never catch the boy—his little body was zooming through the crowded sidewalk like his pants were on fire. She knew she should have put her passport in the hotel safe, and she planned on putting it there when she returned this afternoon, but now it was too late. *What a disaster!*

☙

"Mia?" A low voice calling her name brought her out of her deep thoughts about how much trouble she was in.

Surely Jax couldn't be back already, unless he'd lost sight of the little thief. But when she looked up, she could barely believe her eyes. Before her stood a sweaty, out-of-breath Jax, securely holding the shirt of the grubby boy who stole her bag, which was dangling from Jax's other hand.

"Jax! You are awesome—thank you, thank you, thank you!" Mia quickly jumped to her feet and threw her arms around Jax, accidentally enveloping the boy in the hug as well. He wiggled to free himself, and Mia stepped back to give him some space.

Jax blushed and then looked down at the skinny kid and

said, "He has something he wants to say to you." The boy continued to struggle against the strong grasp of his captor, looking everywhere except at Mia, a defiant scowl on his face.

The people around them began chattering amongst themselves at the spectacle. It was unusual to be able to catch one of the many pickpockets roaming the streets, and they wondered what the young man would do with his little criminal. Arms now crossed with a stern look on her face, Mia waited for the boy to say he was sorry. Instead, he finally looked at her, and her heart broke at his muttered words—vocabulary that she had managed to keep in her limited Mandarin repertoire.

"*Wo yao chi fan*." His rebellious stare contradicted the plea in his voice. He shuffled from foot to foot, suddenly more a petulant child than a hardened criminal.

Mia looked questioningly at Jax. "Doesn't that mean 'I want to eat'?"

Jax solemnly nodded *yes*, and everything changed in that moment. Her anger turned to pity, and she realized the boy was one of what many described as a street child.

Her hand covered her heart as she inhaled sharply. "Oh, Jax." She had already seen several street children on corners and in the short alleys, but had not been so close to one that she could read the anguish and see the hunger in their eyes, as she was witnessing in this young boy. Her heart went out to him and his situation, living a life that she could only imagine. How could she possibly scold someone who was in such desperate need of protection, food, and compassion?

ᗢ

Together, they escorted the boy to a corner noodle shop. Once Jax explained to him where they were going, the scrawny youngster was willing to overcome his fear of his accusers to get a much-needed meal. Jax ordered for the three of them, and then carried the tray to the table as the small boy watched his every move. As soon as the tray touched the table, the boy almost leapt at his portion of the food. He easily scooped the fried egg that topped the noodles between his chopsticks, and it was gone in one hungry swallow. The boy set his chopsticks on the table, picked up the bowl and began slurping the noodles into his mouth—his eyes darting around the room to ensure no one would take away his bounty.

The boy was dark-skinned, had unkempt hair, and burn scars up his left arm and one side of his neck. His clothes were more than just soiled; they were filthy. Even his sneakers were missing laces and blown out on one side. Jax asked him a few questions and with some prodding, found out he was a part of a group of children who belonged to one man who made them steal and beg for money.

"Slow down, son. No one's taking it away from you," Jax assured the boy in a low, calm voice. "*Wo you wenti. Ni you-mei-you mama, baba*?"

The boy kept the bowl to his lips but peered over it to solemnly shake his head that he didn't know if he had parents or not.

"He must not remember his parents," Jax said to Mia. "I'm going to ask him why he doesn't run away."

With Jax's next question the boy's eyes widened in terror. He put his bowl down and shook his head frantically side to side.

"Whoa, there. Calm down. *Hao de, hao de.*" Jax assured the boy all was okay until his fearful look receded, and he picked up his bowl again. "I shouldn't have asked him that—these criminals threaten the children with all sorts of atrocities if they run away. And they believe them because they've seen them follow through with other children."

Mia wondered if the boy had originally been a child who, instead of being delivered to the welfare institute after he was found abandoned, ended up in the clutches of criminals who used his innocence and youth to their advantage—or maybe he was even stolen from his family. She stomped her feet, her cheeks flushed with outrage. "We need to take him to the police so they can find that scumbag and arrest him."

"I wish it were that simple. It's different here. With enough of a bribe, the man will walk away free. And when—*not if*—he finds this boy again, he'll get the beating of a lifetime."

"Are you serious? How can we just let him go back to that kind of life? Where does he sleep? Does he even go to school? How will he ever get away if we don't help him?" She looked at the boy again as he slurped the very last bit of noodles and broth from his bowl. From the register, the shopkeeper watched the trio closely.

Jax explained that most street children slept in doorways or makeshift tents under or around the overpasses and didn't go to school. In China, a child had to be registered with the family planning office to attend school, and that wasn't possible if they didn't have a legal parent or guardian. If the street children were successful in begging for money that day, they were allowed to eat. If not, then they were motivated to try harder the next day to curb their growling stomachs and avoid a beating.

"I heard there's a place in Shanghai that takes in children they find begging in the streets. Robert said it's only a ten-day shelter, but some children have been allowed to stay there longer. The officials are supposed to try to find where the kids come from and return them to their province, but due to the high costs of investigating and travel, they usually don't follow through. Another problem is that it's often the family who sets the kids out on the street or loaned them to someone for begging purposes. They have to be careful because for some, returning them to their homes would only be temporary."

"That's terrible, but at least they're making some sort of effort. Jax, do you think we could go to that center? Maybe it would help to lead me to information about my family."

"I'll find out if they allow visitors. As far as I know, they don't get foreign support like the orphanage does. Maybe we can offer to help raise resources. If we can find a way to explain the center to this little guy, we might just talk him into letting us take him there to help him find his family."

They watched the boy frantically stuffing the slices of kiwi into his mouth. They hadn't ordered it, but the shop owner had brought it out and set it in front of them, making the boy's eyes huge with anticipation. It was sad to see how hungry he was, and Mia hoped he would let them help get him to a better situation.

Tipping wasn't customary in China, but Jax said he wanted

to leave something behind for the kindness the shop owner showed to the boy. He pulled out his wallet, selected a few bills, and laid them on the table. A grimy little hand folded around the bills, and the boy was gone like a flash. Again.

"Wait!" Mia jumped up and called after him, tripping on the protruding doorframe and losing her balance.

Jax grabbed her by the shoulders to keep her from falling. "Mia, he's gone—let him go. If he's away from his station too long, he'll be found out. Even if we tried, we'd never catch him again in this noontime rush." Jax reached for the bag Mia had left on the bench seat, grabbed her guitar, and together they exited the restaurant to be immediately enveloped in a mass of moving people.

"I still want to go to that protection center." Mia glanced at her watch and gasped at the time.

"Jax, I gotta go. I'm late for an appointment!" She didn't want to leave yet, but she did want to get back to the real reason she was in China, especially considering she had just met someone who was living a life that could have been hers, had she not been taken in by the orphanage and adopted by her parents. She had to know how she was found—and how close she came to being a street child.

Jax's shoulders dropped as he sighed. His pouty little-boy face moved Mia, and before even considering the consequences, she blurted, "Do you want to come with me to the orphanage?"

Jax's eyes widened with surprise. "Do you think it'll be okay? I'll go with you if they'll allow it, but I've heard they're pretty strict about who they let in."

"I'm not sure what the director will say about it, but I'm

willing to give it a try. Maybe I'll say you're my brother."

That got her a chuckle from Jax as he quickly flagged a taxi, and they jumped in. Mia passed her hotel card over the seat to the impatient driver. He took a quick peek, threw the card back over his shoulder, and took off.

Mia scooted all the way to the other side of the backseat to put plenty of room between them, but Jax still managed to let his knee buddy up to hers, causing her pulse to accelerate and her palms to sweat before they quickly moved apart. Soon they were thrown together again, as the driver maneuvered his car in and out of traffic. Mia held tightly to the door, once again amazed at the way the Chinese fearlessly took on the task of driving. With her fingers gripping the door, she tried to appear unfazed.

"So Jax, how do you know the language so well if this is your first time to China?"

"Actually, when I got here a few months ago, I would have been embarrassed for you to hear me speak Mandarin. I was a stubborn kid and refused to focus on learning the language my parents had pushed on me all my life. They could never understand that I thought, dreamed, and spoke mostly in English. Actually, my past mediocre language aptitude disappointed them."

"I can relate. You should have seen me when I was younger—I used to make up every excuse in the book to avoid my tutoring lessons. I hated learning Chinese, and I gave my parents a really hard time." She grimaced at the memory.

Jax straightened up, pulled his shoulders back. "But I got to China, and all of a sudden the words I'd heard spoken at home for all those years starting making sense. I sort of woke up and realized that I knew a lot more than I thought I did. Since then, I've been studying like crazy to catch up. It's awesome to know another language—especially the one that everyone expects you to know anyway."

"I know what you mean. Usually in the first few minutes of meeting someone, I'll get asked if I can speak Chinese. It's so embarrassing."

"Well, I wish I could go back in time and appreciate my parents more for their efforts. I'd apologize for being a stubborn idiot. Oh, and I can't wait to see them again and rattle off a conversation totally in Mandarin. I can just see the look on their faces. It'll be priceless." The corner of his mouth lifted.

Mia laughed at his mischievous expression.

"And at least the Mandarin that did sink in helped me to get this internship. If someone else had been chosen, I wouldn't be sitting here with you." He stole a sideways peek at her and then looked straight ahead.

CHAPTER SIX

MIA and Jax arrived at the hotel after a terrifying taxi ride wherein the driver swerved, wove, and honked his horn every few blocks. She wished Jax hadn't told him to hurry, sealing their fate to be thrown around even more than usual as the driver hurtled through traffic to get them to the hotel in record time.

In front of the hotel, Mia climbed out and stood on weak knees as Jax paid the driver the twenty-yuan fare. She was still shaking from their close call with the old man that crossed in front of them on his three-wheeled bicycle, struggling to pedal the heavy load of melons he was hauling. She was sure they skimmed the bike's back tires as their driver nonchalantly pretended not to see the old farmer in the intersection. At the least, he must have heard his passengers release the breaths they were holding in the backseat as they prayed the old man would not be mowed down.

With a few minutes to spare and no sight of Xiao Jo outside, Mia asked Jax to wait in the lobby while she went to her room to drop off her guitar. She was embarrassed to admit she had held her bladder all morning in fear of the infamous public squatter toilets and was about to make a puddle around her ankles. She contained her cool exterior on the way up to her floor, but once in front of her room, she danced from foot to foot as she dug for her key card.

Finally in the door, she threw her purse and guitar on the bed and dashed to the bathroom for twenty seconds of the purest relief she had felt all morning. After washing her hands and pulling a brush through her hair, she vowed not to drink anything else for the rest of the day.

Remembering her earlier close call with disaster, Mia went to the closet and quickly read through the safe's instructions, then placed her passport and the majority of her cash inside. Just as she was headed back out the door, she saw the light on the bedside phone flashing.

Crap. I have to hurry! Xiao Jo is probably waiting for me! Mia picked up the phone and pressed the button to retrieve her message.

"Mia, this is Xiao Jo. I apologize—I must cancel our appointment at the children's home. I will call you tomorrow after I have rescheduled." Xiao Jo's message seemed muffled and barely understandable.

Mia hung up the phone and buried her face in her pillows. When she ran out of air, she sat up and punched her frustration into the downy padding. She was anxious to get back to the orphanage and find out more about herself. Now what was she going to do for the rest of the day?

She remembered that Jax was waiting downstairs, and she bolted off the bed, grabbed her bag, and went out the door.

Back in the lobby, Mia walked up behind the sitting area

where Jax was waiting, totally engrossed in his cell phone. For a few seconds, she stood watching him to analyze what made him so different from the other Asian guys his age. She wasn't sure what attracted her, but there *was* something, or she wouldn't have been standing there wishing she could spend a few more hours with him before sending him on his way.

"Jax?" She called his name softly so that she wouldn't startle him.

He stood up and turned around, a smile on his face. "Hey—I was just talking to Robert. He said if you're sure you can handle it, he can make a few calls and probably get us permission to visit that protection center in Shanghai. He'll let me know what he finds out. Are you ready to go? Is your guide here?"

"Yeah, I'll go with you to Shanghai if he can get us permission. It can't be much worse than the orphanage." *So much for ending things after today.* "But I'm not going to the orphanage. My guide called and said the appointment is cancelled, but she didn't say why." She exhaled a long sigh of frustration.

"Oh. That blows. I know you were really looking forward to going." He sat back down and looked up at her with sad eyes. "Now what? What are you going to do for the rest of the day?"

"Oh, I don't know. Don't worry about me. I'll find something to keep me busy." Mia didn't want Jax to feel like he had to hang around and entertain her, though admittedly, she hoped he wouldn't leave right away. She could see he was thinking hard and wondered if he was trying to come up with something to keep her from going back up to her room and leaving him to spend the afternoon alone.

"What about some more sightseeing? We were interrupted from your souvenir shopping, remember?"

"Um, I don't think so, Jax. I don't think I can get into the bartering mode again." As much as she hoped to spend more time with him, she just didn't want to go through the stress of finding appropriate gifts and the arguing for a fair price she knew it would require.

He stood there for a few more seconds. Mia was amused that he was so obviously wracking his brain for another idea, anything he could tempt her with to keep her for a few more hours. "I know! I have the perfect way to spend the afternoon, and it doesn't have anything to do with shopping. But you gotta let me surprise you. I promise to have you back before dark. I'll have to, because I'm due at work for the evening shift."

"Well, I guess so." Mia hid the smile his invitation brought—she didn't want to look too eager for his company. Mom wasn't there but if she were, she'd either be proud of Mia for her self-control or suspicious of the quick friendship Jax and Mia were forming. That reminded her, he'd better have her back to the hotel by eight o'clock so she could make her Skype call to her parents. It would be just like her mom to hop a plane and come all the way to China to find out where she was and what was keeping her from contacting them.

ଔ

Back outside the hotel, Jax apologized that they had to get back in a taxi to get to their destination. He promised it would only be a short drive, and then they wouldn't have to take another ride for a few hours. He pointed out the difference in the colored taxis as they waited for what was known as the best cab service, with the safest and most senior drivers. Soon a yellow Volkswagen Passat taxi pulled up, and Jax guided her towards it.

"*Ni yao qu nali*?" The driver asked them where they wanted to go as Mia climbed in and scooted over to make room for Jax. The short, stocky man peered at them through the mirror, the ashes on the end of his cigarette threatening to drop into his lap. Mia looked at the driver's identification card on the glove compartment door, matching it to the eyes looking back at her in the mirror. *Not old but not quite young, either.*

Mia wondered what sort of life the man lived. Did he have a son? Had his wife ever given birth to a girl? *Is being a driver considered a good job in China?* Maybe her birth father was a driver? She liked to meet people and daydream the stories attached to them.

"Tongli," Jax quickly replied. Settling back on the seat, he smoothed the wrinkles on the white cotton seat cover around them. He used the electric button to open his window wider, looking embarrassed as he waved a cloud of cigarette smoke towards the opening.

"I'm sorry, but you've probably noticed there are lots of smokers in China. I'd say something to him, but I suspect smoking is probably the only diversion from boredom he has, and I don't want to take that away from him. Do you think you can stand it for a few minutes?" Jax looked hopefully at Mia.

"Of course I can. It's really not a big deal, and I doubt I'll get lung cancer from a few minutes of secondhand smoke," Mia joked to break the awkward moment. It really wasn't so bad. The driver also had a bundle of small white flowers hanging from the mirror, and the breeze pushed the flowers' strong aroma to the back to mingle with the tobacco scent. Mia chalked it up to another experience to remember from this trip, and she admired Jax for having compassion for the driver.

They talked about the scenery around them, and before long they arrived at the end of a long pedestrian street where hordes of people were walking under an elaborate concrete archway marked with engraved Chinese characters.

"What is this place, Jax?" Mia's curiosity was piqued as the investigative part of her brain refused to just sit back quietly any longer.

"We're at *Tongli* water town. And I'll tell you all about it, but first we have to find the boats. I want the setting to be perfect. I've been waiting on just the right time to test my knowledge—so allow me, m'lady, to be your official tour guide."

Mia laughed at his excited expression as he practically dragged her down the sidewalk towards the entrance to the canals. She'd never seen a guy so anxious to describe the history around him, and she hoped she could keep a straight face despite the fact that he reminded her of a little boy wanting to show off his shiny new bike.

She was excited, too. She had heard about water towns in

cultural camp but had not even thought to visit one on her current trip, so she was glad that Jax had thought of it—and anyway, she needed a diversion to take her mind off the orphanage and the sudden cancellation.

Jax tightened his grip on her elbow and guided her past the small stands of souvenirs and drinks, and the lines of pedicabs and drivers competing for passengers. The drivers were muscular, probably because they spent their days with two to three people sitting behind them in the rounded cabs as they pedaled them from one end of *Tongli* to the other.

"Most of the foreigners here don't know where to go to get on the boats, so we won't have to wait long." He yanked her to the side of the path just as one of the rickshaws rushed by, too close for comfort. *Why am I always almost getting run over?* she wondered as she rubbed the place on her arm that Jax grabbed.

The walkway was lined with small restaurants, their red banners hanging outside to draw attention. Beside the shops and tables were ancient Chinese weeping willow trees shading most of the areas, creating a very artistic yet natural atmosphere. Everywhere Mia looked was a mixture of old and new, with literally hundreds of people gathered to enjoy the famous water town.

They arrived at a bamboo gate with steps leading down to the dark, murky water and a wooden boat. On it sat an elderly man talking to a bird tied to the stern of his vessel. The weathered dark skin of the man made it impossible to guess his age, but the Mao pajama-style dark shirt and short pants gave Mia the idea he was very old. The man seemed comfortable with the hot sun beaming down on his bald head and bare feet.

A Fu Manchu mustache would have made the perfect accessory to the grandfatherly face, but it was hairless.

A young boy standing at the gate took Jax's money, gave him change, and beckoned for them to climb into the gondola.

"*Si shi wu fen zhong,*" *Forty-five minutes*, he reminded them as they climbed in. Mia looked back at the boy and wondered why he wasn't in school. He only looked about 11 or 12 years old. He was quite the little businessman, taking their money and hurrying them down the steps. Once they were seated, he waved to the old man and uttered something that neither Mia nor Jax could understand, but was probably something like the local dialect version of "Aye, aye, Captain. Take them away."

Mia scooted over to allow Jax to squeeze in beside her, and as the old man put his long stick in the water to guide them through the canal, she felt a tranquil sensation settle over her. "Finally—some peace and quiet," she muttered to herself. It was a welcome feeling after the last few days of chaos.

Jax broke the silence as he began to recite what he could remember about the famous water town. Unlike the loud, guttural language she had heard spoken all around her in the city that morning, Jax's voice was calm, soothing Mia into a state of contentment.

"Small Oriental Venice is one of the nicknames of *Tongli,*" he began, ignoring the smile slowly spreading across her face. "They consider it quaint, with a population of around fifty thousand. The town's surrounded by five lakes and many famous bridges. In the old days, there were many of these water towns, since the canals were the most popular way to travel. Now there are only a few left that are preserved as close to their original architecture as this one."

Mia sat up straighter to get a better view. "Tell me more! Why are there so many small staircases leading down to the water?" Since he was so eager to be her tour guide, she was going to make him earn his title.

"In the old days—and still for some poor families today—the canal was used to wash clothes, take baths, and even clean their vegetables. Many of the houses didn't have running water until recently, and some of them still don't have it. Ironically, even when they don't have fresh water or an indoor toilet, almost everyone owns a cell phone." He paused for emphasis.

"You may see some people emptying their honey pots from the night before—" he whispered as he pointed to the other side of the canal at a group of local women gathered at some stairs leading to the water "—and if you do, the proper etiquette is to look the other way." At Mia's confusion, he explained the pots were containers that held the evening waste for those without indoor plumbing.

Their gondola glided through the water, and Jax took a break from his speech to let the old man give his rehearsed show for tips. At the man's sharp whistle, the bird dove into the water and emerged with a fish, which the man took from him and tucked into a small basket at his feet.

That's probably going to be the man's supper tonight, Mia mused as Jax handed the man a yuan coin. She studied the proud bird, feeling pity for the animal's captivity.

"The bird is a cormorant. It has a rope tied around the foot to keep it from escaping and a piece of rubber around its neck to keep it from swallowing the fish it catches," Jax explained.

As they passed the various ancestral halls and ancient buildings, Mia daydreamed about the families who might have lived in them years ago. Many of the houses bragged spacious inner courtyards that at one time had been used for Chinese opera shows and family gatherings. Some girls might have been isolated in the upper levels of the houses, becoming women after having their feet bound to better their chances of securing a valuable husband. Some daughters would have been sold off to be groomed for marriage of sons in the households of their buyers, and then there were the many concubines—mistresses—who secretly resided in quarters close to the honorable wives. The historical plight of women in China had Mia's imagination so engrossed that she almost didn't hear Jax continue his tour monologue.

"We're passing mostly personal homes now, owned by famous Chinese people. That one over there is Tuisi Garden and was built sometime between 1877 and 1908 during the Qing Dynasty. *Tuisi* means 'a place of retreat and reflection,' and it was built for an Imperial official who lost his job—fired is how the story goes, but I don't think it was ever said what he did to deserve it. Anyway, he was exiled here to contemplate his actions and regain his dignity, but he eventually became a self-imposed recluse."

"From what I've heard, he got the better deal, to be banished to this beautiful place rather than keep working with power-hungry officials," Mia added.

Jax nodded. "You can't see from here, but the garden includes a bunch of buildings all set on less than a fifth of an acre. See the grove of trees way in the back? They surround what they call the 'intellectual garden.' The garden was designed to be a place for the man to think about his actions, but it was also a common meeting area for friends, artists, and other officials to gather and drink while they discussed so-called important issues."

Important to whom? Mia mused. She knew from experience that men would gather in the name of business when anything but business was on their minds.

"There are also many temples here, but the most famous of the attractions are three bridges. They are named *Taiping* (peace), *Jili* (luck), and *Changqing* (celebration); and for hundreds of years, they have been known as sacred places by the locals. During many special events, especially weddings, the people ceremoniously march across the three bridges to bring peace, fortune, and happiness to their lives.

"How romantic! I wish I could see a bride and groom here today," Mia whispered, fearing a loud voice would shatter the magic of the moment.

"Mia, look!" Jax pointed ahead at the bridge looming over the water in the distance. Climbing the many steps to the top of the *Jili Bridge* was a procession of well-dressed people, being led by the beaming bride and groom in all their finery. The bride wore an elaborate white wedding gown, similar to the one Mia had picked out of a magazine a few years ago when she and Jenny were planning their weddings to their future unknown husbands.

Her mom had collected bridal magazines for months, and one rainy afternoon the girls cut out all their favorite styles to paste into scrapbooks. Jax might not have found it entertaining that the groom she had cut out of the gossip magazine was a Bradley Cooper look-alike, while Jenny had stuck to strictly obsessing over famous singers. She didn't even care what genre of music it was; as long as they were popular enough to be on the radio, they met her checklist of qualifications.

Again regaining her attention, Jax explained that the brides usually wore a traditional red wedding gown to one event, and the white Western style at another time during the wedding.

"I thought white was the color of mourning here in China?" Mia asked.

"It used to be, but the younger generations are moving further away from the older traditions; they want to be like the rest of the world. If they don't have strict parents, they'll try to squeeze as many new customs into the ceremony as they can. You'd be surprised at how many of our traditions they've picked up—they even throw the bouquet to their bridesmaids!" Jax explained. "But they also include some of the older traditions to please their elders and those in the afterworld. A long time ago, you would have seen the bride being carried out on the back of a woman who was paid to be her good luck guide. It was always a mother of many children. The family hired her to arrange the bride's hair and escort her to the wedding so that some of her fertility luck would rub off on the bride."

"I guess since the one-child policy came into play, they don't need that custom any longer." Mia would have liked to see the bride dressed in the Chinese-style red wedding gown, but she was happy to observe the bridge tradition. *Seeing actual events unfold is so much more interesting than just studying about it!* She studied the beaming face of the young bride.

"Jax, thanks for bringing me here. This is just what I

needed. But how did you learn so much about the history here in such a short time?"

"All those Sunday dinners with my grandparents finally paid off. I've heard them and my parents talk about some of these things all my life. As for the local history, when I knew I'd be coming here, I studied everything I could so that my time here would be more than just a job. I know I don't look like it, but down deep I'm just a history geek."

Jax lowered his voice to a whisper again as they drew closer to the humpback bridge. "This bridge and a few others like it in China are supposed to be popular places for mothers to abandon their unwanted children. Since it's said to be lucky, they believe it is a final gift they can give their child as they leave them to find their new path in life."

Mia couldn't think of a response to Jax's story about the bridge. She felt sad that so many women chose to believe abandoning their babies was their only alternative to an unwanted situation. But perhaps it *was* lucky—and if she had been left there on that bridge instead of the train station, she would possibly be more successful in her quest for information about her birth family. She felt depressed at the thought of the many children who had probably lain on the stone steps of the so-called 'lucky' bridge.

"I think it's time for us to go, Jax." She was relieved when the wrinkled old man pulled the boat up to another set of stone stairs so they could depart, and he could take on his next set of waiting customers. As they climbed out of the boat, the sounds of their voices were drowned out by the barrage of wedding firecrackers bursting behind them.

CHAPTER SEVEN

JAX and Mia spent another hour strolling through the town before arriving back at the line of taxis waiting for passengers. It had been a busy day, and Mia felt tired, but she still didn't want to say good-bye. On their way out, they had passed several small families gathered at tables or sitting on blankets, sharing picnic dinners from baskets or large bags. Mia studied each family that included little girls, wondering what made the parents choose to raise their child rather than abandon her in a quest for the coveted boy. She knew from being the only girl in a family with three brothers that they weren't *that* special. *I have some stories that might change some minds around here,* she thought mischievously.

"Hey—I know you must be hungry; you hardly ate anything at lunch. Why don't you come with me to the hotel I work at, and I'll treat you to dinner before my shift begins? I promise you'll enjoy it. The Shiradan has the reputation for serving the best cuisine in town. And I swear to get you back to your hotel in time to call your parents."

Mia stood, contemplating what she should do, but her growling stomach answered for her. She and Jax both laughed, and she agreed to accompany him to his hotel—only the dining room, of course. *I sure won't go to his room,* she joked to herself. It would have been very hard to turn down the banquet he described; other than the one meal she'd eaten at the orphanage, she had basically been living on noodles and cookies for days.

Jax waved a taxi over, and they were on their way once again. Mia was relieved that the driver was more subdued, and she welcomed the change of pace. It gave her the opportunity to enjoy the passing scenery of the bustling city life. Mia was still amazed at the number of bicycles and electric scooters everywhere, vying for their space in the bike lane, and some even bravely taking on the challenge of maneuvering on the main road in the mass of cars and trucks. The expressionless faces of the people going by made her wonder what they were thinking on their commutes to and from work.

"I can't wait to show you the hotel. It's really nice; it's the most popular hotel for foreigners and Chinese nationals visiting Suzhou." Jax sounded proud to work there, and Mia was impressed, even if he was only an intern.

After a few minutes of heavy traffic, they arrived in front of The Shiradan Hotel. Even the entrance was impressive, with the front façade built to look like a pagoda, and Mia thought Jax was lucky to stay there. He got out of the car and reached for Mia's hand to help her out. They entered the enormous lobby together, and Mia looked around her at all of the beautiful sculptures, fountains, and silk rugs. Around her other guests passed, most dressed elegantly or in smart business attire. Mia looked down at her skirt and her dusty sandals.

"Um, Jax, I'm not really dressed appropriately to have

dinner here." She didn't want to embarrass him in front of his coworkers.

"Don't worry. I'll tell them we were out exploring the city and didn't have time to go back and change. It really isn't a problem. And anyway, you look great."

Her confidence wavered, but now that they were there, she didn't want to give up the opportunity for a good—and hopefully free—meal. And at least she was wearing a skirt, even if it was a bohemian look. *How nice it would be to stay in a hotel as posh as this one, instead of the cheaper Chinese hotel,* she thought and then immediately felt bad for thinking like a spoiled child.

Jax led Mia into the main restaurant area. The food on the buffet looked delicious and familiar, and she couldn't wait to pile up a plate. The sight of the mashed potatoes, steamed vegetables, and green salad made her mouth water as Jax guided her to a table. She was so relieved that her dinner would consist of more than Ramen noodles, and she was even going to get some much-needed protein. Her brothers always teased her that she ate like a football player and never gained an ounce, but she'd try to at least appear a bit ladylike for Jax's sake.

"I have to check in with my manager. Will you be all right here for a few minutes?" Jax didn't want to leave Mia, but he explained that he needed to confirm that the front desk was doing okay without his help.

Mia hoped he didn't hear her stomach growl again as she answered, "Sure. I'll just listen to the speaker. Who is this group, anyway?"

All around her ladies were chatting, eating, and supposedly listening to the speaker who struggled from a podium to get their attention. Mia heard American and European accents from all over the room, and the women were dressed in various styles, decked out with pearls and other attention-grabbing jewelry.

"Okay. Don't laugh. This is the Tai Tai Club. In Mandarin, a wife is called *tai tai*. This group's made up of women from different places around the world, who are here accompanying their husbands on work assignments. They get together for activities, or to plan and carry out charity projects. In their communities, they're known as expats—short for *expatriates*."

Mia was surprised that she hadn't seen any of the women in the last few days. "Wow—I didn't know this city had all these foreigners living here. You go on ahead, Jax. I'll be fine waiting here." She couldn't wait to listen in to see what exactly the ladies were up to while living in China.

"Thanks for understanding, Mia. Now I need to find Robert and explain why I'm late." Jax hurried off.

While the speaker—a woman from England, Mia guessed from the accent—explained the next Tai Tai Club field trip to Shanghai for shopping, Mia was close enough to the table beside her to overhear a much more fascinating conversation between two ladies.

"Well, they said they didn't have anyone to care for her in the hospital, so I offered to pay for an *ayi*. They ignored that offer and instead sent her home with the social worker. That child needs constant medical attention! If something happens to her, I'm going to be furious at the director."

The blonde American woman sounds really ticked off, Mia thought as she leaned in to listen more closely.

"Do we have enough to pay for her surgery if they can get her up to the required weight?" her friend asked.

"I don't know exactly what the cost will be, but we have to be close to it, and if we don't have it all, the Happy Fund guys will surely help us out. But first we have to convince the directors of her dire situation." The blonde woman stood and headed for the buffet line.

Mia was startled to realize they had to be talking about a child from the orphanage. She couldn't let the opportunity to find out more pass her by, so she decided to fill her plate before Jax returned. She was sure he'd understand as she jumped to her feet and hurried towards the buffet line.

Now directly behind the woman, the aromas enveloping Mia almost made her forget her initiative to introduce herself. But the woman made it easy when she turned around and smiled.

"Hey, how are you?" Her Southern accent was very pronounced, and Mia wondered where she was from. Mia followed her actions as the woman picked up a plate and a set of cutlery rolled in a fancy white napkin.

"Hi. I'm fine, and you?" Mia wasn't sure how she was going to move the conversation along to talk about the orphanage without sounding like she had been eavesdropping a few minutes earlier.

"Just fine. Are you new here?"

"Sort of—I'm here visiting from the States. But how did you know I wasn't a local Chinese?" Mia asked. The woman was being very politically correct by not assuming Mia was a local Chinese just because of her appearance. Mia purposely skipped the rice and noodles on the buffet and instead concentrated on any food *not Asian-inspired* to fill her plate.

"I didn't know, but you're here in the same room as the Tai Tai Club, and when you answered my 'How are you?' with such good English, I thought you might be visiting from somewhere. Oh, sorry. My name's Resa—I've lived here for a few years. Are you here with family?"

"Um, not really. My friend works for the Shiradan, and he invited me to dinner." She looked all around the room to see if Jax had returned yet. "But I guess he got busy in the office. He hasn't come back yet. Oh, sorry—my name's Mia." She hoped for an opening to pick the woman's knowledge of the orphanage.

"Oh. I bet I've met your friend. I come here all the time for different events and sometimes for Sunday brunch. Would you like to sit with us while you wait for him? No one likes to eat alone." The woman was really friendly, making Mia's goal to engage in serious conversation much easier.

"Sure, I'd love that—thank you so much!" They both finished filling their plates, and Mia followed Resa back to the table she shared with her friend.

"Julie, this is Mia. She's visiting Suzhou and has a friend who works here at the hotel. She's going to sit with us while she waits for him to come back."

"Hello, Mia. Where are you from?" Julie was also blonde but spoke with a German accent.

"I'm from Lynden, Washington." Mia answered. The woman had no idea the history behind that dreaded question that she had experienced all of her life. Most people who asked it were actually trying to find out where she was born, and her answer of being from Washington always left them confused. But she felt that if they wanted to know where she was born then they should ask that, instead of beating around the bush.

"Oh, I've been there once. It's a great place for a quiet getaway, especially if you like Dutch architecture." Resa waved the waitress over and asked for another Coke. Mia asked for a glass of water with lemon to complement her plate of prime rib, baby carrots, and creamy potatoes.

"So, I understand you both are expatriates. What do you do to keep busy here in Suzhou?" Mia attempted to turn the conversation towards a subject that would lead to talk of the orphanage. She didn't want to be too abrupt and just ask; she felt it needed a subtle approach.

"Oh, we find a lot of trouble to get into—or it finds us, I might say." Julie chuckled and winked at Resa. "Most of the locals here think we *tai tai*s do nothing but pamper ourselves, but believe me, there's more to us than shopping and getting massages."

Resa held her hand up to stop conversation. "Here's a shocker: we even cook our own meals most nights and do a lot of the household chores. Many of the foreigners have house help, and we do, too, but we like to feed our own families—when we can find appropriate groceries, that is," she added.

For a few minutes, the ladies entertained her with stories of their treks to the stores to find chickens without heads and feet still attached, and their experiences of their many language translation bloopers that ended in comical results. In between bites, Mia found herself laughing at their colorful stories of life as expats. She was so engrossed in Resa's story about the Shanghai knock-off market and the negotiating skills she had honed that Mia almost forgot she had a motive for joining the conversation.

"You said you're not into massages and shopping, so what else do you do in your free time?" she asked when the two paused for a moment.

Resa set her glass down and took a deep breath. "We volunteer in one of the local orphanages. We go a few times a week and help with the children. They have a lot of needs there, but most of all we give the babies the affection and human interaction that they crave and the nannies don't have time to give."

"And really, they give us much more than we give them. It sounds like a cliché, but it's true—we're lucky to know and be able to interact with them," Julie added. "But we also assist the nannies with their workload so that they are not so overwhelmed. We feed the babies and dress them after their baths. And we help with the weekly bed changing. It's exhausting work, but worth it to know we are filling such a huge need, and it's only right that we should do something to help the community we're living in as guests."

Mia was fascinated at the thought of the volunteers holding the babies to give them the affection they were so lacking, and she was sure the overworked orphanage staff had to appreciate the extra hands. The conversation was slowly leading where she wanted, but she wished they'd talk about the baby they'd been discussing earlier when she had overheard them.

"Do you ever have children there in need of serious medical care?"

"Oh yes," answered Resa. "We've raised funds to send many of them to the hospital to have surgeries. We've had heart babies, cleft lip and palate babies, and even spinal bifida children. We were just discussing a child who is in dire need of heart surgery. The biggest issue is that she hasn't met the weight requirement needed to survive the operation, but ironically, her heart condition is the obstacle keeping her from gaining the weight. She's such a sick little girl—I fear that she has developed pneumonia. We're very worried about her, and feel like she should be in the hospital, being watched closely."

"Why isn't she? What's the problem?" Mia's heart felt heavy that a child wasn't only missing her mother but also suffering such a debilitating health issue.

"We're not sure," Resa answered. "But we're going to talk to the director tomorrow and find out why Xinxin is still not under professional medical observation."

Caught by surprise, Mia forgot herself and exclaimed, "Xinxin? I saw her yesterday!" Immediately after blurting it out, she remembered that she hadn't yet told them that she had visited the orphanage.

"Oh? Are you part of another volunteer group? I thought you were only visiting China? And Xinxin isn't there—she's staying at the home of the orphanage social worker. You probably saw another baby," Resa said.

Now that she had slipped and given too much information, Mia decided to just come clean. "I went to the orphanage to visit because I lived there for a few years before I was adopted by an American family. While I was there yesterday, I saw a baby girl and the director said her name was Xinxin. She really looked sick, too."

"I guess we'll find out for sure where Xinxin is tomorrow. But hey—that's really great that you've come to find your roots," Resa said. "Did you also ask about your birth parents?"

"I do want to know about my birth family and plan to ask. Even if they didn't want me, I need to know who I am. I love my adoptive parents and never want to replace them—I just want to be at peace and move on with my life—but first I need the answers. Actually, I was supposed to go back to the orphanage today, and I hoped to get some information, but my guide cancelled on me for some reason. I don't know when I'll be able to go again."

"Well, Tuesday's our next volunteer day. Why don't you go with us to work with the babies? I'll call the director and get it cleared. I'm sure she won't have a problem with it. Are you staying here at the Shiradan?"

"No, I can't afford a place like this. I'm staying at a Chinese hotel near Walking Street."

"Oh. Well, just leave us the hotel name, and we'll pick you up."

"Yeah, and we can use the extra set of hands after bath time," Julie added. "I'd love to hear more of your story; the subject of adoption has always fascinated me."

Before Mia could answer, Jax arrived at the table and looked around at the trio. "I see you're in good hands, Mia. I'm sorry I took so long, but they needed me for an unexpected rush at the front desk. I'm glad you started eating without me."

Mia looked up at Jax and smiled. His dinner invitation had gotten her one step closer to finding out more information about her birth family.

CHAPTER EIGHT

JAX arrived at Starbucks at eight o'clock sharp and sat quietly outside at a small table, hands folded in his lap to hide his nerves. He kept his mind occupied by watching the window washers on the skyscraper across the way. The unfathomable courage they showed, sitting on buckets at the end of the ropes being gently let down the buildings, astonished him. They resembled spiders as they gracefully found their way to the windows they needed to clean.

He was relieved Mia had agreed to meet him that morning. He needed every moment with her he could wrangle, if he was to make her like him as much as he liked her. They had met a couple more times in the week and a half since their first meeting, and something told him she was fighting an attraction to him. He didn't understand why. *Is she just not into me?* Lost in his thoughts, he didn't see her approach until she stood before him.

"Good morning, Jax! Where's our coffee?" she teased. Her energy and cheerful greeting turned the heads of several businessmen quietly sitting around them. One man lowered his newspaper to watch Mia and Jax, unashamed at staring so blatantly.

"Um, I don't know what you like to drink here. Let's go order together." Her beauty once again blew Jax away; and that morning, with her long hair pulled to one side and braided with a colorful band at the bottom, she looked young and fresh—and he felt proud to be seen with her. He stood, and she led the way into the coffee shop, unknowingly swinging her short paisley skirt from side to side, mesmerizing him as he followed.

At the counter, Mia ordered a chocolate muffin and a venti caramel macchiato with cream, while Jax stuck to a traditional cup of coffee and a plain bagel. She made a face at him as he pulled out his wallet to pay.

"All these choices, and you just want plain coffee and a bagel?" she teased.

"Too many options overwhelm me," he answered with a big smile. "I'm a simple kind of guy." He'd had the same thought that morning when he agonized over what to wear and realized it wasn't much of a choice, considering most of his shirts and jeans looked a lot alike. He wanted to be stylish, but he didn't believe in collecting an excess of anything.

After they received their drinks, they went back outside to enjoy the mild morning weather. Mia chose a small table at the edge near the sidewalk, though Jax warned her that they would be in the prime begging area, and she should be ready for the tin cans that would soon be jangled at them. He told her that Starbucks customers were frequently approached as they were having breakfast or reading the newspaper, in the hopes the interruption would net the beggars a few coins.

"So what do you want to do today?" he asked, hoping whatever it was, it would take up the entire day. He wanted to spend as much time with her as possible, and he didn't need to report for work until six o'clock that evening.

"I have some posters I need to put up around the city." Mia bent down to her satchel and pulled out a black folder. Opening it, she removed a sheet of paper and laid it on the table.

"What's this?" Jax asked as he picked it up to examine it closer. The main focus of the poster was an enlarged photo. It was a child of about three or four years old, though it was hard to tell because of the sadness weighing on her face.

"That's me," Mia said. "That's the photo my parents received on my adoption referral. I want to hang these around the city, and maybe someone will remember me and come forward. I've listed my finding place, the date they say I was found, and the clothes I was wearing. And I've put an e-mail address for them to write to."

"Wow, Mia. That's a long shot; this is a very big city." Jax felt bad but wanted her to know it would be a miracle if the posters generated a lead in her search for her birthparents. Looking at the poster hit him hard with the realization of how sad it must have been for her to grow up not knowing where or who she came from, or why she wasn't wanted by her birth parents.

"I know, Jax, but I've got to try. My parents and I worked together to make these up at home, and Dad got a Chinese guy at work to translate it into characters. I want to make sure I've done all I can possibly do to find my birth parents while I'm here. I want to leave with no regrets."

"Well then, let's do it—but you know your birth family may not have a computer or understand e-mail. Why don't we write my mobile number on all these? If they call, I can take down their information for you."

"That'd be great. I was worried about that, but since I don't have a Chinese phone, and my so called guide-slash-translator has disappeared off the face of the earth, my e-mail address was my only option." She pulled two pens from her bag and Jax wrote his phone number on the first sheet, then together they added it to the rest of the pile. While they worked, they brainstormed places to hang the posters.

☙

It was a long, hot trek around the city, but they finally hung all the posters except for the few Jax planned to take to the train station. It was so far out of town that he promised Mia he would get a Shiradan driver to take him the next morning.

Mia felt confident they had chosen some excellent locations for the flyers, which were now hanging at several local food markets, restaurants, and even the police station. The curiosity of the local people certainly knew no boundaries, for each time they stopped to hang a poster, the crowd gathered around to read it, exclaim and point at Mia as if she were a celebrity. It got to be so embarrassing that she began to stay back far enough that they wouldn't know it was her, while Jax finished the tasks.

At Walking Street, they hung a poster at each end and one in the middle before stopping at the same noodle restaurant where they had taken the street boy on their first meeting. Mia looked around, hoping to see him, but he was nowhere in sight.

They were hungry and tired from the walking, and Jax ordered bowls of noodles and deep-fried bananas sprinkled with honey glaze for dessert. The table was silent as they dug in to refuel, then finally sat back to enjoy the sweet treats a bit more slowly.

"So you've been here awhile now. What do you think of China?" Jax asked, expertly balancing an entire slice of banana between his chopsticks.

"Hmm… It's not like I expected, but it's definitely a world away from my small town." Mia chuckled and used her fingers to pick up a piece of the sticky treat and popped it into her mouth.

"What did you expect to find, rice paddies and small villages? Because they're here. Just say the word, and I'll take you there. I can have you riding an ox through the fields in no time." Jax raised his eyebrows high, as if daring her to take his challenge.

"No—well, maybe something like that. I sure didn't expect to see so many modern clothes, gadgets, and stuff. I mean seriously—does everyone in China own a smart phone? I even saw a billboard advertising the iPad. From what I can tell, they aren't behind the States at all, except for their social welfare system. They have a long way to go on that subject."

"You're right about their competition to stay ahead of the game with technology. Last year, they even shut down fake Apple stores selling fake iPads. People were buying them by the thousands and thought they were getting the real thing! But tell me about your hometown. What's it like? Do you love it there? I've always wanted to live in a small town, at least to try it. On television it looks awesome, everyone going fishing and hanging out at the square or going to community picnics. Is it like that?"

Mia laughed at his depiction of small town life. "Not exactly. Sounds to me like you've been watching too much *Gilmore Girls*. Lynden's a Dutch town; many of the people who live there are Van–something or other. Dad used to joke that if we really wanted to fit in, since Mom was adamant we all take Sunday naps when we were kids, we needed to change our last name to Van Winkle."

Jax laughed. "Mia Su Van Winkle? That has a nice ring to it."

"Yeah, whatever. The town's tiny but really beautiful. There's a lot of farmland around, but it's most famous for the Dutch style of buildings and houses. My family isn't originally from there, and Dad says the historical families will never let us forget it. When my mom first brought me home, she got questions from the ladies around town that still ruffles her feathers to think about."

"What sort of questions?"

"Oh, strangers would ask her if my father was Chinese. And so-called friends of hers asked her if she knew who my real father was—as if it was some deep dark secret."

"That's lame," Jax answered, shaking his head.

"Oh, don't worry. Mom would always tell them that she sure *did* know my real father and slept with him every night. That usually shut them up, but over the years she's had some crazy questions directed at her about me. She's even been asked several times why she didn't adopt from her own country."

"Wow, that's harsh. How does she answer that?"

"Usually she tells them because her daughter was in China. Then she turns it around and asks them if *they've* adopted from *their* own country." Mia chuckled as she thought about her sassy mom. "I overheard her once telling Dad about when she was at the park with me, and a woman turned to her and said, 'Oh, she's so pretty. What is she?'"

Jax laughed. "Oh, I bet your mom was all over that one."

"Mom says she just gave her a look of complete confusion and said, 'She's human, of course. Isn't yours?'"

"That does sound a lot different from growing up in Seattle. I blended in all right; I definitely didn't have the issues you had. Luckily, I look just like my parents, so that saved me from experiencing the constant curiosity you did."

"Well, I definitely went through a lot of bullying. One year, my parents took me out of public school and put me in private Christian school for a while, but it was worse there, so I transferred back to my old school after one semester. My mom wanted to homeschool me that year, but Dad insisted I needed to learn how to face adversity before I left home. I eventually learned that bullies got tired of teasing me when they didn't get a reaction, and by the seventh grade I had a great group of friends that usually ran defense in sticky situations."

"Well, you turned out okay, despite your battles with bullies. Goes to show you must be pretty tough."

"I don't know. It wasn't so bad. Overall, I had a great childhood, and I love our small town—it's so quiet and peaceful.

And over the years, we've come to realize that most of the people who ask inappropriate questions just don't know any better because they're not involved in adoption. As for my trials, everyone has memories of the difficulties of growing up—mine just happened to be because I'm Chinese in a white middle class family, and I grew up in a Dutch town of rich people with funny names." She flashed an impish grin that tore at Jax's heartstrings.

"Um... Switching subjects, I have something to ask you. Saturday night, there's an event at the hotel. It's mandatory that I attend, so will you be my date? I mean—um—unless you have a boyfriend back home that might get jealous or something? I guess I should have found that out earlier."

Mia chuckled when Jax suddenly looked as if he had swallowed something sour. He wasn't good at hiding his emotions—or his jealous streak.

"Jax, stop. I don't have a boyfriend—at least, not anymore. What kind of company event is it?" She could have lied and said she still had a boyfriend, but that just wasn't her. She didn't want to keep encouraging Jax, but she was finding it hard to cut off their friendship.

"I'd rather surprise you. Come on—I promise it'll be fun and something you've probably never done. Just say yes, Mia, please!"

Only a heartless dictator could say no to someone looking at them the way Jax was looking at her. Mia felt her resolve crumble. "How can I say yes if I don't even know what to wear, Jax?" She hated wearing formal attire and hoped Jax would at least give her a hint at how miserable she was going to be.

"Let me handle that. I'll take you shopping Wednesday morning and help you pick the perfect outfit. I'll even buy it for you!" Jax sounded excited that she was about to agree to go.

"Okay, Jax. I'll go with you. And you can take me shopping, but I'm paying for my own dress. You can just be my own personal Chinese haggler and help me get a good price." She laughed as she gathered up her things to go. She was going to have to talk to Jax about his infatuation with surprises—she was a girl who needed to have all information at her fingertips at all times. *Maybe that's why I can't stop searching for my birth parents until I have my answers*, she mused.

CHAPTER NINE

"*DUI bu qi.*" A man growled an apology at her as he shoved past, bumping her with the luggage he dragged along behind him. Mia was waiting outside the hotel as she'd arranged with Resa, but she wished she'd made arrangements to meet somewhere else. Early mornings at the hotel were the busiest time of the day with people checking in and out, businessmen hurrying through, and tourists trying to get directions. It seemed as if she were in the way no matter where she stood.

Resa had told her they'd be driving a blue Buick van and would pick her up at eight o'clock sharp. When Mia returned to her hotel the night before, she was surprised that Xiao Jo still hadn't returned any of her messages. She couldn't imagine what had happened to the girl, or why she wouldn't answer her phone, even if she couldn't accompany her to the orphanage. And why didn't she set her up with another bilingual guide if she couldn't finish the assignment herself? It was peculiar for the translator to be so unprofessional, especially when the girl knew that Mia had traveled halfway around the world to get there. If she didn't hear from Xiao Jo that day, Mia planned to e-mail the website to inquire what was going on and maybe even ask for a refund of her money. *I should have known better than to book a stranger from the Internet*, she berated herself for the third time that morning.

The night before, Jax had escorted her to her hotel, and he'd even insisted on walking her into the lobby to make sure she was completely safe. Mia knew she shouldn't encourage him, since he was living in China and long-distance relationships didn't ever work out, but every time she told herself it was the last time she'd see him, she somehow got wrangled into another date. She wanted to kick herself for being so weak.

An embarrassing admission for someone her age, but Mia had only had one serious relationship in her life—and it had left her with a broken heart. She was still recovering and had promised herself she'd never open herself up to that kind of pain and humiliation again, but she just couldn't make herself avoid Jax. His enthusiasm for life was contagious, and being around him was a salve to her unsettled soul. She told herself it would be over soon enough when she left China, and she looked forward to the mysterious event on Saturday.

As Mia waited, dozens of blue Buick vans came and went. She didn't know how she was going to pick out the one that carried her new friends, but finally the van arrived. Resa opened the door and waved Mia over. Julie moved to the back to allow Mia to sit in the middle seat, and she wrangled her guitar case in and shut the van door.

"Did you already have breakfast? We have fresh muffins we're bringing to the *ayi*s." Resa pointed to a plastic container tied with a red ribbon, lying on the floor between their seats.

"Thanks, but I had some fruit from the hotel dining room.

That's really nice of you to bring the staff goodies." Mia wondered if the muffins helped pave the way for the foreigners on the turf of the Chinese nannies.

"Well, I convinced the other volunteers a long time ago that it isn't bribery; it's a way to bridge the cultural gap by offering kindness. Everyone likes a treat now and then, and if it brings a smile to their faces, it's worth the detour and small amount of money it costs. I used to only bring them for the director, but then I realized that she gets all of the favors from visitors, and the nannies rarely get anything. So now I carry them straight to the room the staff takes their breaks in," Resa explained with a playful twinkle in her eye. Mia noticed that she wore a colorful chain of plastic infant link toys around her neck, obviously something to use to interact with the children.

As their driver took them further into the older part of the city nearer the orphanage, the fleeting scenes of local life all around her mesmerized Mia. They weaved through the narrow alleys, and she watched people going about their routine chores, and she wondered if they were aware of the institution that housed so many orphan children, just blocks away from them. *Do they use the nearby orphanage as a threat or reminder to keep their own sons and daughters in line? Or do they just pretend it didn't exist so that they won't feel any responsibility to assist in any way?*

She watched what appeared to be a grandmother walking behind a toddler riding a small scooter, hands out protectively in case he lost his balance. The pedestrians parted for the couple as they slowly made their way up the sidewalk, the child receiving pats of encouragement from strangers walking by.

Julie brought Mia out of her daydream with a question of her own. "Have you found out anything about your birth parents yet?"

"Absolutely nothing I didn't already know when I came here," Mia answered with a frustrated sigh. "I know I was found in the train station and then brought to the orphanage. I lived there for three years before my parents adopted me. Oh—they did tell me one thing I didn't know, that I was in foster care for the year before my adoption. My parents were told that I wasn't ever in foster care, but I even met the woman they said was my foster mom." She chuckled at the memory of the plump woman furiously stuffing her mouth with the delicacies at the luncheon. "That was awkward."

"That's good news, because the foster parents know a lot more than they get credit for. If the director doesn't want to or can't tell you anything more, your best chance is to question the foster mother about what she's heard." Resa slapped her hands together, then she quickly sobered. "I also wanted to tell you that when my driver called the director yesterday and asked if you could accompany me today, Director Zhu hesitated. Then she said you could come but none of the administration staff members can meet with you."

Mia frowned at that bit of news. "I can't understand why she won't let me bring up the subject of my origins. Why does it all have to be such a big secret? It's my right to know who I am, but she won't even meet with me. That's really strange, don't you think? My time here is running out. I only have a few more weeks, and I've haven't learned much more than I already knew." She laid her forehead against the side window and gazed out at the busy street life. She was so close, and yet millions of miles away from finding out who she was.

Julie said cheerily, "Well, at least you get to interact with the children today. They're going to love that you brought your guitar! And we'll ask the driver if he can find out who the woman they claim was your foster mother is. What did you say her name was? Mr. Wang usually sits in the guard shack while we are working, and many times on the way home he surprises us with information about the children or the orphanage staff, stuff we'd never find out from the directors."

"They introduced her as Lao Ling," Mia said, tracing the drawing on her guitar case with her finger.

"Lao is a title of respect, so hopefully there isn't more than one foster mother with the surname of Ling," Resa said. "But anyway—Julie, remember that time I asked where that little girl with the burn scars was, and the staff all said they didn't know? When we got in the car, Mr. Wang knew the whole dramatic story and told us the details. We already knew that the little girl had been abandoned at age five after she was badly burned at home and that a charity organization paid for all of her reconstructive surgeries. After her recovery, she was put on the adoption list and matched with a family. What we didn't know was that just before the adoption was final and it was time for the adoptive parents to come to China to get her, the biological parents showed up and reclaimed her."

"How did they pull that off without being arrested for abandoning her? What about all of the hospital bills that they didn't have to pay?" Mia sat up straighter. She couldn't believe that such things could be ignored.

"Chinese law states that parents can be arrested for child abandonment, but most times, the officials look the other way, especially if they're given a monetary incentive to forget the details. Also, if the orphanage directors or staff members have some connection to the family, they'll coordinate the reunion without involving the authorities. I've heard many times from the *ayis* in the baby room that some of the children's parents hang around the gates to occasionally check on the children they abandoned." Resa shook her head at the injustice of it all. "It took me quite some time in China before I learned about the high percentage of children who are abandoned because their parents can't afford the critical medical care they need. To many foreigners, it might seem cruel that a child in need of heart surgery is found underneath a bridge in a box, but to the Chinese it's a gift of love, that they would choose to leave their child for a chance at saving his or her life. When I think of the little burned girl, part of me always cheers that the child was reunited with parents who obviously loved her but couldn't afford the medical care she desperately needed."

Resa's thoughts on the issue of abandoned children forced Mia to realize that maybe it was a possibility she was abandoned out of love—not the rejection she had feared for most of her life.

As they turned down the last alley leading to the orphanage gates, Resa explained to Mr. Wang that she wanted him to quietly find out about the foster mother who had lunch with Mia on her first visit to the orphanage. Mr. Wang agreed that he'd see what he could dig up, and he stopped the van for them to climb out. Resa and Julie picked up their backpacks filled with cookies and baby supplies, and the trio entered the gates, to immediately be surrounded by children with hopeful eyes and open hands waiting for snacks.

Mia lingered back and studied the scene before her. As Resa and Julie handed out cookies, she was relieved to hear the laughter and see the spontaneous smiles she had expected to see on her first visit. It amazed her to see what a difference a little gesture of affection and a small treat could make in a child.

They stood in a concrete area that the ladies called 'the courtyard.' It was surrounded on two sides by buildings and bordered on one side by a tall wall with jagged glass lined up along the top, obviously to keep intruders from climbing over. The wall had colorful cartoon characters painted in scenes, but in the courtyard there didn't appear to be toys or anything for the children to play with, they simply jumped around and chased each other. Next to the courtyard was a fenced-in play area, padlocked from the outside, the swing set and climbing gym just out of reach to the children.

Most of the kids appeared between five and ten years old, with an even balance of girls and boys—though with the chopped-off hairstyles, she was using the colors and patterns of the clothing to guess the genders.

One boy about five years old reached for his cookie and then gently guided another small girl to Resa for her own treat. Mia had to swallow the sudden lump in her throat at the show of kinship between the two children.

Resa and Julie finished handing out snacks while Mia sat on the curb with her guitar and began to play a favorite children's song. She softly sang the words to "Old MacDonald Had a Farm" and like a pied piper, her voice drew the children in. Smiling and clapping, they did their best to dance and mimic the animal noises, while taking turns touching the guitar to feel the vibrations. After two songs, Resa beckoned to her that they needed to get going. Mia stood and slung the guitar strap around her shoulder, much to the dismay of her crowd of fans.

"*Ta hui lai, ta hui lai.*" Julie assured them that their new hero would be back.

"Okay. Come on, Mia. We need to get up to the baby room. It's bath day, and they'll be waiting for us to get started." Resa led the way up the several flights of slippery recently mopped stairs, through the hallway and into the two adjoining rooms that the infants and toddlers shared.

Following their lead, Mia kicked off her shoes and slipped her feet into a pair of cloth slippers. She assumed it was to keep the street germs out of the room and was impressed at the precautions implemented by the staff. They entered the room and set their bags on the cabinet next to the outdated television, Mia cringing at the high volume blaring out the drama of the Chinese soap operas. Three toddlers sat in walkers that were tied to the enormous metal playpen behind them to keep them from rolling about. *How do they learn to walk if they aren't allowed to practice?*

Julie and Resa both immediately lifted babies out of cribs and beckoned to Mia that she could do the same.

"*Mifan*?" Resa asked a passing *ayi* about rice.

"*Deng yi huir.*" The young woman told her it'd come later and continued her fast pace around the cribs with the scraggly broom in her hand.

"It looks like the rice and bottles are late again. We'll have to feed them before the *ayi*s bathe them, so we still have some time to play. Our goal is to give every baby some individual attention and stimulation before we go. So don't spend too much time with one child—get to as many as you can," Resa instructed Mia, speaking above the wails of hungry children.

Another *ayi* walked around laying clean clothing at the foot of each crib and bed. "*Ta shi shui? Zhonguo ren*?" She asked Resa who Mia was and if she was Chinese. The perfect English coming from Mia's Asian face had obviously confused the young *ayi*.

Resa explained that Mia was Chinese, but lived in America and was here to visit. The *ayi* studied Mia as she continued to lay out the diapers and shirts.

Before Mia could decide which child to pick up, the bowls of rice and milk bottles were wheeled into the room on a large metal cart. As the *ayi*s began propping the bottles on rolled sheets in the cribs, Resa put the child she was holding back in her bed and picked up a child with a cleft lip, taking her to the small sitting area to feed her personally. Julie chose to keep the baby she had in her arms, and she joined Resa on the short blue pillows that served as couches.

"You can feed the toddlers rice, if you want," Resa told Mia. She pointed at the rice still steaming on the cart. "Usually we try to get the cleft babies fed first because they have a difficult time forming enough suction to drink their milk before it is taken away. We use a squeeze-pause-squeeze method. It takes a bit of practice and can be really messy until you get the hang of it. You should have been here the first time I tried to feed a cleft palate baby. After two minutes of feeding her, everything came flooding out her nose and all over her face. I felt so bad, but the baby just stared at me and waited to be cleaned up, without even making as much as a whimper."

"Why does China have so many babies with cleft lips and palates? I hear about organizations like Smile Train that come over to do surgeries for the babies. I even helped with a fundraiser once that paid for a dozen surgeries." Mia picked up a bowl of rice and carried it over to kneel in front of one of the walkers. All three children began to cry and hold out their hands when they saw the food, and Mia wished she could feed all of them at the same time. Instead, the *ayi* who had asked if she was Chinese pulled up a stool and sat between the other two toddlers, alternately shoveling rice in their mouths from the same spoon and bowl. *I'm fast—but not fast enough for their satisfaction!* Mia thought.

"The cause of cleft lips or palates hasn't been proven yet, but there are many theories. Some scientists believe it's caused by various negative environmental factors or by genetics. I've even heard it's because many Chinese mothers are too poor to eat foods high in folic acid. Or sometimes it can come early in the fetus stage if the mother has some type of infection or virus."

Mia was struggling to get the rice into the bobbing mouth of the boy she was feeding, and her incompetence was making her smear much of it on his tiny face. The rice was steaming hot, but each time Mia would stop to blow on it, the boy became almost hysterical in his hunger, bobbing his open mouth back and forth to try to get closer to the spoon, making Mia wonder how long it had been since his last meal. She did her best but felt sorry that her inept hands made it slower to fill the toddler's empty belly. Beside her, the *ayi* didn't take any time to blow the heat from the food; she quickly and expertly fed it to the two children.

"Do they always share bottles and utensils?" Mia asked, though she knew what the answer was going to be. In that setting, the children shared everything.

Resa soon stood up and put the satiated baby back in her crib and then began to go around to other cribs to replace the bottles into the frantically seeking mouths of the babies who had dropped them. Julie joined her, and they explained to Mia that the babies only had a very short time to drink the milk before the bottles were picked up and taken away. If a baby knocked the bottle away from her mouth, and no one got around to replace it, she or he might lose the chance to eat until the next meal.

So this is what I went through when I was a baby? Mia felt a twinge of resentment at the bland, colorless room and the strict schedule the babies were expected to follow. *Isn't feeding a hungry child more important than staying on task every moment of every day?* The analytical part of her brain reminded her that institutional life was different from real life—this wasn't meant to imitate a home, and schedules kept things running smoothly. However, the emotional side of her refused to believe it was fair to leave even one child hungry for one minute.

The volunteers and *ayis* finished feeding the children and began to undress them. Resa and Julie were fast at getting the children down to only a diaper, but again, Mia struggled to keep up. She didn't want to hurt the baby by being too rough, though judging from how one *ayi* pulled the shirt over one small boy's head, they were used to abrupt treatment.

"Don't forget to pull off their socks," Julie reminded Mia as she passed by to get to the infant in the next crib. Babies were already being bathed and returned to their beds, crying for the comfort of clothing, causing Julie and Resa to work more quickly.

Mia stood still in front of the tiny room that doubled as a kitchen area and bathing room. As she stared at the process of washing the infants, she was taken back in time to a memory she didn't even know she carried.

The unbearable cold felt like needles on her skin as her clothes were stripped roughly from her body. The ayi *reached down and grabbed her under the arms, dangling Mia in front of her as she carried her to the washing room. She was passed to another* ayi *and then dumped into the huge sink of hot water. Mia screamed at the scalding temperature, and a few seconds later, she felt the shock of water dumped over her face, as her hair was washed, and her body was quickly scrubbed. Shaking and wailing from fear, Mia was picked up and handed off to another* ayi, *to be taken to the next station where she was roughly dried. Powder was shaken over her body, the cloud choking the breath out of her. The* ayi *picked her up and returned her to her bed, where she was quickly dressed in several layers until she was bound almost too tightly to even roll over, the prison of clothing only allowing her to stare at the same dirty water spot on the ceiling above her bed until she was able to comfort herself to sleep by humming a familiar song.*

"*Zenme le*?" A soft voice brought her out of her flashback

and back to the reality of the moment. The *ayi* who had asked about her was standing next to her, concerned at the look on her face. Mia stood still, rubbing at the imaginary goose bumps up and down her arms.

"She's asking what's wrong, Mia," Resa translated as she hurried to dress the baby she leaned over.

The *ayi* laid one hand on Mia's shoulder, giving her a reassuring squeeze. Mia appreciated the woman's gesture of compassion as she fought to bring her emotions under control.

That was the first memory she'd ever recovered of her time in the orphanage. Perhaps more would return, but after the distress that one evoked, Mia wasn't sure she wanted them to.

Resa joined Mia and the *ayi* next to the bathing room. "Are you okay, Mia?"

"Yeah, I'm fine. This is the same way they did baths when I lived here. I just remembered it." She turned away from the bathing room, wanting to hide from the memories it invoked.

"I'm so sorry, Mia. I know it seems cruel and abrupt, the way they do the baths. We have to remember the *ayi*s have a lot of children to bathe before the scheduled sleeping time. If they're behind in their duties and one of the directors walks by to find some children still being bathed when they're supposed to be taking their afternoon naps, then the room's staff will be disciplined. I know it's like an assembly line, and I wish it weren't so, but they don't mean to be callous."

Mia moved away from the doorway to the bathing room. The scene was too disturbing, and she didn't want to witness it any longer.

Resa continued, her cheeks flaring pink, "I remember my

first winter here, when I came in to find all the babies strapped down in their beds so tightly they couldn't turn over or move at all. I was outraged, but someone finally explained to me that because the rooms were so frigid with the winter chill, the straps were to keep the infants from kicking off their covers. I was embarrassed at my ignorance—it was done to protect them, not hurt them."

"And this young lady is Tingting." Resa gestured toward the *ayi* who still had her hand resting on Mia's shoulder. "She's the sweetest *ayi* in the room. She's also one of the few who will take the time to comfort a crying child instead of scolding it into silence."

"*Ta feichang hao*!" Resa said for Tingting's benefit, telling her she was very nice. Tingting smiled, showing off a dimple in her right cheek.

Tingting looked about fifteen years old, with round rosy cheeks and eyes much too wise for her age. Like Mia, she wore her hair long, but she kept hers pulled back in a loose ponytail. She didn't appear as tired or stressed as the other nannies in the room, and she went about her work with a measure of peace and grace that the others didn't possess. Mia wasn't sure whether it was because she didn't work as hard or just because she chose to enjoy her work with the children. Either way, Mia felt genuine warmth from the young girl and determined she was someone she would enjoy getting to know.

As she took another look at Tingting's face. *Have I seen you before?* Then she remembered—the young woman was one of the three who had been watching her the first day she arrived at the orphanage, following quietly as she was shown around.

Mia smiled at Tingting and then moved to the crib with the diapered baby struggling under the set of clothes that were dropped on her face. She picked up the clothing and began to dress her. She didn't care if they were in a hurry; she was going to make sure that one baby felt a bit of gentleness before she went to sleep that day. As she guided the tiny arms through the sleeves and pulled the split pants over the makeshift diaper, she softly hummed a lullaby to calm the baby girl.

CHAPTER TEN

EXHAUSTED and with her back aching from all the bending to dress the babies, Mia climbed into the back of the van. She politely gave Resa and Julie the two middle seats—but she also wanted to sit in back to allow herself some privacy to take in all she had witnessed during their visit. On their way out, they had asked an *ayi* about the baby girl, Xinxin. The *ayi* took them to the observation room, and they arrived just in time for Mia to feed her a bottle. It was alarming to see how hard Xinxin struggled to suck the milk through the nipple, and she broke out in beads of sweat from her efforts. Resa explained that because her heart was failing, even as simple a task as sucking a bottle was a major effort to the sick infant.

Xinxin was much smaller than the average nine-month-old, her disability stunting her growth. When they walked into the room, she gave Resa the sweetest little wave and smiled weakly to her only visitors of the day.

Resa and Julie were both concerned that the director had allowed Xinxin to go home with the social worker, instead of being hospitalized. The young woman had never had children and also didn't assist in the care of infants at the orphanage.

When Xinxin had showed signs of gasping for breath all through the night, the social worker feared Xinxin would die and cause trouble for her, so she had brought her back to the orphanage.

On their way out, Resa detoured straight to the director's office, and when she joined them at the van, she triumphantly informed them she had obtained permission to take Xinxin to the local hospital for a full examination.

"Do you have plans on Monday, Mia?" Resa asked as she snapped on her seatbelt. She pulled out a small bottle of gel sanitizer and generously squeezed it over her hands and wrists, then offered it to Julie. With so many unrecognized rashes and ailments in the baby room, they always took precautions to avoid bringing home the unwanted germs.

"Not really. I haven't heard back from my guide whether she's able to get me another meeting with the director, and that's Jax's busiest workday, so I doubt I'll be seeing him."

"Would you like to come with us to take Xinxin to the Shanghai Children's hospital? We won't be able to do much sightseeing, but you'll see a lot of real local life that way. No pressure if you need to do something else."

Mia realized she would really like to go and see what happened with an orphan in a hospital. Most of all, she hoped they would be able to help Xinxin. She immediately accepted the invitation, and they planned for her to be picked up again in front of the hotel.

"*Tai Tai*?" The driver peered at Resa through the rearview mirror. "I know where foster mother lives. I can take you if you want. Only few minutes from here."

This news startled Mia, and she hoped that Resa would offer to take her there to question the woman about what information she had to help Mia find her parents.

Resa smiled. "Great job, Mr. Wang! Let's go by there right now, and you can translate for us. Ladies, we'll meet with her, find out what she knows, and then we can stop by Yang Yang Dumpling House on *Shi Quan Jie* for lunch. Sound good?"

Mia had never imagined that meeting these ladies would have catapulted her into such an adventure with the orphanage, and she was thankful to Jax once again for unknowingly assisting her in her search for the truth.

ঙ

Mia wasn't sure what she expected Lao Ling's house to look like, but the building was quite different from what her imagination had been conjuring up on the way from the orphanage. Mr. Wang had said he knew where the woman's *house* was, not *apartment*, so she was a bit surprised when they entered the parking lot surrounding four blocks of twenty-story buildings.

From the street, the gray, institutional-like structures would have been colorless if not for the many displays of clothing flapping outside most every window. Mia wondered how the garments remained clean after drying surrounded by the thick smog. A few of the tenants had made attempts to bring a small part of nature into their lives, building platforms outside their windows that held various small green plants and trees. Mia could only imagine how hard it was to lean out to water and prune them. *Parents here must have to watch their children very closely, even in their own homes, because of those windows.* Just looking at the open windows on the tall buildings caused her fear of heights to send a chill up her spine.

The littered parking lot had several rows, containing hundreds of parked bicycles and electric scooters, all precariously leaning left or right, as if with one gentle push they'd fall like a line of dominoes. She saw a few children squatting in a circle on the pavement, the biggest boy in the group tossing dice in the middle and directing some sort of game.

Mr. Wang parked directly in front of what appeared to be the back entrance to the building. He stepped out and immediately lit a cigarette, as if he couldn't wait another second for his boost of nicotine.

As the ladies exited the van, they found themselves standing at a small fruit and vegetable stand. An elderly woman had bought a yellow fruit that Mia didn't recognize and was peeling it for the child waiting at her feet. The toddler wore red split pants decorated with Christmas trees—a strange choice, considering it wasn't a common holiday in China. The little girl stomped her feet impatiently, her tiny shoes emitting high-pitched squeaks as each one hit the solid ground. No one but Mia seemed to notice the irritating noise, so she assumed that squeaky shoes must be a common fashion statement for Chinese children.

Resa and Julie's blonde hair and pale faces immediately earned the attention of most everyone in the vicinity of the van, causing a small crowd to begin gathering around and a buzz of chatter in the air. Obviously the residents were not used to foreigners visiting their homes. The two didn't appear to notice the attention as they followed Mr. Wang to the entrance of the apartment building.

The driver strutted like a proud peacock as he dropped his cigarette on the sidewalk and led the procession of ladies past the group of curious men leaned against the building—all smoking—to the open door. "She lives on seventh floor. I don't know if she there."

"Mr. Wang, where's the elevator?" Resa asked, looking all about the main lobby area.

Mia took in the scene of half a dozen young men—painters by the look of their clothing—curled up on bamboo mats taking their noontime nap against the walls, out of the midday heat. They didn't move an inch, even through the commotion the ladies were causing. She admired their ability to tune out the world and sleep on command. She was proud that her people—as she was starting to think of them—were some of the hardest workers she had ever seen in her life. She also liked the idea of adults taking naps during the workday. It seemed to her that everyone would have a much more productive afternoon if they napped like the Chinese, instead of fighting through the afternoon haze of fatigue like most Americans did.

"No elevator," Mr. Wang answered gruffly, leading them to the dim stairwell.

The group slowly climbed the concrete stairs until they were finally at the designated floor. Mr. Wang turned right and led them past several apartments. The atmosphere reminded her of summer camp, with doors propped open as an invitation for others to visit, providing Mia the perfect opportunity to get a glimpse of home life for the average family in China—something she had always wondered about.

Through one door, she saw a couple of men sitting on a small, flowered couch, bare feet propped up on a coffee table, both watching a small, outdated television, with the ever-present cigarettes in their hands. On the screen, Mia glimpsed the outlandish costumes and heard the screeching of a Chinese soap opera. At the next door, they passed two young children kneeling on the floor over some sort of art project, colored pencils scattered about them. A feeling of content emanated from the room as behind them a woman who must have been their mother scooped steaming rice out of a large crockpot.

Mia wished they could spend more time walking up and down the halls, observing the interesting scenes, but Mr. Wang stopped in front of a closed door marked A8.

He knocked loudly and waited. Within seconds, they all heard a woman call out, and Mr. Wang answered back something unintelligible to Mia's ears. When he was granted permission to enter, he turned the knob and opened the door to find Lao Ling rocking a small baby against her chest, and the orphanage *ayi*, Tingting, sitting across from her on the couch, a look of surprise—mingled with a touch of alarm—across her face.

CHAPTER ELEVEN

RESA spoke first. “Tingting? How did you get here so fast? What’re you doing here?” Mr. Wang quickly translated the question for her.

Mia could sense her confusion. Tingting looked as if she were caught with her hand in the cookie jar and hesitated so long to answer that Lao Ling began to explain to Mr. Wang that the *ayi* had come by to check on her latest foster child. The old woman looked down at the chubby face of the unsettled baby and began to repeatedly thump his back—something Mia had seen other Chinese women doing to infants, a soothing method of some sort, so different from the gentle touch her mother had used on her.

Tingting bobbed her head in agreement at Lao Ling’s explanation of her visit, as Mr. Wang translated it to the others.

Mia wasn’t so sure about the story; Resa had just explained to her in the ride over that foster home visits were usually only done by a social worker from the orphanage. However, since the baby had just obviously had cleft lip surgery, judging from the stitching around the mouth, Mia accepted the explanation. It was only logical that in the first days after the surgery, it would be important that the babies be kept from crying so that they didn't pull the stitches out. Mia thought the child was lucky she would receive constant attention from the old woman, even if only temporarily.

Lao Ling barked some orders at Tingting, causing the girl to rise quickly to put the kettle on for tea—*The all-weather drink*, Mia thought. The old woman looked around at her small home, gesturing for the foreigners to sit. She wore a different apron than she had when Mia first saw her—a white one with broad black zebra stripes. She pulled a baby rattle out of one of the pockets and began waving it back and forth in front of the baby as she held on to him with the other arm.

There was only one small couch other than the rocking chair, so the three ladies remained standing as Mr. Wang immediately chose the couch. *So much for chivalry.*

The apartment contained one large front room, with a small sitting area on one side and a kitchen with a window open to the parking lot on the other. On the opposite wall were two doors, one open to a tiny bedroom and the other closed, probably leading to a bathroom. In the kitchen was a wooden table, only big enough for two at the most, but Mia didn't see a refrigerator anywhere. The few counters held various food supplies, including a bag of rice that sat next to a hot plate where Tingting placed the kettle to boil. She assumed that the local people probably had no use for an oven, but she did wonder how the woman got by without a refrigerator.

The room was sparsely decorated; one wall held a framed picture of Chairman Mao, and the other a decoration made of an intricately knotted red rope with tassels. A basket beside the door held several pairs of the flimsy slippers like those they had worn at the orphanage.

They all removed their shoes and chose a pair to wear through the living room, Resa and Julie laughing and pointing at the way their too-long American feet hung over the heels of the dainty slippers. Lao Ling waved at the driver to scoot over for Resa and Julie, and she used her foot to push a short, three-legged stool out of the corner and towards Mia.

Wondering how to present the important questions, Mia stayed silent and waited for Resa to broach the subject.

"Mr. Wang, can you please ask Lao Ling what year she was a foster parent to Mia?" Resa gave an encouraging smile as she spoke to the driver but looked at the old woman.

With what seemed like an extraordinary amount of vocabulary, Mr. Wang translated Resa's question to Lao Ling, and then waited as the old woman returned her lengthy answer, her voice shaky with nervousness.

"She says you do not tell the orphanage officials you come here, or she get a lot of trouble. Because she really cared for Mia, she tell you what she can." Everyone nodded in agreement and appreciation to the old woman for her courage.

Mr. Wang continued, "She doesn't know years but say Mia was three or four years old when she come live with Lao Ling and husband. Orphanage boss said she would only keep girl for few days, but it almost a year and then she get adopted by American family. She say Mia very quiet when she came from orphanage, and her eyes carry much sorrow. Lao Ling was told the girl was found in train station when she a baby and lived at different orphanage until she come to Jiangsu to prepare for adoption—but she didn't believe this story because girl cry for parents in sleep, and how she miss them if she abandoned as baby?"

In the pause of translation, everyone turned to Mia—pity in their eyes.

"Please, go on. I need to hear everything she knows," Mia firmly encouraged. She didn't want the heavy emotion in the room to disrupt the woman's memory, and she sure didn't want to be pitied.

The old woman rocked the baby back and forth, thumping his little back as she gave another spurt of information for Mr. Wang to translate to Mia.

"She say you beautiful child, even with chopped-off hair and dark circles under eyes. Everyone watch you because of beauty. Orphanage boss tell Lao Ling keep you indoors and not bring you outside. That made Lao Ling suspicious, but she don't ask questions. She say you easy child to care for. Most days you sit in corner, humming songs. She say you love music and happy when singing."

As the conversation flowed, Tingting sat on a chair in the kitchen, nervously picking at her fingertips as she listened intently. The baby the old woman held began to quiet at the sound of the steady voice in his ear.

Resa cut in. "She knows more. I feel it—she is holding something back. I think she's afraid to share her secrets. Tell her anything she tells us will remain in confidence, and that we want to give her a gift for caring for Mia."

That meant cash would be exchanging hands for the information, but no one cared if it reaped the results Mia longed for.

As Lao Ling processed the message from Resa, translated by Mr. Wang, her nervousness overwhelmed her. Even holding the baby they could see her hands start to tremble. A line of sweat formed on her upper lip and she stood and handed the baby to Tingting, directing her to take him outside for a walk. The *ayi* grudgingly exchanged her slippers for a scruffy pair of sandals and left through the front door, the baby beginning to cry again at being relocated to a new, less comfortable shoulder.

When the door closed behind Tingting and the baby, the old woman took a deep breath and continued her story. Mr. Wang listened intently and turned to Mia.

"Lao Ling hear that a man and woman come to orphanage soon after you come to her home—that they looking for daughter. She don't know if you are daughter, but maybe could be you. Long ago, many children taken from parents who not fit to raise them. If you, then she say your parents maybe criminals or too poor to care for you. She hear orphanage boss refuse to listen to country peasants. But couple stubborn and spend many days and nights outside gate, until one day it only woman, and then weeks later she also leave and never return."

Mia couldn't hold back any longer. "But what if it *was* me they were looking for? Maybe I wasn't abandoned, and I just got separated from them somehow. Didn't anyone care that it might be my parents—that they might be good people whose child was lost? And why can't I remember even being here?" So many questions, and Mia knew it would be a miracle if they were answered to even a fraction of her satisfaction. It was so unfair to be robbed of the information that would help her piece together her early years in China.

Mr. Wang uncomfortably translated Mia's words to the old woman, and then everyone became silent until once again Lao Ling began to speak.

"She say tell you she know someone can maybe help find out if parents look for you. If she do this, it must be secret, or she be in very much trouble." As Mr. Wang translated the message, the woman looked at each face with an expression of seriousness that would tolerate nothing less than complete obedience.

As this was translated, everyone sat up straighter, alert and ready to hear more. Resa immediately opened her purse and removed 1000 yuan—the amount equal to what the woman earned for three months of caring for one foster child—and handed it to Lao Ling with words of gratitude for her compassion for the orphans of China.

The old woman folded the bills and discreetly tucked them in her apron pocket, then continued to give Mr. Wang more information to repeat. "There is man who work as teacher far from here. He collect spit from other Chinese girls to find birth families. She no promise he help, but will ask. He has assistant in this city, she not know names but call them *The Finders*. She tell them you need help. If they decide you safe case to take, they contact you at hotel."

Mia felt a glimmer of hope and rushed over to hug the woman. Unaccustomed to such affection, the older woman blushed and waved her away quickly. She gave her last message to Mr. Wang to convey, "She says maybe not help but is all she can do for you."

The finality of her tone was the sign it was time to leave

her alone. She had already put herself in a risky position, and now she just wanted the foreigners out of her home, as far away as possible. She stood up and went to the window. From her apron pocket she pulled out a pair of old-fashioned eyeglasses, perched them on her nose and peered out over the parking lot. She searched below for a moment, and then yelled at Tingting to bring the baby back in.

With a dismissive wave she said good-bye and herded the ladies towards the door, Mr. Wang following behind, looking exhausted from his temporary job as a translator.

As the group put on their own shoes and shuffled through the doorway, Lao Ling gave one more message to Mr. Wang to convey. "She say at lunch the orphanage boss gave you, she scolded for bringing up memory of keeping you hidden inside. She hope she can trust you to keep quiet, or her family will suffer, and you never find truth."

Resa assured the old woman that no one would breathe a word about their visit or the information she had given them, they all thanked her repeatedly and continued their exit.

CHAPTER TWELVE

MIA stood in front of the full-length mirror, smoothing down the layers of the dress and studying the reflection of the colorfully clad young woman before her. It was so much fun picking out the costume. Jax had taken her to an area of town called Wedding Street. There they explored shop after shop of dresses—wedding gowns, formal gowns, and even traditional Chinese gowns. Jax had explained to her the area was very popular for foreigners and locals alike, as you could get a custom-fit gown at amazingly cheap prices compared to the rest of the world. The best part was that they would alter it as you waited—same-day service!

When she saw the multi-colored garment in the window, she knew it was just right for her to play the part of a dressed-up peasant. It must have been meant to be, because when she slipped it on, it was almost a perfect fit. Only the bottom had to be altered as they waited, for Mia didn't want to be stepping on her hem all night.

Before deciding to go as a peasant, she had wracked her brain to come up with a creative idea for the fundraiser. Jax called it a *P-party*, meaning everyone had to dress as something beginning with a *P*. She wasn't sure what he would show up as, because he said he wanted to surprise her. *I hope he likes my outfit.* She whirled around, admiring the blue and purple swirls of color and the way the chiffon floated around her. The headband of flowers and her low, strappy shoes complemented the outfit and made Mia feel very feminine. She applied her makeup a bit more generously than usual, added a sheer layer of lip gloss and hoop earrings, and was ready to go.

Promptly at seven o'clock, she was waiting outside and had thwarted several inquisitive looks from other hotel patrons by the time the shiny black sedan pulled to the curb and Jax stepped out. He had borrowed a Shiradan driver and car, as if climbing out of a grungy taxi would have taken away from the drama of his costume.

Mia covered her mouth and laughed when she saw how he was dressed. His costume, obviously tailor-made, consisted of knee-length black pants and a white frilly shirt covered by a tattered vest. The sword pushed into his belt and the black leather patch over his eye were the perfect touches needed to transform him into a swaggering—*and sexy!*—pirate. She felt a tingle start in her belly as she studied him from head to toe.

"You look awesome, Jax!"

"Thanks, Mia. You look beautiful—like an exotic flower." He blushed all the way to the tips of his ears. "Sorry, that sounded so cheesy." He opened the car door. "Now get in the carriage, wench." Obviously trying to make up for his previous unmanly comment, he held the door as she climbed in for their ride to the Shiradan.

Both nervously made small talk, and Mia wondered why

it was unusually awkward between them. *Must be the costumes.*

At the Shiradan, Jax escorted her through the entrance and into the midst of an already waiting group of expats standing outside the banquet room.

"They open the doors at seven thirty," a hostess said as she offered them a glass of champagne from her tray. They both accepted, mainly to have something to carry that would hide their awkwardness.

On a table outside the banquet doors, a large poster caught Mia's attention.

"That's Xinxin!" she exclaimed, pointing at the child's face. The picture was almost as touching as seeing her in person, and Mia felt a surge of longing to see the infant.

"Yeah, she's one of the children the club is raising funds to help. I looked at these earlier today when they were setting up. There are at least twenty children pictured tonight, all needing some sort of medical intervention." They strolled beside the table, looking at the individual posters displayed and reading the placards placed in front of them. Mia discovered at least four children who needed cleft palate surgery, and another few waiting on heart operations. One was an older child, named Xiao Li, who balanced on a set of crutches. Her expression was pained but hopeful, causing a ripple of pity in Mia.

It was hard for Mia to fathom that medical care wasn't provided to the destitute. In China, being poor and sick was a deadly combination. It made her sad.

Around them, other guests were arriving quickly, and the costumes were causing a ripple of excitement through the crowd. There were a few princesses, of course, and one looked more like a queen in her regal red velvet outfit and her crown of diamond-studded jewels. Most everyone she saw was a foreigner, with only a few Asian faces interspersed in the crowd. Once again, Mia felt like she stood out too much, and she led Jax to a corner where they could observe the costumes without drawing attention to themselves.

Jax pointed out a man with a ridiculously large box strapped around his middle. "That's Mr. Cotter, the headmaster of the international school. I think he's supposed to be a parcel—the English word for *box*. And if you can't tell, he's from England."

Behind the man, a couple arrived, causing a stir in the crowd. An Asian woman—she looked Korean to Mia—wore a white sheet expertly draped as a toga, her tan skin the perfect complement to the creative gown. She wore golden sandals and stunning jewelry, but the best parts of the costume were her dramatically kohl-lined eyes and her wig, a shoulder-length black mass of curls embedded with short snakes. There was no doubt that her costume was meant to be Medusa, and Mia wondered how that fit the *P profile*.

"She's Medusa. She came as a *partner* to Poseidon, the mythological god," Jax explained, clearing up the confusion. The young woman was so beautiful—no one else in the room could have pulled off the costume like she did. Mia admired the woman's confidence in her heritage and the proud way the tall Caucasian man escorted her through the hall to stand in front of the display of children. They both generously gave to the donation jars, and then moved on to talk to a couple dressed as Pocahontas and the Pied Piper.

Mia giggled to herself to see a policeman escorting a

prostitute, and a pussycat following a prisoner decked out in black-and-white striped pajamas with ankle shackles. *What a creative way to raise funds for charity!* she thought as Peter Pan walked by her, looking uncomfortable and a bit ridiculous in his green tights.

Jax and Mia each took a turn posing for the photographer stationed in front of the banquet room. Jax whispered to him that they needed two photos printed, so that both of them could have a memento of the evening. The photographer promised he would have copies ready for every guest by the time they left the party.

The doors finally opened, and Jax escorted Mia into the banquet room and to the employee table near the stage. The room looked beautiful, the tables covered by fine burgundy cloths with centerpieces of complimentary wine chilling in silver decanters. Extravagant drapes hung around the edges of the room, and low lighting illuminated an intimate dance floor. To one side of the room were four long tables with various items labeled for the silent auction; all were prizes donated from the businesses of the attending guests to raise funds for the needy children. Several of the pieces of donated art caught Mia's eye, but she knew she wouldn't be able to transport any of the items in her luggage, so she moved on.

Jax and Mia sat down, and introduced themselves to the other Shiradan employees already sitting at the table. Robert and his wife, Anthy, were extremely friendly, and Mia immediately felt comfortable. The elegant woman—originally from Indonesia, she told them—entertained Mia with stories of living at the hotel and the characters she had run into over the years. Another couple from Norway joined the group, and it was difficult for Mia to understand their accent, but she did her best to make a good impression and participate in small talk for Jax's benefit.

The room filled quickly, and soon almost two hundred guests were conversing at every table, standing in corners and raising the volume to a frenzied level. Mia spotted Resa and waved to her, and the woman came over with her husband—also dressed as a pirate but not nearly as swashbuckling as Jax.

"Hi, Mia! I didn't know you'd be here." Resa looked completely out of her comfort zone dressed as a pirate's wench, and Mia almost didn't recognize her because of the long black wig she wore.

"Hi, Resa. Wow—you look so different." They talked for a few minutes, confirming their plans to meet on Monday morning, and then Resa excused herself and her hubby to go help with the voting boxes.

The band began to play, and Jax asked her to dance. Mia stood and took his hand, but under her breath she prayed that she wouldn't look like an idiot. Other than her high school prom, she had never before danced at a formal event. Luckily, her dad had insisted when she started high school that a girl needed to learn to dance properly to a slow song—so to the chortles of laughter from her brothers, he had spent hours one Sunday night teaching her. The joke was on them, however, because when her dad felt like she had finally gotten it, he made them take turns leading Mia around the family room. She smiled as she remembered that to pay them back for their orneriness, she had managed to stomp on their toes a few times before they let her go.

Much to her surprise, Jax was an accomplished dancer, and he gracefully led her around the dance floor. Together in their pirate and peasant costumes, they made a striking couple, turning several heads as many of the women wondered who she was.

"Mia, you are the most gorgeous peasant I've ever laid eyes on," he whispered in her ear as he took her for one more twirl around the floor. The feel of his hot breath against her skin sent an electrifying tingle all the way up her spine.

"Aww, you probably say that to all the village girls." Mia smiled over his shoulder, content in his arms. His appreciation for her appearance was much more welcome than that of the obnoxious German businessmen who had been ogling her earlier as she waited outside her hotel. She had pretended she couldn't understand them so that they would move on.

Three slow and one fast dance later, they returned to their seats, and Mia excused herself to the ladies' room.

After a few wrong turns, she found the restroom and entered a stall. A few seconds later, she was adjusting her dress and getting ready to open the locked door when she overhead a whispered conversation going on just a few feet away. "Guess who Sadie said is here? Can you *believe* she came with him? That's the ultimate insult to his wife—she's just rubbing it in his wife's face in front of all her friends that she's his newly appointed Chinese mistress." The woman spoke with an Australian accent. *Or is it British*? Mia couldn't really tell the difference.

Well, I can't walk out there now, thought Mia. *This is awk-*

ward. She sat down on the lid of the toilet to wait them out, hoping they would leave so she could get back to Jax.

"Have you seen her yet?" asked the other woman, obviously wanting to get the total scoop of what the temptress looked like, how old she was, and whatever else she could ferret out.

The second woman is definitely American. Mia fiddled with her purse, impatient for them to leave.

"No, but Sadie said she's really young and pretty—she's dressed as an exotic princess, and *of course* he stuffed himself into a prince costume. She's going to get quite the surprise when she finds out the rich man she thinks she has stolen will go broke paying alimony and child support for his three children. And I hear his company's about to end his assignment and send him home, anyway. Her prince is quickly going to revert back to an average frog. When will these local girls ever learn?" She let out a shrill, catty laugh.

The two sounded like they were going to be there for a while, and Mia remembered seeing a lounging area inside the door. Jax was probably wondering what had happened to her and could come looking, so she decided she couldn't wait any longer for them to finish their gossip fest. She unlatched the door and briskly walked to the sink to wash her hands.

She looked up just in time to see the shocked faces in the reflection behind her, one woman pointing at her and leaning over to whisper to her friend.

Mia tossed her hair back and lifted her chin. "Don't worry—I'm not her. I'm an American, and I don't mess with the husbands around here." She dried her hands and walked out of the bathroom, head held high, and a smirk of indignation on her face. She left them with their mouths hanging open and their cheeks flaming at being caught at their gossip.

At the table, Jax stood as soon as Mia approached. "Everything okay, Mia?"

"Yep. I ran into some interesting company, but nothing worthy of a replay." Mia winked at him and sat down beside him. She had no intentions of spoiling the evening by repeating the episode she'd overheard.

Robert stood and led the way to the dinner buffet as a passing waiter popped the cork on what would likely be the first of many bottles of wine passed around. The group returned to the table, plates piled high with a delicious array of cuisine. Mia and Jax were the first ones to dig in, not letting etiquette get in the way of their rumbling bellies.

An hour later, the president of the Tai Tai Club took center stage and began announcing the silent auction, while the band got ready behind her to crank it up louder. As the winners claimed their prizes, the early-to-bed crowd slowly made their way out of the room, calling good-bye to their rowdier friends staying behind to party late into the night.

By midnight, the conservative elite crowd was transformed to a group of wild partiers. The room was filled with smoke, noise, and bodies, moving to the thump of an invisible but loud bass. Mia had only seen one man so far who'd been so drunk he had to be helped out and to a taxi, leaning on the shoulders of his two buddies as his wife followed. However, she didn't think many others were far behind him.

"Jax, can we get out of here?" Mia shouted into his ear. They had done their share of dancing, mingling, and even participated in the voting of the *P* King and Queen. The stunning Medusa won first place—well deserving the title of queen of the party.

"Absolutely. I thought you'd never ask. Let's go get some coffee." Together they made their way through the crowd and out into the lobby area. At the table of printed photos, they competed to find their photographs. Mia spotted them first and grinned at what a cute couple they made in print. She tucked the photos into her bag and thanked the photographer.

"Don't forget to give me one of those photos, Mia." Jax elbowed her.

"What do you need one for?" she teased. She had every intention of giving him one for a keepsake.

"Um, remember, I told you about Adam? We Skype a few times a week, and he keeps ribbing me about you, calling you my 'phantom girlfriend.' I need the photo to prove you're real."

"Jax, I am not your girlfriend, but you know he's just yanking your chain, right?"

"I know—but I want him to see you, especially on my arm as my date. Then maybe he'll shut his mouth."

As soon as they stepped into the night air, Mia relaxed, and they walked arm and arm down the street to find a taxi. It was late and not many taxis were around, but there were some filthy but engaging children begging Jax to buy a rose for his date. He relented and pulled out one yuan each for the two young girls who should have been home in bed, instead of out earning a living. They both ran off with their coins to look for the next unsuspecting pedestrian. Mia and Jax continued to walk.

A few blocks later, they lucked out as a taxi pulled up

beside them. It was a quiet ride to Starbucks, both of them a bit drowsy from the wine and overwhelmed from the excitement. Mia sat close to Jax, leaning her head back on the arm he draped around her shoulders.

At the coffee shop, they ordered their coffee and found a seat in the dining room. When the girl brought out their order, she smiled but didn't ask why she was serving a pirate and a gypsy. She set the drinks down and walked away, giggling.

"So, Mia, I have something I've wanted to tell you all night but was waiting for a private moment."

"What? Tell me." Once again Mia thought about how she hated surprises and wished he'd come on out with it. She leaned down to blow across the top of her coffee, hoping to cool it down faster.

"This morning someone called my number and said they think you're their daughter." His voice was low and calm.

Mia jumped up so fast, she knocked Jax's coffee cup over. He quickly righted it before too much dribbled out the top, and he grabbed a stack of napkins to soak up the liquid creeping towards his lap.

"Oh, sorry Jax. What did they say? Did you get their name? Where are they from? Why did they abandon me? Why didn't you tell me?!" She punched him in the arm, unable to hide her frustration and curiosity. *Doesn't he realize how big this is?* She had so many questions; she didn't know where to start.

"Whoa there—hold on—they didn't tell me any of that information, and I didn't feel like you'd want me asking that stuff without you. They're going to meet us tomorrow at the Humble Administrators Garden. I told them to wait at the main gate at noon. You do want me to go with you, right?" He looked worried that he may have overstepped his boundaries.

"Of course I want you to come, Jax. Oh—I can't believe this! Is this really happening? Am I really this close to finding my birth parents? Finally—the agony of not knowing might be over." She was so relieved she almost began to cry but stopped herself. She didn't want to show that much weakness in front of Jax.

"Aww… Mia, don't look so sad. This is a *good* thing. You can finally solve this mystery—and who knows, maybe it'll open a whole new chapter in your life."

Mia was silent, allowing the thoughts to swirl around her in her head. Her life would change tomorrow—for the worse or for the better, she didn't know, but at least the truth would be unveiled. She stood and told Jax she was ready to get back to the hotel; she was mentally and physically exhausted. They left the coffee shop, and Jax flagged a taxi.

Minutes later, the car pulled in front of Mia's hotel, and Jax climbed out and held his hand for Mia to take. Just as she put her second foot out of the cab, she tripped, losing one of her shoes in her untimely moment of clumsiness.

Jax grabbed the sandal from between the car and the curb and bent down to slip it back on her foot. "Jeesh, Mia, what are you trying to do? Turn yourself into Cinderella? It's well past midnight, but here's your slipper—now does your prince get a kiss for returning it?"

Mia laughed and quickly kissed Jax on the cheek, thanked him for a wonderful night, and said good-bye. As she looked over her shoulder to give him one final wave before disappearing through the glass doors, she thought she saw disappointment on his face. She wasn't sure if it was because she hadn't invited him in or because she had diverted a possible lip invasion with the quick kiss-on-the-cheek move.

Mia sighed. She wanted their first kiss to be special, with her mind totally on him—not still reeling from the news about meeting her birth parents.

She looked out the window at the perfectly aligned stars and gave a silent thanks—it had been an amazing night with an even more amazing guy.

CHAPTER THIRTEEN

MIA refused to let the gray, overcast sky ruin the day for her. She had waited years to find the truth, and to be honest, she was a little bit peeved at God for allowing this day to be so gloomy. Still, she and Jax were determined to make the most of it, and they sat together on a stone bench outside of the famous garden, watching the many locals and tourists preparing for a day of exploring the famous garden.

Vendors were already loudly hawking their goods, trying to get a jump on competition with each other for bottled water, fans, street food, and postcards. Anyone who knew Suzhou knew *Zhuōzhèng Yuán*, the Humble Administrators Garden, so Jax thought it the best place to meet Mia's birth parents. Jax's friend and spur-of-the-moment translator, Guifeng, stood a short distance behind them to give them privacy as they waited for the couple to arrive.

The couple was almost an hour late, causing Mia to chew her already short nails to the quick. Her foot thumped against the bench sporadically as she searched each new face in the crowd. *Will they look like me? Will I be able to recognize them? Will they cry when they see me? Oh man—I should have brought my birth mother some flowers...*

The anticipation was about to send her over the edge, and she couldn't stop checking her watch. Jax continued to reassure her they'd come—and finally, they looked up to find a couple walking towards them on the sidewalk, the man holding what appeared to be one of Mia's posters and looking around as if he were lost.

"Guifeng, I think that's them. Will you go talk to them and see?" Jax asked his friend.

Guifeng approached the couple and after a few words, the man nodded his head that yes, he was the person who had called. His small wife shuffled along behind him, pulling a small, tattered suitcase. One wheel on the luggage was giving her a hard time, flipping round and round, causing the woman to keep stopping to straighten it out. Mia got the feeling she was using the wayward suitcase as a diversion to avoid eye contact. *She must be shy. I sure didn't inherit that from her. I've never been called timid.*

The woman was thin, with stringy hair cut at shoulder length and curled up at the ends from the humid weather. Judging by her dusty clothes and ragged shoes—and her husband's equally drab outfit and untrimmed hair—they had to be a very poor family. Mia didn't care about that; she just wanted to know them and get an explanation of exactly why they couldn't raise her.

Guifeng led the couple over to Mia and Jax, and then beckoned for everyone to follow him to a picnic area just inside the garden gates. A huge ancient tree provided a canopy over the table, an added convenience in case the weather turned nasty.

"*Zuo xia.*" He gestured for them to sit down, while he remained standing at the end of the table.

Everyone awkwardly sat and quietly looked around at each other. Sitting straight across from the people who claimed to have given her life, Mia took her time to examine them closer. They didn't appear very emotional, and that puzzled her. If they cared enough to come forward, she would think they would be feeling something at the reunion of a long lost daughter. But in Chinese culture, it wasn't common to publicly display emotion, so that could make sense.

She searched the woman's features to see if any mirrored her own but couldn't find anything even remotely similar to hers. She wished she shared the high cheekbones of the woman; they gave her a very elegant profile. She wanted to find a resemblance, but even their skin color was different. Mia was a darker brown, compared to the lighter tone on the woman. Where Mia had long, graceful fingers, the woman's were short and stubby. As for the man, she felt a moment of guilt that she was glad she didn't share any of his harsh, unattractive features.

Jax nudged Mia. "How do you want to start this, Mia? You have the floor. I'm here strictly for emotional support. This is your moment."

"Please tell them thank you for calling," Mia started. "I want to know their names, and ask them why now, after all these years, they have decided to come forward."

Guifeng quickly translated her words to the couple and gave them time to respond. The woman started to speak, but the man put his hand up to silence her. He removed the dangling cigarette from his lips and gave his somber answer to the young man.

"His name is Bowei, and his wife is Shui. He says they searched for you for years after you were lost in the train station. He claims your mother put you down for only a moment, and someone must have picked you up, for when she returned, you were gone. He wants to know if you live in America and if you have a rich family?" At the sudden blame thrown on her for losing the girl, the woman lowered her eyes and stared only at the top of the stone table.

Well, this isn't the joyful reunion I've imagined for years, Mia thought to herself. She had hoped for embraces and tears—apologies for the pain their irresponsibility caused her, or explanations that would absolve them of guilt. Yet this felt more like a job interview than a child meeting her parents. She didn't feel any sort of connection to the people, and it puzzled her that they didn't show any urge to touch her or to celebrate in finally finding her. It was too weird.

"Yes, tell him I live in America. Then ask them where and when I was born, and if they have any photos or valid birth documents." Not that Mia could verify their answers, but she felt it important that she note her real birth date and hometown. As Guifeng spoke to the man, Jax rubbed her hands to warm them. It had started to rain lightly, and though the tree kept them from getting wet, Mia felt chilled and was starting to tremble. Other tourists and vendors around them were quickly pulling on raincoats and disposable slickers and bringing out their umbrellas.

"Mia, what do you think?" Jax whispered. "Do you get a good feeling from them? They look kinda sketchy—is there any way for them to prove they're your birth parents?"

"I don't know, Jax. Maybe they're just nervous to meet me. I don't remember them, but that's not unusual. I don't remember anything from my time in China."

Guifeng turned to them again. "He says you were born in Wuxi in 1990, but their documents are at home. He wants to know if you have any money he can use to get a hotel room for him and his wife, that they have traveled a long way and are very tired."

What? That doesn't make sense. Mia scratched her head in confusion. She wasn't responsible for their travel to Suzhou—they had obviously already been there when they saw the poster. Why would he ask her for money like that? She *had* been born in 1990, but that was listed on the poster so wasn't a new revelation.

At the mention of money, Bowei's wife beckoned for him to follow her to a spot just outside of earshot and began talking to him, her face a mask of anger. They argued for a few moments, and Bowei returned, his wife following behind, her cheeks flushed red.

"It's okay." Mia felt sorry for the woman and formed a sudden unexplainable dislike for the man who claimed to be her father. His face was set in a stern grimace, and he wouldn't even look at his wife again, despite her pulling on his sleeve for his attention. He continued to puff on his cigarette while staring across the table at Mia, inconsiderate of the smoke that wafted around her head, making her eyes water. "Ask him why they were at the train station the day I got lost."

Guifeng asked the question, and they waited for a response.

Bowei took his time, taking a final drag on his brown cigarette before rudely flicking it onto the sidewalk, just as an elderly couple strolled by. The old man gave Bowei a scathing look for his rudeness, but he was oblivious to the silent scolding. Shui kept her eyes downcast, her hands gripped around the handle of the suitcase propped at her feet.

Bowei stared straight at Mia while he answered, "We were coming to town to buy supplies for our business. We sell almond tea, and the farmers around us were starting to charge too much for the almonds we grind with the raw rice. I thought we could get a better price at the market here. That's why we are here today, but we are low on funds because I had to use more money than usual to get here."

He turned to look at his wife sitting beside him, her head hung low. "She was sick, so we paid for a soft sleeper ticket to allow her to rest comfortably on the train. I hope you can help us get a hotel room for a night so she can recover for the trip back. I have used up the rest of our money for almonds." He gestured to the suitcase that held his supplies.

"Mia, don't give them any money," Jax warned.

"Don't worry, Jax, before I give them anything, I want to see if they'll agree to a blood test. But first I have a major question for them that they should know the answer to if they're really my birth parents."

A flash of lightning lit the sky, followed by a loud rumble of thunder. Suddenly the sky around them darkened, and Mia scooted closer to Jax. She wasn't afraid of much, but lightning storms had always frightened her.

"Guifeng, we've gotta find shelter, but first—I have an

important question for them. Ask them if I was born with any type of disability, disease, or birthmark."

"What? Were you?" Jax leaned over and asked her, his voice low so that they wouldn't hear. "Not that it matters to me—but you look perfect as far as I can tell."

"Just wait. Let's hear what they say." Mia sat back and waited for her question to be translated.

When Guifeng finished speaking, the couple looked at each other, each seeming to wait for the other to reply. They looked back at Mia, studying her every feature and even looking at each of her limbs. Finally, Bowei answered. "No. You were born faultless, except that you are a girl."

Mia's heart fell; they weren't her birth parents. They were imposters—criminals seizing on a way to make some quick money. As she lifted her eyes accusingly to those of the woman, she saw her flinch with shame. Shui knew they'd been discovered. She could see it in Mia's face.

"*Dui bu qi.*" She muttered an apology to Mia, but the tardy words were lost in the sudden onslaught of heavy rain that even the dense tree branches and canopy of leaves couldn't hold back. Bowei turned to his wife and began berating her in their foreign dialect, while Jax jumped to his feet and opened the umbrella over Mia. All around them people ran for shelter, afraid of the series of lightning strikes that were hitting too close for comfort. Every covered area and overhang was suddenly packed with people, squeezing together to avoid the rain pouring down around them.

Jax fumbled with the small umbrella to cover both of them. Mia was quickly soaked, and lightning was striking all around them.

Guifeng didn't wait for further instructions; with arms up in an attempt to cover his head, he ran to one of the pagodas to cram in with the cluster of tourists competing for shelter.

"Let's go, Jax. These aren't my birth parents. They don't know me." She was relieved that the rain disguised the tears on her face.

Jax looked at the man standing across from them, his face set in a defiant scowl. Jax looked ready to tear him to pieces. "Well, you know what? Maybe I ought to kick your scruffy—"

"No, Jax. He isn't worth it. Come on. We need to go. I'm getting soaked." Mia pulled on Jax, breaking him away from the steely glare he was shooting at Bowei.

Jax didn't say anything else. He put his arm protectively around her and quickly led her towards the taxi line. Mia didn't spare the man and woman even a farewell wave. They deserved nothing for their charade.

Mia and Jax hopped over an already gigantic mud puddle and climbed into a cab. With one last look at the bedraggled couple—quickly becoming soaked without the protection of rain gear or an umbrella—Mia turned her head and shut her eyes. She felt a sudden burst of pity for the pathetic woman. She was obviously an unwilling accomplice in the man's scheme to con her. *Just another dead end*, she thought as the driver sped away from the busy park and the people who had added one more bad memory to her story of abandonment.

Mia felt hopeless. She was almost at the end of her savings, and so far, other than the truth about being fostered, she had learned little. She had probably hurt her parents for insisting on the adventure, she was behind in her class assignments, and she was finally feeling like she had made a mistake in coming to China. Her only comfort was Jax's warm arm around her shoulders as she held her tears back all the way back to her hotel.

CHAPTER FOURTEEN

MIA awoke the next morning with a pounding headache, but since she didn't want to miss the trip to take Xinxin to Shanghai, she took two aspirin, drank an entire bottle of water, and jumped in the shower. As the hot water soothed her aching body, she thought about the call to her parents from the night before. She had told them about the phony couple, and her father was outraged they had tried to take advantage of her that way. He felt they should have been arrested at the least, and he had to rein in his fatherly instinct to go after them and knock some heads together.

Her mom was very worried and told Mia she wanted her to come home early—*right now* was her exact request, if Mia remembered correctly. As usual, her father was able to stand strong and insist that their daughter was responsible enough to keep herself safe. He understood that the search was very important to her and she couldn't walk away not knowing what had happened with her birth parents or why she had been abandoned. She only had one more option, but she worried that perhaps *The Finders* wouldn't want to help her, would think she was too risky, or would be unable to help her. Mia was running out of time. The previous day's episode with the couple was a low moment for her, but it was a new day, and she was determined to go forward with an optimistic attitude.

Still wrapped in a towel to cool down from the steaming shower, she took a few minutes to check her e-mail and wasn't surprised to find yet another message from Collin. He just wouldn't give up, and Mia was determined to remain stubborn. She wasn't even going to give him the satisfaction of opening the messages. *Let him suffer like I did when I found out the way he was talking about me to his frat buddies.* He had broken her heart, all so he could act like the big guy on campus and brag about having an Asian girlfriend. That alone would have been insulting but bearable, but when she had read his Facebook wall and saw the remarks about sharing her all around, that was the last straw. She wasn't going to take any more racist comments, and she sure wasn't going to allow another man to call her his little China Doll ever again.

In grade school, she had to deal with the *ching-chong* chanting and kids making squinty eyes at her, but since high school she had put up with bigoted idiots and repeatedly had her heritage thrown in her face with sexual innuendo and insults. She had hoped that when she reached college, the students would be mature enough to treat her like everyone else and not brand her because of her Asian features, so Collin's betrayal had really hurt.

She was done with dating—finished trying to find someone who liked her for what was inside instead of on the outside. Going forward, she planned to buckle down and finish school without letting her social life interfere. As for Jax, she really liked him a lot—*Maybe too much*—but she had to face that it would soon be over when she returned to the States and her regular life.

She finished reading through her e-mail and quickly dressed, packed a few snacks in her bag along with a bottle of water, and headed down to the front of the hotel to wait for Resa to pick her up. She was ready to take on the day. A good night's sleep had given her back her resolve that being there wasn't a mistake, and she told herself not to give up so easily.

The van soon arrived, and the door opened to find Resa in one seat and a Chinese woman sitting next to her holding Xinxin. Mia climbed to the backseat and settled next to another young lady she hadn't met before.

"Mia, this is the *ayi* the orphanage sent to care for Xinxin on the way to the hospital," Resa explained. "We really didn't need her, but I guess they wanted some sort of representation. And beside you is Gigi, one of our group translators. She accompanies us when we embark on complicated endeavors, as my Chinese skills are only what I consider 'Survival Mandarin.'"

Gigi smiled and held out her hand to Mia to shake. "I am originally Shanghainese, but I lived in Texas for over ten years, until last year when we came back to China." Her English was impeccable and Mia instantly liked her easygoing manner. Unusual for a Chinese woman, Gigi wore her hair in curls, wildly framing her face. In her white linen pants and the oversized Chanel sunglasses propped on her head, she made quite the fashion statement.

"The *ayi* has never ridden in a car or van," Gigi whispered. "She has been in a large bus, but she usually gets around on a bicycle. So she is a bit nervous."

Mia glanced at the *ayi*, who was more than a bit nervous—terrified was more like it. Mia felt sorry for the *ayi* as she whipped her head back and forth to locate the cars and trucks weaving around the van, each horn blare making her jerk in fear. On her lap was tiny Xinxin, dressed in multiple layers as if she were going on a winter hike through the mountains, instead of facing the unusually warm spring day forecasted.

"Why is Xinxin so bundled up?" Mia asked, worried about the little girl, whose hairline was already damp with sweat. "And shouldn't she be in a safety seat?"

Resa nodded her head, "Yes, she should be in a safety seat, but they aren't common here in China. I wish I had one. I've actually asked a new family who is moving here from the States to bring one for me to use, but I wasn't expecting to need it so soon. As for the extra clothing, they believe that sick children should be bundled in layers for any kind of weather." She took a moment to remind Mr. Wang to drive very carefully with the child in the car. He nodded his agreement in the mirror and opened the window on the passenger side to allow some air to flow through.

Mia pulled her water bottle out of her bag and offered it to the *ayi*, but it was declined; Resa had already given her one, which sat propped untouched in the drink holder attached to the bucket seat. Mr. Wang kept switching from watching the highway to peeking in the mirror to see what was happening behind him with the foreign ladies and the latest orphan child. Mia wished he would keep his eyes on the road but knew it was a lost cause to remind him, so she said a prayer that he'd keep the van under control.

As the vehicles on the highway moved around them too quickly and recklessly, Mia worried for the safety of the child propped in the *ayis* lap. Soon they were nearly to the toll gates separating Suzhou from the Shanghai highway. They all settled back to wait patiently as Mr. Wang raced to the shortest line.

Sitting in line at the toll crossing, Mia was amused to see a caravan of three vehicles pulled to the side of the highway. Surrounding the cars appeared to be a family, including grandparents down to the smallest child toddling around. The family looked like they were all in an uproar because one of their chickens had flown the coop—*Well, flown out of the back of the van, at least.*

Two men and one woman chased the chicken round and round the cars, trying to surround it for someone to reach in and grab it. Even the elderly woman got into the action, swatting at the chicken with her purse as it ran by her, flapping its wings and squawking for freedom. A little boy and the toddler girl shrieked with laughter at what they thought was some sort of game as their elders raced around frantically.

"I hope that chicken gets away." Mia pointed out the window to the fiasco, just as one of the men left leaning against a vehicle and smoking a cigarette to join the chase.

Gigi laughed with her. "That's probably their dinner. They aren't going to let it get away."

They all continued watching as Mr. Wang inched along towards the ticket taker, and they cheered when the chicken hopped the guardrail and disappeared down the embankment and into the grove of trees on the other side. Everyone abruptly stopped running around, defeat showing in the slump of their bodies as they climbed back into their cars to continue their trek without the escaped bird.

Mr. Wang took his toll ticket from the somber young woman at the toll window, and they were on their way again.

"So where do they find these *ayi*s?" Mia asked. Now through the toll gates, they were well on their way to Shanghai, and the *ayi* nervously watched the traffic around her as she bounced little Xinxin on her knees. The *ayi* was darker than most of the people Mia had seen in Suzhou, and she wondered where the woman came from. She thought the *ayi* looked about twenty or thirty, but it was hard to tell because of the sun damage to her face. Dressed simply in dark pants and a dark shirt, she didn't appear familiar with Xinxin, so Mia doubted she was a regular *ayi* at the orphanage.

Gigi took the opportunity to speak to the *ayi* and ask her a few questions. They talked back and forth for a few moments, and then Gigi turned to Mia.

"She is from the countryside and usually farms the land with her husband. Crops were bad last year, so when she heard she could get work at the orphanage, she put her name in. They called and asked her to do this short assignment," Gigi explained. She went on to tell them that the woman had never had any children of her own, but she had helped others in her small town to deliver babies and sometimes took care of the children when their mothers needed her.

Mia wondered if the woman had been a witness or even a party to infanticide in the villages, but she wouldn't dare offend her by asking the question, no matter how much it burned in her mind.

Xinxin started to fuss a bit, and the *ayi* pulled a bottle from the bag at her feet. She leaned Xinxin back on her arm and began to feed her the lumpy concoction, but Xinxin struggled from the exertion needed to successfully pull it through the nipple. Her tiny dots of sweat became large beads, and Resa finally interrupted.

"Gigi, tell the *ayi* I insist she take that sweater off Xinxin, that to get too hot is dangerous for a little heart patient." Xinxin's cheeks were scarlet with exertion.

The *ayi* argued with Gigi, but Resa reached over and began pulling the sweater off the little girl. Evidently unaccustomed to being around foreigners—especially insistent ones like Resa—the *ayi* gave in and helped to strip the layer of extra clothing off Xinxin.

Once relieved of some of the clothing, Xinxin settled down and fell asleep, with half the milk still remaining in the bottle. Mia felt sad the child was too sick to continue the efforts to appease her obvious hunger. She reached out and gently massaged the tiny fingers that dangled over the seat, just within her reach. She hoped her message of hope traveled all the way up Xinxin's arm and to her battered heart. *Hold on, Xinxin. Hold on.*

ᴄᴙ

Mr. Wang pulled in to the parking lot at the hospital and followed the drive lined with flowerpots to the front entrance drop-off. Mia almost hated to arrive—halfway to Shanghai, she had finally convinced the *ayi* to allow her to hold Xinxin, and the baby girl was sound asleep, snuggled on her lap. The total innocence of the child and the severity of her health issue gave Mia a heavy heart, and she wished she could sneak little Xinxin out of the country and keep her as her own. *Perhaps it wouldn't work out in a college dorm room*, she mused, *but knowing Mom, this child would have a family in a minute if it were allowed.*

Xinxin didn't even fuss when she was rudely awakened to be handed over to the waiting *ayi*. She simply opened her eyes and looked around curiously, helpless to voice a choice in any decisions to improve her prognosis. She was especially interested in the men lined up against the hospital wall and the plumes of cigarette smoke wafting over their heads. The men silently watched the ladies climb out of the van and make their way to the door. Unlike what their female counterparts would have done, they kept their curious questions to themselves.

Resa and Gigi, obviously very familiar with the protocol and layout of the hospital, led the group through the doors and to the large open area. To Mia, the facility resembled the inside of a busy train station more than a medical center, with the benches placed around the room and the many windows in which the transactions, appointments, and other tasks were done. Parents and children roamed about everywhere, and the first thing Mia noticed was most babies and toddlers were overdressed in the warm spring air, proving to her it wasn't just country folk that believed the custom of suffocating a sickness away. The children toddling around the room or being held by their parents were too hot, their scarlet cheeks sure signs of their discomfort.

Gigi and Resa talked to a young woman at a small window to request a consultation, as Mia, the *ayi*, and Xinxin waited on a small bench in the open waiting area. Xinxin's medical folder was examined, calls were made, and the two ladies were directed to another window further down the hall. At that window, they were given a piece of paper to indicate which doctor they would see and what the consultation fee would be. With validation in hand, they moved to a third window to hand over the required cash. With their receipt as proof of following the correct procedures, they returned and herded everyone up to the fifth floor to await the heart doctor to examine Xinxin.

Mia thought the first floor contained a lot of people and was instantly overwhelmed at the amount of parents, grandparents, and children in the heart department waiting area. It was total chaos, and at first they couldn't find a place to sit in the crowded room. Entire families were huddled on benches and even spread out on the floor in the three corners. Young children toddled around, their brown bottoms poking out from their split pants.

A nurse or receptionist—Mia couldn't tell—saw them searching for an empty corner and barked out orders for a family to tighten up. A fussy grandmotherly woman bustled around, picking up her large assortment of bags, snacks, and empty drink containers to allow a small but sufficient area for the group to sit.

They sat down. The *ayi* inexplicably handed the baby to Mia and then began pouring water into a bottle of milk powder. She shook the mixture to blend it then gestured for Mia to hand the child back to her. Xinxin fussed at the constant motion but settled down as soon as the nipple touched her lips. Mia got the impression the country woman was embarrassed to be sitting with foreigners, as she kept her head down to avoid eye contact with the many curious people who were chattering and speculating about Xinxin and her entourage.

"Looks like we may be here awhile," Resa muttered. "We should have stopped for an early lunch before coming in. As soon as we leave here, we'll go across the street to a restaurant for some fried rice."

"It's okay. At least we'll have a chance to talk. I have a lot of questions, and you might be the best person to answer them." Mia settled her bag between her feet, uneasy to let it sit on the filthy floor, but unwilling to hold it for a lengthy time.

"What do you want to know? If I don't know, Gigi can probably help us out," Resa replied just as a couple walked through, the father holding a fat, red-faced baby while the mother pushed along an IV pole to keep it close to the line attached to her child's head.

"Since you've worked at the orphanage for a few years, you probably know more accurate answers than I can find online. Believe me—I've studied the subject of orphans for a long time—but I find such confusing information. In my case, I was abandoned at a train station, but without a note or any type of explanation. I can't imagine a parent not wanting to explain such a desperate action. If it were me, I'd want my child to know why I couldn't keep them. Were any of the children you work with found with notes?" Mia reached into her bag and pulled out a tissue and handed it to the *ayi* to wipe away the sweat from Xinxin's brow, collected there from her struggle to drink her milk through the nipple. *I wonder why she doesn't cut a bigger hole in the nipple. Even with no baby experience, I can figure out that much.*

"Well, Mia, like you, I hear many stories, and I really don't have a way to determine the truth from rumors. However, Gigi sponsors Xiao Li at the orphanage, and probably because she is Chinese, she was allowed to view the girl's file and read a note that was found with her. Gigi, will you tell her what you saw?"

"First, what do you mean by *sponsor*?" Mia asked. She was intrigued by the idea of mentoring an orphan child, and she reached over to stroke Xinxin's leg.

"The orphanage has a program to bring in extra funds, and it entails sponsoring their children. For a monthly fee, if you live locally, you can choose a child and help with the costs for their rearing. As a sponsor, you can also have the children to your home for holiday visits and take them out on excursions. On Chinese New Year, the sponsor brings gifts for their child. Most of the sponsorships are by expatriate Asian residents, the rich Koreans and Japanese from the local women's clubs. Recently though, they've allowed a few volunteers from my group to sponsor some of the children, and Gigi chose Xiao Li."

Gigi explained, "Xiao Li is nine years old and has osteogenesis imperfecta— brittle bone disease. On her first day of school last year, she broke her leg. She recovered and went back to school, just to break the other one a few months later! Now she isn't allowed to leave the orphanage and has to take her studies there."

"Oh—I think I saw her picture at the fundraiser Saturday

night! That's so sad for her." Mia couldn't believe the extent of some of the children's problems, and that they had to deal with so much pain.

Gigi shook her head in dismay. "When I arrived at the director's office to sign the sponsorship papers, she allowed me to look at Xiao Li's file. She was also found at a train station, but she had a letter pinned to her shirt. The note was very tragic—it was written by her mother and explained that because of their financial situation, her husband had committed suicide. She went on to say she couldn't afford to help her daughter, so she was going to follow in his footsteps." Mia could hear the compassion in Gigi's voice for Xiao Li's mother.

"Xiao Li is quite a character," Resa cut in. "Last December, we had a party during the Christmas season to acknowledge the foster parents and children they cared for. Xiao Li had just had surgery a few weeks before to have rods inserted into her legs for support, and she was recovering in a foster home. I didn't want her to miss the party, so I insisted they bring her. The social worker tried to convince me it wasn't possible, but I was adamant. The day of the party, I was in the classroom when I heard a commotion in the courtyard. I looked up just as four *ayis* were carrying Xiao Li—or trying to maneuver her, I should say—through the door, body cast and all. Xiao Li was giggling and waving at me, happy to see all her friends and get gifts like everyone else."

Gigi laughed with Resa and added, "They didn't tell us she was in a body cast or we wouldn't have insisted. It was sort of lost in translation. We have no idea how they got her in a vehicle to bring her over, but we hope they didn't lay her in the bed of a truck!"

"That *is* funny—and I'm glad she got to attend the party. It sounds like she was happy to be there." Mia said. "What about the rumors that finding places are sometimes invented for the benefit of adoptive parents who wish to have a remnant of their child's history?"

"According to what I've read on blogs, news articles, and adoption forums, many people believe the orphanage administration fabricate finding places," Resa answered quietly, hesitant to participate in spreading a rumor that could potentially cause trouble for her as a volunteer.

"But why would they have to make it up? Why not tell the truth?" Mia asked. As she waited for an answer, an elderly woman approached her with a baby over her shoulder, bellowing to ask what a foreigner was doing with a Chinese child. They ignored the woman, and she moved away, still staring at them as she retreated.

Resa looked at Gigi, prompting her to give her input. "It is also rumored throughout China that out of the thousands of children reported missing each year, some of them were abducted and taken to orphanages. Each child is worth a finding fee, based on age and gender—and healthy children are worth more. In those cases, they would have to create a story about the child being found."

Mia had heard snippets of this sort of crime, but so far she had never heard it from a trusted or proven source. "That's terrible. Do you think that really happens that way sometimes?" She looked at Resa for an answer.

Resa hesitated, expression conflicted. "Yes. I do."

The nurse announce Xinxin's name, and Gigi stood quickly. They gathered their belongings and followed the nurse to a small examining room. She mumbled a few words and then left them alone again.

"The doctor will be here shortly," Gigi explained, as she dropped the folder of records on the counter and gestured for the *ayi* to sit in the only seat. The woman gladly took the chair and perched Xinxin on her knees, allowing the little girl to look curiously around at her new environment.

Mia also looked around the room, dismayed at the condition of the walls and the cold metal examination table. *Isn't the Shanghai Children's Hospital rumored to be one of the best in the area? Perhaps all of their money goes to pay for high caliber physicians and medical staff*—at least, she hoped that was the case.

They waited for another half hour before the doctor arrived. As soon as he walked through the door, he reminded Mia of Jerry Lewis in his nutty professor routine—complete with thick glasses, a wrinkled white lab coat and bowl haircut, nonchalantly flipping through Xinxin's short medical file.

Through Gigi's translations skills, Resa explained to the doctor she wasn't even sure what heart disease Xinxin was afflicted with, but she knew her condition was too serious for the baby to be at the orphanage. She asked for a complete examination and a recommendation as to what the medical plan for the child should be. She reminded Gigi to tell him that the volunteer group would be covering the medical costs—so money would not be a problem.

The doctor listened to Xinxin's heart and took vital signs. Then he turned to Gigi and explained that to give a complete assessment, Xinxin would have to be admitted and he didn't have any available beds at this time.

"What? No available beds in a hospital this big? Something doesn't sound completely right." Resa looked towards Gigi, her eyebrows raised.

"First of all, we'd need to get permission from the director to leave her here." Gigi reminded Resa. "And then we'd need to see if this *ayi* will stay with her. Don't forget every patient has to have a full-time caretaker with them. Then if we can arrange that, you know we'll have to pay a deposit to the hospital to cover upcoming charges."

"Yes, I know all that. Tell the doctor if he can find an empty bed, there will be a bonus for him. While he is *looking* for space, we'll call the director and get permission. This is what Xinxin needs, so we can find out what it will take to correct her heart issue and move on to the next stage, which we hope is surgery."

The doctor disappeared, and Gigi called the orphanage. The director balked at leaving the child, but as Gigi relayed all the responses to Resa, she refused to back down. The director finally gave permission, and Gigi hung up and began the process of explaining to the *ayi* what was needed from her. They offered her fifty yuan a day for her services—a fortune for a woman from the countryside, and she quickly agreed to stay. They all settled around the room to await the doctor and his hunt for an available bed.

Xinxin again became the focus of the group, and she entertained everyone with her sweet attitude and abundant smiles all around. Mia felt her heart melting as the baby girl reached for her finger, holding it tight as she gazed in her eyes.

"How do you avoid getting attached to the kids you advocate?" she asked Resa.

"I don't. I care about all of them, but I broke my own rule and became overly attached to a few. In my first few months at the orphanage, I fell head over heels with a tiny little boy who was only a few months old and quite sickly. I called him Squirt, and I was determined to help him gain weight to survive. Each day I came in and coached him through the feeding time, and he came to know my voice. If he'd hear me in the room elsewhere, he'd move his head all around trying to find me until I came to him and held him. The *ayi*s began handing him to me while telling me it was 'my baby.' I thought he was improving, but one day I came in and he was gone—his crib empty and his mat rolled up. I was devastated, and it took me a long time to get over it. I learned a valuable lesson that I'm still trying to follow: Expect the worst, but celebrate the accomplishments. I have to go into each case reminding myself it might be their fate to only live a few months or years on earth." Resa closed her eyes, pushing back tears.

"That's so sad. I could never do what you do, because I'd want to bring them all home," Mia said.

"That's a sentiment I often hear, Mia. To be honest, sometimes those words get under my skin. Of course you would do what I do—because you wouldn't let the opportunity to make a small difference in the life of a child go by. Right? And yes, I do want to bring them all home. I've thought about adopting many times. But I know that if I adopted one of the children I've met, then I'd spend most of my time focusing on that child. There wouldn't be enough of me to give the kind of time and energy I do now to the many more children who need me."

"I completely understand. And yes—you're right. If I had the chance to work with these children every day, I would. No matter the toll it would take on me personally," Mia responded.

The doctor returned, and Resa took the opportunity to hand him a wad of bills, folded to hide the amount. At this stage in the child's severe condition, money was no object to get Xinxin the care she needed. With that exchange completed, he then informed them he had found an empty bed, and Xinxin could be admitted. He also told them she was scheduled for a thorough exam in three days. They thanked him and followed the nurse to her station for the proper paperwork.

Mia was fascinated at the way things worked in the Chinese hospital compared to what she had always experienced at home. She followed along, observing every transaction.

At the admitting window, Resa received the slip stating that she needed to pay the hospital a deposit of two thousand yuan. She and Gigi moved down to the payment window, paid the deposit, and beckoned for Mia and the *ayi* to follow them back up to the heart floor.

At the nursing station, Mia was captivated by the old-fashioned nursing uniforms, consisting of stark white dresses and vintage nurse caps. *Where did they even find those anymore?* she wondered as she fought to keep a grin from erupting. She felt like she was dropped into the year of 1950 as the young nurses bustled around to help the foreigners.

Resa presented the stamped receipts, and they were shown to the room where Xinxin and the *ayi* would be staying for the next week or so. The room contained three normal adult-sized beds, fitted with tall metal sides that could be pulled up. The white sheets on the bed might have been fresh, but it was too hard to tell because of the multitude of stains. Two of the beds were already occupied by children, with family members scattered throughout the room. Someone had rigged a clothesline across the sill in front of the window, and colorful washcloths and clothing added the only color to the dismal room. Various dishpans, food containers, and other items littered the sill under the line of drying laundry.

"Where will the *ayi* sleep?" she asked, looking around the room for a chair or cot. One older woman misunderstood and beckoned to her to take the lone chair in the room.

"She'll have to squeeze in with Xinxin," Resa informed her as she motioned for Gigi to accompany her out the door. Mia wondered what would happen if Xinxin had surgery. *Surely no one could sleep with her while she was recovering from a painful operation—could they?*

While Mia stayed behind with the *ayi* to entertain Xinxin, Resa and Gigi went down to the mini market on the first floor. When they returned, Mia helped them unpack the bag of supplies. In the tiny cabinet beside the hospital bed, they crammed a few bottles and a can of high quality milk formula to help fatten up their little patient. They also managed to squeeze in the diapers, washcloths, a dishpan, soap, and shampoo. They had even found a plastic toy mobile to hang over the bed to entertain Xinxin. Resa also bought several bowls of instant noodles and some cookies for the *ayi*. They left her a bit of money to buy bottled water and provisions from the food cart for the next few days and wrote down their cell phone numbers.

By then, they had been at the hospital for close to five hours, and everyone was tired, hungry, and sad to leave Xinxin behind. Mia squeezed her tiny hand and quickly left the room before she could get emotional. With one last wave, Resa and Gigi joined her, and they made their way back down to the parking lot to find Mr. Wang.

On the way home, Mia asked Gigi how she had gotten involved in volunteer work in China, and the girl entertained her with stories from her childhood in Shanghai. Her family had seen hardship but was blessed by success later in life. Gigi had met her husband while away at college, and together they had built a flourishing life. After several years of living in the United States, she was glad to return to China and felt it was her duty to help those in her country less fortunate than she was, those who had not found a way out of poverty.

"Gigi is a godsend. Besides her unlimited compassion and her sense of humor, her knowledge of this mysterious culture and her bilingual skills make her one of our most valuable assets to the team."

"Since you grew up in Shanghai, have you heard of the Shanghai Mei Street Children Protection Education Centre?" Mia asked Gigi.

"Oh, yes—though it's fairly new, I think maybe just a few years old. Just recently these types of places have been opening in different provinces. It wasn't there when I was young, but I've heard about it in the last year. It is the government's attempt to make an effort to help the thousands of children who are abducted each year—at least the ones who are found on the streets begging. They can't do much about the children who are sold to childless families; they are harder to find."

"Do you think those places really help the children?" The centers fascinated Mia.

"I believe it's a safer place than the streets, but they have a reputation for only doing what they have to do to meet the minimum standards set by the Minister of Civil Affairs. Originally the intent was to offer counseling and educational services, especially to teach the children Mandarin so they'll have a chance to do something with their futures. But China doesn't want to spend the money it will take to put the resources in place. Not much of an effort is made to take the children back to the provinces they came from, and some don't even know or remember their hometown anyway. Many are never reunited with their families."

"I have to see this place. Jax is supposed to be working on getting permission for us to visit," Mia said.

"I will also see what I can find out about visitors, if you like," Gigi offered.

"That would be great, Gigi. Thank you." Mia didn't know what she could do to help, but she was definitely interested in learning more about the centers. She leaned back against her headrest, suddenly exhausted from the long day and all the new experiences she had encountered. She spent the rest of the ride back to Suzhou daydreaming and quietly contemplating the strange country that had once been her own, albeit briefly.

CHAPTER FIFTEEN

MIA had been in China for two weeks, and she couldn't believe how fast the time had gone by. Even so, she had visited the orphanage a few more times but still hadn't been able to secure a meeting with the director. Xiao Jo seemed to have fallen off the face of the earth and wasn't even answering e-mails. To stay busy, she and Jax spent most every afternoon together, exploring Suzhou and getting to know each other.

A few days before, he had introduced her to the famous Tiger Hill—a site with over twenty-five hundred years of history that Jax insisted she had to see before leaving China. He told her that a famous king was buried there along with thousands of swords from his collection, and legend had it that a few days after his burial, a white tiger appeared to guard his tomb, hence the name Tiger Hill. Mia was glad they went, as the park was stunning. The area around the famous hill was groomed close to perfection and contained some of the most beautiful designs of rock gardens and horticulture she had ever seen. Like everyone around them, Jax insisted they take their pictures in front of the leaning pagoda, a seven-story tower that leaned north at a precarious angle.

Later they traveled to Jin Ji Hu, the lake on the east side of the city. It was a great day, and after devouring a picnic lunch, Jax even taught Mia how to fly a kite—something Mia judged to be a passion of the Chinese, from the competitiveness of those around them trying to get their kite to the highest elevation.

Finally Jax and Mia had enough, and they stopped to relax on their blanket in the grass, staring up at the sky dotted with hundreds of colorful kites of every shape and size. It was the best moment of the day, quiet and peaceful, just enjoying the increasing camaraderie they had discovered between them.

"Mia, you didn't tell me how it went at the hospital. I wasn't going to ask until you offered, but how was it?" Jax reached over and grabbed her hand.

"Well, it was sad. I didn't want to bring it up because I am always giving you depressing reports. I felt so bad leaving Xinxin there with a woman who she obviously didn't know, to face God only knows what in the operating room. I could only wonder where her mother was, and how awful it had to be for her to abandon such a sweet baby girl. I know she must have done it out of love—she probably thought it was the only way to get Xinxin the help she needs for her survival. But it was terrible to walk away from her. Jax, when I turned around in the doorway, she was waving bye-bye with a confused look on her face."

"Man, that's heartbreaking. You have to wonder how many babies in the orphanage are there because their parents can't afford the medical care they need. It's a shame, but what a selfless act of love."

"I just hope they can help her. I haven't heard anything about her lately, but I'm praying for her every day. But let's stop talking and thinking about Xinxin and the orphanage and just appreciate all this." She waved her hands around at the scenery.

They both grew quiet, watching the people stroll along the boardwalk. Unlike Mia's experiences at the lake during her childhood summers, everyone there gathered *around* the lake instead of *in* the lake. Jax said it was forbidden to get in the water, though he wasn't sure exactly why. The lake was simply an artistic backdrop to all of the rolling hills, sidewalks, sculptures, restaurants, and shops. Even so, the hundreds of visitors proved that it had to be just as entertaining outside of the water as in it.

At the sidewalk shops, Jax helped her negotiate prices for cheap souvenirs to hand out to her neighborhood kids at home. They got the Chinese version of ice cream, and Jax even bought her a frilly parasol to use to mimic the other girls who were ferociously protecting their skin from the sun as they walked along the paths winding around the lake. Mia held it for a while but soon felt silly and folded it into her bag, explaining to Jax that she loved the sun and didn't care if her skin turned even browner. He laughed and agreed with her that it really didn't matter, and he already knew her well enough to guess she wouldn't like that the umbrella was so girly.

Before the end of the afternoon, Mia had counted seven brides with grooms and other wedding attendants posing for photos in various spots on the grounds, all dressed in traditional white gowns, so happy on the day that marked the next step in their lives.

Jax had the entire day off from work, so when they finally tired of Jin Ji Hu, he took her for dinner at another well-known but small restaurant to sample more *baozi*. Her favorites were the ones with a meatball surrounded by tasty soup encased in the dumpling. Jax taught her how to poke a hole in the dough with her teeth and suck out the juice before feasting on the meatball and dumpling. Mia ate until she was ready to pop. He tried to convince her that the *cai bao* were the best, but she didn't like the taste of the tofu steamed in the dough.

Finally they returned to his hotel and found their way to an alcove in the lobby area, pulling the hanging beads closed to give them more privacy from other patrons. Unable to tolerate the shoes pinching her feet any longer, Mia slipped them off and folded her legs beneath her. She picked up her guitar and softly played the chorus of a favorite song, watching Jax's face as he listened intently. Five minutes and then ten went by, both of them at peace with the quiet music and each other's company.

Mia finally stopped strumming and leaned back against the red satin couch. "Jax, do you believe in ghosts?"

"What? That's random. Where did that come from?" Jax chuckled.

"Never mind. Anyway—it's not fair that you know so much about me already, and I feel like I don't know anything about you. Tell me something nobody else knows." She felt that the story of her search for her birth family was the only personal subject they ever broached, and she wanted him to know she was interested in his own history.

Jax furrowed his brow in mock concentration, then slapped his knee. "Oh. My name—why do you think my parents named me Jax?"

"I'm sure I have no idea, Mr. Hu. Please enlighten me," she teased as she put her guitar in the corner. She lifted her feet into his lap and felt a rush of pleasure when he picked one up and began to rub it. She hoped he wouldn't notice her chipped red polish or that her second toe was a smidgen longer than her big toe.

"Hmm, what do we have here?" Jax pulled one of Mia's ankles closer to scrutinize a tiny tattoo. "What does the butterfly symbolize?"

"It has to do with my birth mother. But it's a long story, and tonight I want to hear something about you. Why did they name you Jax?"

"Okay, fine. I hope I tell this right. It's been a long time since I've heard it."

"Quit procrastinating and tell me already!" Mia kicked at him playfully.

"Yikes—the sexual tension in here is getting thick." He laughed and stilled her foot to begin massaging it again. "Okay! When my parents immigrated to America, they came to San Francisco. My mother said they were walking down a side street on their way to find Chinatown, and she saw a group of white girls circled together playing a game on the sidewalk. Mother and Pop were exhausted from carrying all of their worldly belongings in four huge suitcases, so she decided it was a good place to rest—meaning 'a good place to be nosy.'"

Mia laughed at the impression he gave her of his mother scurrying around like a busybody.

Jax beamed at her, then continued, "So she set her two

suitcases down and sat on one to watch the girls play the game while she waited for her feet to stop throbbing—she didn't have her own personal masseuse handy, like *some* people." He winked and shot her a sly grin, his thumb making tiny circles in the sole of her foot.

"So anyway—the street game was nothing she was familiar with, and it fascinated her to watch the little girls bounce the small ball while expertly picking up little metal stars poured from a cloth pouch. Even though she couldn't speak their language, she said they were nice to her; they smiled and said hello. Months later, when Mother began to take English lessons, she described the game to her teacher and was told it was jacks.

"Over the years, she faced a lot of discrimination, but because of the girls she saw playing the game of jacks, she kept hoping the next generation would be more accepting of Chinese immigrants and their families. To keep that memory of those carefree children who welcomed her to their country, she gave the name Jax to me. My father lengthened it to Jaxson to make it sound more American. At that time, he was all into memorizing American history, especially the presidents, so it worked out well for him."

"What a wonderful story! Your mom is really clever. Wait—you've never told anyone else that story?" Mia asked, squinting at Jax suspiciously.

"No one's ever asked!" Jax laughed. "I guess it's not that interesting. Or *I'm* not that interesting."

"Oh—you are, believe me. And you're a great storyteller. At least your name has meaning and wasn't just chosen randomly from a list of popular American names. Most of my friends tell me they don't know why their parents gave them the name they did. But what do your parents do for a living, Jax? Do they still work?"

"Um, yeah. My parents are workaholics. I swear they don't know how to slow down—and they never let me relax either. It's always work, work, work or study, study, study. When they first arrived in California, they began their own tailoring business. They started small, actually worked out of a rented closet-sized room in a bad part of town. They constantly tell me the stories of how they came from nothing and built a flourishing business. My mother is a seamstress, and she took in small jobs altering formal gowns to make ends meet while Pop was pounding the pavement to find customers for his suits."

Mia watched the expression Jax wore as he talked about his parents. She could sense some bitterness, but also a measure of pride. She could see why he'd be proud, as she was also captivated by the description of their humble beginning. She knew from stories she'd heard that years ago, immigrants from China had to work a hundred times harder than the average business owner to launch their futures.

Jax continued, "A few years later, they heard there was more of a chance for them to be successful in Seattle—not as much Chinese competition there at that time—so they moved. After years of being poor while they worked hard, Pop was able to get a steady flow of Seattle businessmen as regular clients. Eventually he even bought his own building downtown—a huge accomplishment for small-time Chinese immigrants way back then. They did that for years and were comfortable, but about ten years ago they opened a Chinese antiquities store.

My father and his brother in Beijing are partners, importing Chinese furniture and other items to the States for resale. Pop was really disappointed when I told him I wasn't going to join the family business but instead planned to follow the hotel management route. He just can't understand I want to make my own way, create my own life." Jax lowered his eyes and released a long sigh.

"So—I spent my teenage years at the notoriously boring House of Hu after school, arranging furniture, polishing wood, and making deliveries in the summer. But I did it without too much grumbling—had to, because they constantly laid a guilt trip on me by telling me the store was paying my way to college."

Mia laughed at the thought of Jax running around with a can of furniture polish and a dust rag in his hand, flexing his muscles as he manhandled heavy antiques into the back of a truck.

"That sounds like a great first job to me. It sure beats bagging burgers or mowing grass," Mia joked.

"It was all right, I guess. I agree it's definitely better than working in a fast food restaurant or sweating outside in the Seattle summers. And when I started high school, they promoted me to assistant manager because I set up a website and put us on all the social networking sites. They had never heard of PayPal—can you believe that?" He chuckled. "Going online doubled our profits, and my parents thought it was the greatest thing ever. My buddy Adam took over as delivery boy, and until I came here, I took care of most of the online business. But I had to teach my mother how to do it before my last year in college, because I knew I'd be looking for an internship."

Jax smiled. "That was easier said than done—my mother was terrified of the computer. But now she thinks she's an expert and even has her own Facebook profile. I'm glad it's too much trouble to access Facebook from China, because she'd drive me crazy."

Mia sat straight up. "Oh crap—Jax. I just thought of something! My mom has probably shopped in your parent's store! Our house is decorated with Asian stuff, and I know Mom got some of the pieces in Seattle. Wouldn't that be such a coincidence? I can't wait to ask her."

"Oh yeah, that would be a riot. Hey, Mom—you remember that lady you overcharged for that fancy Chinese screen last summer? I've spent the last few weeks chasing after her daughter."

"Jax! Shut up! You have not been chasing me! We've been keeping each other company in this crazy city. We're *just friends*." Mia blushed as Jax wagged his eyebrows at her.

"So, tell me more. What's your favorite music? Who's your favorite artist?" Mia was anxious to change the subject to something safer.

"My favorite is whatever music you create with your cute little fingertips and that silky voice," he answered, dramatically batting his eyelashes at her.

"Oh! You're such a flirt!" Mia threw the small couch pillow at his head as he ducked and held his hands up in mock surrender. She loved that their friendship had made the turn past awkward and into playful.

"Okay, seriously. I like Train and Mumford & Sons, but

my favorite is John Mayer. Last year I saw him put on a concert in Seattle, and man, does he put on a good show! If I were as talented as you, I'd have jumped on stage with him and started singing."

Mia sat up, picked her guitar off the floor, and began to strum again. "I love John Mayer, too. But people say my style is most like Colbie Caillat. Here are a few chords of a melody I started on the flight over, and it's been floating around in my head ever since, begging to be finished. Don't laugh at me."

She closed her eyes and concentrated as she sang, *"Is it you that visits me in my dreams? Not your face I see—but with your voice, it seems. You sing to me and bring me peace. Is it you that visits me in my dreams? Is it you; is it you; is... it... you...?"*

"That's beautiful, Mia, and so haunting. You've got talent, girl. When did you learn to play?"

"My parents say I've been singing since the day they brought me home. One of my older brothers plays guitar, and any time he'd get it out, I'd sit in front of him and listen with rapt attention. One day he handed this guitar to me and told me he wanted me to have it because it was the one thing that would bring a smile to my face. I began learning that day, and within a few weeks could play a whole song—I was only about six. Since then, I've become more dependent on it to help me release my emotions through music, because I never wanted to tell my parents how much it hurts to grow up feeling like I was thrown away."

She lowered her eyes to hide the tears. Nothing was worse than crying in front of someone, and it was something she had fought all her life. She was known in her family as the tough little soldier; her mom always said she must have not been allowed to cry as a toddler, because no matter how upset she was when she was little, she refused to let anyone see her shed a tear.

"Hey—I'm sure it wasn't like that. They probably couldn't afford to keep you or pay for medical care they thought you needed. Or maybe you were a second child and they were forced to give you up. I bet you were loved very much. Who wouldn't love you? You're amazing. Why can't you see that?" He grabbed her hand, and using his finger, he swirled little circles in her palm.

"You don't know what it's like, Jax. You *know* who you came from. When I was a little girl I used to look in the mirror and wonder who I got my nose from, or if my eyes are like my birth father's, or if my birth mother has lips like mine. I don't know a single person in the entire world that shares my blood or my features. I don't even know my real birthday! It's disturbing! Even with my entire family around me, loving me every minute, sometimes I feel so alone and different. It's like a hole inside of me that can't be filled; it just burns from the emptiness, the constant question of who I am." Her lower lip trembled as she tried to bring her emotions under control.

"Come here." He tugged on her hand, and she scooted a few inches nearer to him. "And… even closer." Despite her resistance, he continued to pull until she was securely in the circle of his arms.

Jax pulled her so close Mia could feel his heart beating wildly next to hers. For a few minutes, he held her tightly, until she stopped trembling.

Mia felt him hesitate, then he leaned in, and gently kissed

her. When she didn't reject him, he brought her even closer until she was cradled on his lap, and kissed her again—deeper and harder. With his hands twisted in her silky black hair, she lost herself in the spicy smell of his skin.

Mia couldn't believe they were kissing—she hadn't planned on allowing that to happen. But she couldn't make herself stop Jax. She felt light-headed and warm all over, and she didn't recognize the little electric shocks that were making their way down her arms and to her fingertips—a magical feeling that she wanted to go on forever.

Jax finally released her lips and smiled, his dimples shining bright. "Mia, you and I are going to write our own personal love song. Get me some paper and a pen." He pretended to frantically search all around him. Mia erupted in giggles, glad that he had found a way to make the moment perfect, and at the same time embarrassed that he had broken her resolve to keep the relationship on a friend level. She knew it was now out of her control. Fate had brought her and Jax together, and there was no stopping them. She'd just have to deal with the aftermath later.

CHAPTER SIXTEEN

MIA entered the hotel, walking briskly towards the elevator, anxious to get to her room and into a hot shower, before she crashed in bed. It was almost eleven o'clock, and Jax had just escorted her back to her hotel. The day had taxed her physically as well as emotionally. Even though she was still scolding herself, she couldn't wait to relive the kiss over again in her dreams, but she first planned to pen some lyrics while it was fresh in her mind. She was a bit embarrassed at her lack of willpower. Good thing they had been in a semi-public place, or who knew how far they would have gone? *But then, maybe a short fling here in China is just what I need,* she thought with a smile.

"*Qingwen*?" Just as she pushed the elevator button, she felt a touch on her shoulder and heard the hesitant voice vying for her attention.

She was surprised to find Tingting beside her, looking hopeful.

"*Wo yao shuo hua—keyi ma? Wode fanyi zai zhi li.*" Tingting asked if she could talk to Mia and pointed over to another young lady sitting in the lobby area, waiting to translate.

"Um... okay." Mia was perplexed about the sudden visit

and wondered if something had happened to the woman who claimed to have been her foster mother.

"*Zenme le*?" Mia asked what was wrong as they walked towards the translator.

"*Deng yi xia*." Tingting answered for Mia to wait as she guided Mia over to the group of couches and gestured for her to sit.

They sat down together, and Tingting introduced the other girl as Feiying. About the same age as Mia, the girl was pretty in a mousy sort of way—short hair pushed behind her ears and eyeglasses that were too big for her small, oval face. She wore a boxy skirt and jacket, something like a flight attendant would wear—much too mature, and unflattering for her age. On her feet was what Mia's friend Jenny would have teasingly called 'grandma shoes.' Feiying was definitely a no-nonsense type and immediately jumped into the conversation to begin translating.

"Tingting asked me to come help her speak to you. She would like to apologize for the late hour, but can you spare a few minutes? Would you like to go up to your room?" Feiying fired the questions at Mia more quickly than she could form responses. She just nodded *yes* to everything and led them to the elevator and up to her room.

As soon as the door closed safely behind them, Mia gestured at the small table and chairs next to the window for the girls to sit down.

"Is something wrong with Lao Ling?" Even though she had only met the woman a few times, the thought of something happening struck a chord of panic in Mia's heart.

After translating the question to Tingting and awaiting her answer, Feiying assured her nothing was wrong with the old woman, and explained that Tingting only wanted to come and extend her friendship—and offer to be of any assistance that she could to Mia. She explained they had been waiting for her in the lobby for a few hours.

"What does she think she can do to help me? Does she know a way I can find out more information about my birth parents?" Mia questioned, excited at the prospect of another lead.

As Feiying relayed the questions, Tingting shook her head *no* and explained that while she didn't know anything right now, she'd keep her ears open in case the other *ayi*s mentioned any details. She paused and brought out a small silk box, extending it to Mia.

"What's this?"

"*Xiao liwu.* A small gift that Tingting wants to give to you—she says that you are special, and when she saw this it reminded her of you. She would like for you to accept it as a token of her friendship."

Mia took the box and gently opened the fragile top. Inside was the most exquisite necklace she had ever seen—a white flower carved from some sort of stone, hung on a braided black silk rope. The style complimented Mia perfectly: sort of bohemian but still delicate.

"Oh, how beautiful! But it is much too expensive; I cannot possibly accept such a gift." Mia was embarrassed that she didn't have anything to reciprocate with.

Without even waiting for translation, Tingting knew from

her face that Mia was reluctant to accept her token. She reached over and took both of Mia's hands in hers. Looking into her eyes, she softly spoke a few words for Feiying to convey.

"The flower is a lotus and is made of jade, a very special gemstone in China that will bring you good luck. Tingting says it would honor her very much if you will accept the gift."

Not sure what the proper etiquette in China was for accepting such gestures, Mia decided to go with her heart and graciously accepted the necklace. She could tell by the look on Tingting's face that it was very important to her, and she didn't want to disappoint her.

"Okay, I'll keep it. I really love it. Thank you, Tingting!" She did her best to express her delight to Tingting with her smile, then stood and threw her arms around the girl in an American-style bear hug. The embrace was awkward but sweet. *I'll teach these people how to openly show affection if it kills me,* Mia thought, a mischievous grin plastered on her face.

"*Jiaopian jiating, ma*?" Moving quickly on to her next subject, Tingting asked if Mia had any pictures of her family.

"Oh, sure. I have lots of pictures." Mia first took the jade necklace out of the box and put it around her neck, then stood in front of the mirror to admire it for a minute. It was so dainty and beautifully carved—it would probably be her favorite piece of jewelry for a long time. She pulled out her iPad from the desk drawer and opened her picture file. She sat on the bed with the girls gathered on either side of her, and led them through her photos, narrating each event and naming each person she pointed out.

Tingting looked especially interested in the pictures that

included her brothers. "*Tamen da bizi!*" She laughed, making fun of what she considered big noses on what Mia protectively thought were the most handsome faces in the world. Mia didn't get offended—as she knew that 'Big Nose' was a common title for foreigners throughout China. Tingting scrolled down through more photos, then asked if she had any sisters.

"Nope. I'm the only daughter in a family of boys, all older than me. It can be tough at times, but mostly I feel protected. My brothers always look out for me, but sometimes it can get hard to have any privacy. They feel like they've gotta interrogate every boy who ever attempts to talk to me. They still treat me like I'm twelve." Mia smiled as she remembered the first time her brothers met Collin and how nervous he'd been. She'd thought they were going to send him down the road with his head in his hands when he slipped his arm around her in front of them. She had to whisper to him to remove it before he lost it permanently. Later they laughed about it, but she reminded him to keep his moves out of sight of her family until they had officially approved him as acceptable boyfriend material.

She wondered briefly what they would think of Jax if they were to ever meet him. She knew one thing: they'd be surprised she was interested in a Chinese guy. But she would never know, because she was going to make sure to leave their romance on this continent.

"*Ni you mei you nan pengyou?*" she quickly asked Tingting, causing the two girls to fall backwards on the bed and erupt in giggles that Mia struggled with most Mandarin but was able to ask quite efficiently if they had boyfriends.

"*Mei you. Mei you shi jian.*" When Tingting got her laughter under control, she said she did not have a boyfriend, that she didn't have time for one. She explained that she worked at the orphanage all day, and most evenings she worked at a small hotel restaurant.

"But why do you work so hard if you are not in school?" Mia was perplexed that such a young girl would work two jobs—when did she just make time to have fun? The girl couldn't have been more than fifteen years old. That was the prime of her youth. *She should be dating, dancing, or something other than caring for babies and waiting tables.*

Feiying explained that Tingting paid for her living expenses and sent all remaining income back to her village to care for her ailing father.

Mia couldn't imagine working two jobs at her age and wondered where the rest of the family was and why they didn't ease some of the burden from the girl.

Tingting saw the dismay on Mia's face and quickly interrupted Feiying to add that her brother also sent part of his pay, so that together they could ensure their father lived comfortably and got the medical care he needed. He'd spent his years as a farmer, and when her mother got sick, all of his savings had gone for medicine and doctors to try to save her. She died, and her father was never able to build up another nest egg—except for what he generously spent to send her brother for an education—so it was their responsibility to make sure he was cared for.

Mia shook her head in disbelief at the responsibility placed on the young girl's shoulders, and she marveled at how mature she was. While at home, most kids her age were getting their driver's licenses and starting to date, Tingting was working to support her ailing father. She recalled hearing that China didn't offer their people the same type of social security that America did, and farmers definitely didn't have a retirement plan to pull from, only whatever savings they were able to put away through their working years. She thought the father was lucky to have two dutiful children to help him in his old age, especially considering the tragedy he had suffered. She felt a rush of admiration for Tingting for shattering the stereotype of girls in China, for the young woman was completely devoted to caring for her parent and probably did a better job of it than some young men would.

Tingting gave Feiying another question to ask.

Mia answered, "Yes, I actually do have some of my early pictures on here because I had to gather them for my high school graduation yearbook page." She explained that in American high schools, at the end of the last year, students could submit photos of themselves at every age to put in the school record book as a keepsake. She opened the file that contained pictures of her from age four to about age seven, and Tingting pulled the tablet onto her own lap so that she could get a closer look.

Mia was surprised at how intensely Tingting perused her photos, especially her earliest ones.

"This was Adoption Day—look how scared I was! I don't really remember it but my mom says I was very upset. I can't imagine being sad to leave the orphanage, but it sure looks like it here." Mia talked as if the gloomy little girl in the photograph was amusing, as usual trying to hide the true emotions the picture evoked. When she looked at it, what she really thought was what a pitiful child she was—missing her birth parents and being handed over to unfamiliar faces, about to embark on a new life in a strange country.

"Adoption Day? I don't understand these words." Feiying asked. She and Tingting talked together for a minute, then looked at Mia for an explanation.

Mia chuckled, and then explained, "Adoption Day just means it's the day my parents got me in their arms, and we became a family. Some people use the term *Family Day*, *Forever Family Day*, or even *Gotcha Day*. It doesn't really matter, but my brothers have pictures of the days they were born. I don't have that, so in the place of those milestone photos, my parents call the day I was adopted my Adoption Day. We don't celebrate it anymore. My brothers made a valid point when I was about eight years old. They asked my dad why I got to celebrate two days—my birthday *and* Adoption Day. We decided I had to choose, and of course I chose my birthday! I never wanted to be singled out as different, anyway, and it only made sense to celebrate the day I was born instead of the day I was adopted. But they still wanted to mark that day as special in some way, so they started a new tradition—they gave me this bracelet for charms."

Mia pushed her sleeve up and showed the girls the bracelet packed full of tiny creations. She usually wore it every day, unless she was going to an event where it wouldn't be safe or just didn't look right. "Each year on my adoption day, they quietly give me another charm to remind me they consider that day as one of the most extraordinary days ever. These charms represent milestones in my life and are a great way to look back and reminisce."

"What do you mean, *charm*?" Feiying asked, her serious face scrunched up in concentration.

"A charm is what they call the little things hanging on the bracelet. I call it my memory bracelet. This is my first one—a panda bear to represent China. The next year, they gave me this American flag to symbolize my new life in the States." She showed the girls the tiny bear and flag, hanging side by side on the silver strands.

"And these little slippers are from the year I was really into the whole ballet thing—which I decided I hated a year later and haven't done since. When I was twelve, I finally got the puppy I had begged for, and this charm looks just like my dog Hoss. He's gone now, but he was the best bulldog ever." She looked sad for just a moment, then picked up the next charm. It had been a long time since she had really looked at the bracelet and let the memories flow over her.

"I got this one when I learned to play guitar, and this is a car to remember the year I got my driver's license. Here is my graduation charm and…" Mia could go on and list many more, but she stopped because she saw that she had lost the two girls a few charms back. They just didn't get it, or maybe her childhood was so far removed from anything they had known that they just couldn't comprehend dancing, puppies, cars, and such.

Tingting picked up the iPad again and studied the picture of Mia with her parents for a few moments longer, her face somber.

Feiying said, "She wants to know what you remember of

your birth parents?"

"I don't remember much, but sometimes I have dreams with Chinese people in them, and I wonder if maybe they are memories from my early life here. I see a woman's face a lot—not clear enough to remember it, just a blur of her eyes or maybe her nose. Mostly I hear a voice, singing in my dreams. When I wake up, I usually can't remember the words, and I always wonder if it has anything to do with my birth mother."

Tingting had one more question for Feiying to ask, and they argued back and forth for a minute before the young girl finally let out a sigh of exasperation and spit it out. "Tingting wants to know if it is painful to think of your mother." The translator's cheeks reddened.

"Well, my mother is the woman who raised me. She stayed up nursing me the nights I've been sick; she was the one who took the extra time to wrap my hair up in the pigtails I insisted on when I started school; she hugs me and does things to cheer me up when I'm feeling low. I can tell her about boyfriend troubles and she'll even join me in ice cream pity parties, despite her constant attempts at dieting."

Mia chuckled at the confused expression on Feiying's face as she struggled to understand her words and convey them to Tingting. While she translated, Mia remembered when she had broken up with Collin. That weekend, she had come home from college, and her mother knew as soon as she saw her face that they needed to make an ice cream run. Together they put away an entire box of Moose Tracks, and her mother agreed with every rant and insult she could muster about the boy she had previously declared as perfect.

"Mom is my best friend, and I wouldn't be who I am today if not for her. But if you are asking about my *birth* mother, yes—it is painful to think about her. As the years go by, I drive myself crazy inventing stories of how and why she abandoned me. I think of her on the holidays, and wonder if she has the coveted son she probably yearned for. I don't feel bitter towards her—I just wish I knew why she didn't want me."

Mia paused to control the tears that threatened to come. "My mom understands I have an empty hole in my heart that needs to be filled with the truth. She helps me to deal with the emotions and even encourages me to remember my birth mother every Mother's Day—a big holiday in America to honor mothers. We usually buy a white lily and set it afloat in our backyard rock pond, and we say a prayer for my birth mother. Mom always takes that time to thank my birth mother for giving her the best gift she ever received: me."

Tingting turned her head away from the others and brushed a tear from her cheek. She cleared her throat and stood to go.

"*Xie xie*, Mia," she thanked her. Then she told Feiying to tell Mia she would see her again soon and to ask her to refrain from mentioning her visit to anyone else.

Mia assured her she would keep their visit just between them and showed the girls to the door. In the hall, she hugged Tingting and thanked her again for the gift. She couldn't believe how nice she was, coming over to extend her friendship and giving her such a lovely necklace. They all waved good-bye, and Mia went back in the room and closed the door behind her, anticipating climbing under the covers and giving in to exhaustion. All she wanted was to lay her head down and close her eyes—and hopefully sleep until noon.

She sat down on the edge of the bed to remove her shoes and noticed her message light blinking on the phone. She dialed to pick up the message and heard a recording tell her in stilted English, then rapid Mandarin that she had a package waiting for her downstairs. A package? *Could it contain a letter from The Finders*? Suddenly energized, Mia quickly slipped her shoes back on, picked up her key card and raced out the door to retrieve the note that she hoped would put her closer to the truth.

☙

"May I help you?" The polished young woman at the hotel desk asked as Mia approached. Alice—as her nametag stated—radiated discipline and commitment from head to toe, her dark hair knotted in a French twist to complete the picture of professionalism. Beside Mia, a businessman waited impatiently with his passport in hand, ready to check in but a moment too late to be first in line. Mia ignored his surly attitude and leaned forward, both hands on the counter in anticipation.

"I'm in room 620, and I received a message that I have a package waiting for me here." Mia felt like a hobo standing there in her dusty jeans and tee shirt, her makeup faded away from the long day, but why should she care? Those people didn't know her.

At Mia's English, the clerk quickly held her hand up for her to stop talking.

"*Deng yi xia*," Alice said, asking her to wait a moment, and she stepped through a door behind her to alert her supervisor to come forward. Mia could hear them communicating back and forth, the other woman obviously disgruntled for being disturbed from whatever she was doing in the back area.

Mia impatiently clicked her short nails on the marble countertop. *What could the package hold? A letter? If it is from The Finders, are they going to help me? Or is it to tell me they feel they can't assist in my search?* She wished they'd hurry up.

Soon a middle-aged Chinese woman came forward, her expression suggesting she was in charge. The bifocals barely perched on the tip of her flat nose added a touch of cartoon comedy to her stoic persona. Her badge stated that her name was Pandora. *An interesting choice for a name*, Mia thought.

"Hello. Can I help you please?" Pandora's English had a British lilt, and Mia wondered if she had studied in Europe.

"I am in room 620, and I received a message that I have a package waiting for me here," Mia repeated, that time to someone who could hopefully understand.

The manager reached behind her and pulled a large yellow envelope from a marked slot in the collection of cubbies. Mia practically yanked it out of her hand, and then rushed back to the elevator and up to her room to open it in private.

Inside, she sat at the table and examined the envelope. Marked simply with *patron room #620*, it had no other writing on the front or back. Using her fingernail file, Mia opened the envelope and pulled out a piece of paper, two cotton swabs, and three small plastic containers with lids, about the size of prescription pill bottles.

She turned the envelope over, and a small adhesive label with an address written in Chinese characters fluttered into her lap. She studied the characters briefly, but couldn't interpret even one of them. *Oh, well. The note should tell me what to do with each item, hopefully*. Thankful the note was in English. She picked it up and held it closer to the lamp. It read:

Client #2414,

We have decided to take your case, though we cannot guarantee results. Follow the instructions carefully, and then leave the resealed package at the front desk for mailing.

Wash hands thoroughly.

Using the cotton swab, swipe inside of your cheek generously and put swab in one plastic container. Attach lid securely.

Using the second cotton swab, repeat process and enclose in second container. In third container, place a few hairs plucked from the crown of your head. Include 1500 yuan for processing fees. Put all containers back in envelope and attach enclosed address label on the outside.

Take envelope to the hotel front desk and request them to mail for you.

If your DNA sequence matches any of those in our register bank of parents searching for lost children, we will contact you. Please keep this process confidential.

Good luck,

The Finders

Mia wondered who the group consisted of and thought about copying the Chinese characters of the address and asking Mr. Wang to track it, but she assumed it was probably just a post office box. She decided she didn't want to jeopardize the trust of anyone who might try to help her locate her birth parents. She quickly went to the bathroom, washed her hands, and dried them on the towel she had left hanging that morning. Then she realized she should have used a clean towel, so she did it all over again, that time drying with fresh linen from the metal rack over the toilet.

She returned to the table, sat down, and carefully swabbed the inside of her cheek, putting each swab in the containers as instructed, noticing her name printed on the top of each lid.

Back to the bathroom again, she peered into the mirror to decide which lucky hairs she would pluck from her head. Which ones would travel to an unknown location and possibly help match her with parents who shared the same color, consistency, and genetic makeup as it did? *You are the lucky winners*, she announced after a careful contemplation. She focused on a few unruly renegades close to her temple and carefully pulled them out to maintain the roots, tucked them into the last container, and closed the lid.

She returned all containers to the large envelope, added the requested processing fee, and attached the label to the front. She carried it back down to the front desk. The lobby was vacant, but Pandora was still on duty and ready to assist. Mia asked first for some tape to close the package, and then asked the woman if she could mail it for her.

"Yes, madam. We will be glad to." She efficiently tucked

the envelope into a large box behind her and went on about her duties, doubtless unaware of the importance of the material that just passed through her hands. Mia hoped that somewhere, sometime, her birth parents had found the same group she had, and that their genetic codes were waiting in a data bank for her to come to them. A million to one chance—but a chance all the same.

Drained from the day's events and unexpected excitement of the evening, Mia slowly made her way back up to her room, skipped the hot shower and went directly to bed. She didn't even have time to contemplate the events of the day—she was out as soon as her head hit the pillow.

CHAPTER SEVENTEEN

SLEEPING soundly, Mia first thought the distant ringing was a part of her dream. It echoed closer and closer, until finally the shrill noise roused her from a perfect fantasy of Jax once again massaging her tired feet—along with a few other body parts.

She turned over and groped for the phone, successfully grabbing the handset, but also pulling the entire phone base and all the table top contents to the floor. She hoped she didn't awaken the guest in the next room with her clumsiness.

"Hello?" she mumbled. The clock on the side table flashed 3:16 AM. *This had better be good. It's probably a wrong room—who would call me at this time of night?*

"Mia! Get up! This is Jax. You have to get out of there—right now!"

"What? What's wrong?" Mia sat up, rubbed her eyes, and tried to blink away her confusion. *Am I still dreaming?*

"My manager just told me a group of policeman were here looking for you about half an hour ago. They must have followed us here earlier and thought you were staying at this hotel; they were probably waiting until night for fewer witnesses before approaching you. He said they looked like criminals in uniforms. I don't know what they want, but I think they're up to no good. They may have gone back to whoever told them you were coming here, and found out where you are really staying. You have to get out of there until we find out what they want." Jax was freaking out so badly that Mia caught his fear and quickly crawled out from under the covers.

"Where will I go? I can't leave in the middle of the night, Jax!" Mia didn't know what to do, but she did know she wouldn't be safe walking in the city alone at that hour.

"I'm coming right now. Get your stuff together and wait for me. I'll take you somewhere safe. Don't answer the door. Okay? Say okay! We have to hurry."

"Fine! Okay—I guess. I don't know what to do or where to go. Maybe they're trying to help me, Jax? Maybe they're good guys?"

"Mia. For God's sake, please! Do as I tell you, and we'll talk about it when I get you out of there. The police are different here in China; they can take you wherever they want, for whatever reason they want—right or wrong. If you try to resist, the hotel staff cannot help you. They're too afraid of consequences to interfere. I've heard a lot of bad stories of corruption around here. Please—get ready. I'm leaving now."

They hung up, and Mia frantically pulled her suitcase out of the closet and began to throw all of her clothes into it. She grabbed her iPad from the table and slid it into her shoulder bag. Picking up her guitar, she started to add it to the growing pile when she heard a feet pounding down the hall. She froze—surely they couldn't have found her already? She set her guitar back down, and not making a sound, she tiptoed over to the peephole; luckily her door was directly at the end of the long hallway, giving her a complete view of all incoming traffic.

What she saw sent a shiver of fear down her spine. Three uniformed men, brows furrowed in serious concentration, were coming towards her door. She had only a few seconds to figure out what to do. *Where will I go? If I don't open the door, will they break it down? Do they have a key?* Mia felt like screaming as she frantically looked around the room for a place to hide.

The bed was too low to the floor to crawl under, and the bathroom was nothing but glass doors all around. They'd look in the closet first thing, so that was out. She was stuck—nowhere to go. She felt like a cornered animal, but then she looked at the window.

Could I—? Her floor was six stories up, and the hotel didn't have balconies, only a five-inch ledge that couldn't possibly be wide enough for her to stand on. *But there's nowhere else to go!* Mia quickly threw her suitcase back in the closet and pulled her bedcovers up to appear as if she hadn't come back to her room for the night. She grabbed her shoulder bag and headed for the window. She didn't want to leave her passport and guitar behind, but there was no more time. She could hear the men, and they sounded like they were almost in front of her door now.

Thank goodness the Chinese don't care much about following safety codes, Mia thought as she easily unlocked the two latches and pushed open the tall window. The opening was at least five feet high, giving her ample room to get through. She looked down for one second and felt a wave of nausea as she retreated back into the room. *I can't do this. It's too terrifying.*

The so-called policemen stopped outside her room and began pounding on the door. Mia looked towards the noise and then back at the window. She decided to trust Jax's instincts, and she quickly climbed through without looking at the ground far below. She hoped no one would spot her climbing around like Spiderman and alert the hotel staff.

Using one hand to grip the side of the window frame, she reached in and pulled the window shut with the other, hoping they wouldn't guess her escape route. With her fingers gripping the metal casing and her toes clinging to the rough ledge, she scooted very slowly to the left, out of view if they looked out. Even as she coached herself to remain calm, her body rebelled and began trembling from head to toe. She concentrated on breathing in and out as she waited, praying they would leave and not look out the window.

They must have had a key card, because she heard them enter the room without breaking the door down. They were a loud group, obviously not caring if they disturbed the other residents of the hotel. Mia heard a sharp twang from her guitar, and the fear ran even deeper at the thought that they might take her most prized possession. *Please, Lord, don't let them take my guitar*, she prayed fervently.

Thankfully, she knew there was no way they could get in the safe, and they couldn't take it because it was bolted to the closet floor, so her passport and the rest of her money would be okay. They'd probably already spotted the suitcase peeking out of the closet and wondered why it was open with her clothing spilling out, but let them wonder. She could only hear small bursts of sounds from the room interspersed with the occasional car or truck speeding by, and a few horn blares. *Traffic is light this time of night,* she mused, trying to keep her mind off the fact that she was standing on a tiny ledge sixty feet above the ground. *Who am I kidding? I'm going to throw up any minute now. I will not cry, I will not cry... Breathe in, breathe out...*

She heard them dumping out the bag of souvenirs she and Jax had bought from the vendors at the lake, the plastic crinkling and the toys hitting the floor. *What are they looking for? Legitimate law enforcement wouldn't be going through my belongings, would they? I don't have anything of value other than my money and the necklace that Tingting gave me, and I'm wearing that. Luckily my guitar was battered and scarred—nothing fancy to the naked eye, but priceless to me.*

All around her, even without turning to look, Mia could see the blinking lights reflecting off the buildings. *Why does every structure in China have to have strings of lights?* She wondered. *And when will they leave my room?* Her fingers were numb, and she wasn't sure how much longer she could hold on. Good thing she kept her fingernails short to play guitar; she couldn't imagine clinging to the ledge like this if she had long nails.

She shifted her weight and realized she should have left the iPad behind, because her bag looped around her neck felt as if it weighed fifty pounds. Already she could feel the sting of several mosquito bites and could only imagine how much they were enjoying their surprise feast. Ignoring the instinct to swat them was almost more than she could stand, and Mia tried to think of something else to get her mind off of them. Forgetting for just a moment to keep her feet absolutely still, she tried to use one foot to scratch at the other. She felt a wave of dizziness and clawed at the window frame to regain her balance.

Miraculously, she got through the tense moment without making a sound, except for the thumping of her heart that sounded as if it would jump right out of her chest.

If Mom knew that I'm clinging to a ledge outside a window on the sixth floor of a hotel, she'd probably faint dead away. Her mother had never been able to stand anything happening to Mia—Mom had cried harder than Mia herself did when Mia took a fall off a horse when she was younger. As Mia was being wheeled into surgery, Dad comforted Mom—as if Mom herself were the one responsible for the break, instead of the frightened horse that had bucked Mia off its back.

Finally, the room on the other side of the window was silent. Mia wanted to wait a few more minutes just to be sure they'd left, but her legs changed her mind. They were shaking violently, and if she didn't get in, she feared they were going to buckle. She pushed the window open with one hand and began scooting over to get in front of it to climb through. Suddenly, her foot missed the ledge, and she faltered, flailing to steady herself. Her floundering made her lose her balance. Before she could regain control, both feet were off the ledge, and she was falling.

The thought surged of how painful the impact would be, meeting the ground from six stories up, but as her body dropped below the ledge, her frantic fingers caught the lower right edge of the window frame. *Where the heck is Jax? And can't anyone below see me? Is the entire freaking city asleep?*

Mia dangled from the window, her arms bent unnaturally

to accommodate the ledge that stood painfully as an obstacle between her and the metal framing she clung to with a death grip. She kicked her legs, trying to find something—anything—to use as a platform. She was losing strength fast, and her fingers were losing their grip on the frame. This realization sent her into an even bigger panic. She was going to fall.

CHAPTER EIGHTEEN

STOP kicking, be still, and breathe! she told herself as her fingers continued to tingle from lack of circulation. *Close your eyes and think of this as the big oak tree in the backyard—you've pulled yourself up before. You can do this. Focus.*

She heard something and stopped moving. A soft voice—where was it coming from? It was the song, the one she'd heard in her dreams many times, the one she couldn't understand. *Maybe this is a dream?* The sudden cramp in her arm told her it wasn't, and Mia closed her eyes and took a deep breath. Calm washed over her, and a vision of her backyard at home, complete with the oak tree and her tire swing, crept into her mind. She remembered a day many years before, when she lost her footing while climbing her beloved ancient tree. She'd fallen from it before and didn't want any more stitches, and that thought had given her the strength she needed to get herself back up on the limb. She knew that if she fell this time, it wouldn't simply be stitches; someone would be sweeping her remains into a body bag.

The seconds were ticking by, and if she didn't do something, she was going to fall. Still seeing the old tree in her mind, Mia gripped more tightly and attempted to kick her right leg up to the ledge. Despite stretching beyond limits she knew she had, she couldn't get it up far enough. She tried again, but it was just too high. *Think, Mia; think!*

She gingerly used her feet to try again to find any niche or object to step on to take some weight from her aching hands. *There!* She couldn't see it, but she was able to wedge the front of her left foot in enough to give her some stability and to shift some of her weight off her fingers. She could feel the blood start returning to her hands. With her left foot secure in its new location, Mia tried again to swing her right leg up to the ledge. Sweat poured from her face at the exertion. *Got it!*

With her right leg anchoring her, she painstakingly pulled the rest of her body back onto the small overhang. Safe again, she lay there for a few seconds until the hammering of her heart slowed down to only a gallop.

Knowing she needed to get out of sight as soon as possible, Mia curled towards the window opening. Using the last bit of energy she could muster, she brought herself into a crouching position and dropped back in, staying quiet in case the policemen were on the other side of her door. Feeling shaky from her ordeal, she crept over to the peephole and looked out, only to find an empty hallway on the other side. They were gone—*for now*—and other than making a huge mess of her clothes and stuff, everything looked like it was still there.

Jax better hurry up, she thought frantically. Mia quickly threw on jeans and a shirt and slipped on her sandals. Running to the safe, she discovered they had somehow figured out how to open it. Her passport and the wad of Chinese bills she had sitting on top of it were gone. Mia felt a shiver of foreboding as she realized how difficult it was going to be to get her passport back. They hadn't noticed the thin black waist pack that held the majority of her American cash, so she removed it and stuffed it in her bag. She'd leave behind all of her bathroom items and the souvenirs, and just take her suitcase, guitar, purse—and, of course, George.

Gathering the items close to her, she perched on the corner of the bed and tried to breathe deeply to calm herself as she waited for Jax. As the quiet settled around her, she was taken back in time, fragments of something she couldn't quite put together flashing in her mind.

One second, she was playing at the feet of an old woman, and the next second, a man with a uniform grabbed her around her waist and carried her away from the small brick house. She kicked and screamed, grabbing at air—grabbing at anything to slow him down. It was no use, and she soon found herself in the backseat of a car, rushing down the road at a high speed. He said if she cried any more, she'd never see her parents again, so she stopped making noise.

She squeezed herself as close to the door and as far away from the scary man as she could. She didn't make another sound, just closed her eyes to shut out their angry faces, and covered her ears to block out their ugly words. She would not cry, never again. Even when the car stopped, she didn't want to open her eyes—if she couldn't see them, maybe they couldn't see her. And if they couldn't see or hear her, maybe they'd let her go, and she'd find her way back home.

The memory stopped there. Mia tried, but she couldn't remember anything else. She didn't like the feeling it gave her, the intense fear and sense of loss that enveloped her. One silent tear slid down her cheek, rolled off her nose, and landed on her clasped hands. *Where is Jax? Why isn't he here yet?*

☙

On his electric bicycle, Jax kept the accelerator turned to the maximum speed all the way to Mia's hotel, thankful it had a full charge for once. He was in what he called a 'controlled panic.' If they had already gotten to Mia, he didn't know how he was going to locate where they took her. If he did find where they took her, he didn't know how he was going to get her released if they had charged her with some ridiculous offense. He didn't know much right then, but he did know that he'd do whatever it took to find her and keep her safe.

At the intersection, an old beggar woman stepped off the curb right out in front of him, rattling her can at him to get his attention.

"*Gei wo qian, gei wo qian.*" She continued to chant her request for money. *Not now, lady! Why is she still staggering around this time of night?* He swerved around her, barely missing her feet and kept going, unnerved that her interruption had cost him at least an extra ten seconds.

A block from the hotel, Jax turned down the dark alley that bordered the back of the grounds. He didn't want to pull up in front, in case the policemen were still there or someone was watching the entrance.

Next to the service buildings were already a few scooters and bikes from the staff, so Jax parked in the midst of the pile to blend in. He turned off the motor, pocketed the keys, and tried to appear nonchalant as he entered through the gardener's gate. Sitting on a bench he saw a young guard, head leaned back against the stone wall behind him, mouth open, emitting a low snore. Jax quietly crept past him, careful not to disturb any pathway stones that would wake the sentry. He hoped his pounding heart didn't give him away.

Looking back and forth, he couldn't find the main rear entry door so instead he went through what appeared to be a staff door. Inside, the silhouettes of the various hanging pots and pans displayed dark shadows across the dim room; the kitchen crew had not yet arrived to prepare for the morning buffet. Jax practically ran through the path among various counters and around the huge industrial sinks and cooktops until he found himself in a large hallway. At least thirty feet ahead were two service elevators, and Jax sprinted towards them. Finally inside one, he pecked at the sixth floor button until the doors closed and the car began to move up. *Please let her still be here, please let her still be here...* He repeated the mantra as if it alone would secure her safety.

Not wanting to wait any longer, Jax slipped through the elevator door when it opened just enough for his body to squeeze through and sprinted down the hall towards Mia's room. He cursed as he tripped over a leftover room service tray that held the remnants of a midnight snack: silver plate warmers and empty wine glasses discarded haphazardly on a large tray on the floor a few doors from the end of the hall. The clatter of the disturbed dinnerware made a huge racket, and the door to Mia's room flew open—and there she was. She catapulted herself into his arms, and he held her, for the second time in less than twelve hours, but this time much more tightly in his relief that she was safe.

"Jax, thank God you came. They were here—I had to hide. I crawled out the window and almost fell. They made me remember something—I thought I was going to die—my legs were shaking—they messed with my guitar—the mosquitoes were attacking me—what do they want?—what should I do?" Mia's teeth chattered as she stammered almost incoherently.

"Whoa, whoa... Slow down. Calm down." Jax rubbed her back and gently pushed her back into the room, shutting the door behind them. "We need to get your stuff and get you out of here. Come on; let's hurry." He didn't want to take the chance that the men would come back for a second look.

"What if they're in the lobby? I don't know if they left or not." Mia was scared; she didn't understand what was going on or why they wanted her. Over the years, she had heard stories about the corrupt government officials and policemen in China, and she didn't want to find out if the stories were true or false.

"We're going out the back way. You'll have to call them tomorrow and tell them to go ahead and check you out. We can't take the chance that someone is watching downstairs for you to arrive. I'd take you back to my hotel, but that isn't such a good idea since they were already there—but I have a friend that'll put us up. It's nothing fancy, but they'll never think to look for you there. Come on; follow me."

Jax picked up her suitcase, and Mia grabbed her bag and guitar. He looked through the peephole first to make sure the hallway was still clear, then led Mia out and to the service elevator. They carefully left the hotel the way that Jax had entered, luckily still avoiding any kitchen or housekeeping staff that would ask questions.

"Climb on, Mia." Jax beckoned towards the electric scooter placed strategically in the middle of the long row.

"Wait. Where are you taking me? We need to think this through, Jax." She moved into the shadows and Jax squeezed in next to her, under the eaves of the security shack. The sleeping guard was no longer on his bench, and Jax needed to hurry Mia towards a decision so they could get off the hotel grounds and to a safer location.

"Well, you can't stay with any of the foreigners I know, because that would draw too much attention from their drivers and house help. You need to stay with someone Chinese so you can blend in until we find out what's going on and why the police want to talk to you. I have a friend who is a painter, would you stay with him?" Jax wasn't sure what to do with Mia to keep her safe. He only knew he had to get her out of public view.

"Jax, wait—let me think for a second."

He stared at her and wondered why she had to think everything through so thoroughly. He wished she could just go with the plan and stop making it more difficult with her reasoning.

"I have an idea. Remember I told you about the orphanage *ayi* named Tingting? She was here when I got back to the hotel tonight, and she said she would help me any way she can. Why don't I try to find her?"

"But do you know where she lives?" Jax asked. "And do you think you can trust her? Maybe she's the one who led the police here!"

"No, I don't think so. I feel she's sincere and honest. I don't know where she lives, but it must be close to the woman who was my foster mother. If you can get me to the orphanage, I can lead you to Lao Ling's apartment, and we can ask her how to find Tingting. And maybe she knows why the police are looking for me—or she can find out."

Jax didn't have a better option so he nodded his approval. "To get to the orphanage, we'll need to take a bus or taxi. My bike won't have enough juice to get us all the way over to the other side of town and get me back. I'll leave it here and come back for it later. Let's go."

After one last look back at the hotel, they were on their way to what he hoped would be a safe place for Mia. He led her out through the hotel back gate, down the alley, and out to a side road to find a bus or taxi, whichever came first.

CHAPTER NINETEEN

THE taxi driver stopped his battered car in front of the alley leading to the orphanage and turned around to ask them for more directions. Mia couldn't tell Jax where Lao Ling's apartment was located, but from the institute, she could lead the way by following her memory from her previous visit. A few turns and fifteen minutes later, she triumphantly pointed at the gray building, and the driver screeched to a stop. Mia and Jax climbed out, paid the driver, and then peered up at the building.

"It's too early to knock on her door," Mia said, looking at her watch.

"It will be five o'clock in just a few minutes, and she'll be awake. We'll just hang around here until then. He sat down on the curb and patted the cement to invite Mia to join him.

"Jax, I just don't understand what's going on. Why would the police want to talk to me, and why would they come into my room without permission?" She tried to act brave, but she felt very intimidated by the Chinese government. She quickly told him about the unexpected memory that their visit—and uniforms—had dredged up.

"That's scary—do you think that really happened to you?"

"I don't know, Jax. Maybe it's just my over-charged imagination. But I can't figure out why the police didn't just come speak to me in the daytime hours—why go sneaking around at night? It's no wonder that my brain is inventing more drama."

"I don't know why they want you, but maybe since you didn't come to China with a tour group or any family, they feel suspicious. I can't imagine what else it would be that would set them off."

As she huddled against Jax in the early morning chill, an old man rattled by them, his back permanently twisted and bent over, pushing a large metal cart.

"Breakfast," Jax answered even before she formed the question. "He sells rice and noodles for only three yuan a bowl to people on the street, at work sites, bus stops, and the local parks. He gets an early start to get his cart to a good location before his competition gets there."

The old man barely gave them a glance as he labored to push his cart up the inclining road, his too-large plastic slippers slapping the pavement with each step. Mia thought it a shame that an elderly person had to work such a hard job just to survive. She wondered if he had grown children—and if so, why would they allow their father to struggle to make a living?

She thought about the many street sweepers she had seen all around the city, using the old-fashioned brooms to clear the leaves, trash, and other debris from roads and even busy highways. They looked like a line of old grandmothers, dressed in flowery shirts, gray or blue pants, and colorful scarves wrapped around their heads. Some of them could be seen lined up working on government property, pulling weeds or planting flowers. *They should be home serving tea or making dumplings, not battling the cold weather and stifling heat of the seasons to earn barely enough money to feed themselves.* She'd been told the women generally only made about three hundred yuan a month. *That's barely forty American dollars!*

Jax bumped her out of her mental rant and pulled her to her feet. "It's time. We need to get off the street before more people show up. Which way?" Mia led him to the back entrance and up the stairs until she was once again standing at the door of the woman who claimed to have cared for her as a child.

Jax knocked and stood aside. He whispered to Mia, "I want the woman to see you first when she opens the door."

"*Ni hao*?" Lao Ling opened the door a crack and peeked out. "Hello?"

When she saw Mia standing there, she quickly opened the door and pulled her in. She beckoned for Jax to hurry in and shut the door. She left them standing there as she pulled a clothespin from her pink polka-dotted apron and hurried over to use it at the window to pin the curtains together for more privacy.

The woman began talking quickly, and Jax and Mia looked at each other, confused.

"Oh, she's speaking the local dialect. I guess I'm going to get a chance to see just how much my Mandarin has improved in the last few months."

Mia frowned. "Oh, no. What if you can't understand her?"

"Don't worry. I'll make her understand this is serious. I'm glad I've been spending a lot of time with the hired housekeepers and custodians at the hotel. This is all they speak."

Bit by bit, he explained to Lao Ling that the police came to the hotel looking for Mia, and she needed a safe place to stay until they could determine the problem. He asked her about Tingting, if she lived close by and would possibly hide Mia for a short time. At that request, a look of panic crossed the face of the old woman before she quickly hid it. Mia followed along and caught the highlights. She noticed Jax left out the story about her hiding outside of her window, as he probably didn't know the words to explain it in Mandarin. He did, however, tell Lao Ling that the police had confiscated Mia's passport.

Lao Ling paced the floor, wringing her hands and stopping to listen at the door every few moments. She pulled a tattered bandana from her apron pocket and mopped the sweat from her forehead. She denied having any idea why the police would be looking for Mia, but she was definitely fearful that somehow there would be trouble for her because of the foreigners.

"*Deng yi xia. Wo hui lai hen kuai.*" She quickly darted out the door with a promise of returning in just a moment. Mia looked at Jax, confused at the old woman's abrupt exit.

"Where's she going?" she asked, alarmed to be left alone in the apartment without an answer of if she would be allowed to stay or if she must go.

"She said for us to wait here and that she would return quickly." Jax assured Mia that Lao Ling was doubtless checking to see if anyone was outside, watching the apartment. He moved closer to her on the couch, slipping his arm around her for reassurance.

"Jax, it's so strange that I was told not to return to the orphanage after I started asking questions about my birth parents. Then my guide dropped me—it's like she just fell off the face of the earth! What is going on? Xiao Jo was so friendly until the director scolded her and Lao Ling on that first visit. Do you think they're hiding something? Am I just being paranoid, Jax?"

Jax hesitated. "I don't know if that's what started this or if you have just set off the curiosity—or suspicion, if you will—of the government. But until we know, we need to keep you safe."

Mia anxiously watched the door and listened for footsteps. As the minutes ticked by, her imagination ran away with possible scenarios. *What if Lao Ling can't be trusted? What if she brings the police? Surely she wouldn't betray me that way?* Jax put his hand on her knee to stop her increasingly frantic foot tapping. Just as she was about to erupt with anxiety, the door opened and Lao Ling returned, Tingting following close behind, her brow creased with worry.

Both Mia and Jax jumped to their feet, relieved that the old woman returned and even more so that Tingting arrived with her. As soon as Mia saw the young girl, she instinctively reached up to touch the jade flower hanging around her neck.

"Mia!" Tingting rushed towards Mia and hugged her tightly. "Lao Ling told me what happened. Don't worry, we will discover what this is all about." She lowered her voice and gestured for Mia to also whisper. "The walls in these small apartments are thin, and no one ever knows who might be listening."

The ease with which Tingting spoke English stopped Mia in her tracks, and she pulled back and looked at her in confusion. "Tingting, I thought you couldn't speak English?"

Lao Ling and Tingting exchanged a worried look, and the old woman nodded her head to the younger woman in a gesture of approval.

"I am sorry I did not tell you the truth, Mia. It is better for me if most people do not know I speak English."

"Wow. You really fooled me. You even had a translator accompany you to talk for you at my hotel—that's taking the charade a little far. Didn't you trust me, Tingting?" Mia felt crushed that she was in the 'untrusted foreigner' category, even though she was Chinese, just like Tingting.

"At first I didn't know if I could trust you. But after we met at the hotel and you showed me your family and told me your mission to find your birth parents, I decided to tell you very soon. Please, Mia, you must forgive me and know that I trust you now, as I hope you do me. But now, let's figure out what to do about this situation."

Jax moved to look out the window, peering from behind the curtain. "Tingting, it's nice to meet you. I agree we need to decide what to do. First, have you heard anything at the orphanage that would lead you to believe that Mia's questions about her birth parents have started trouble?"

"The top director came to our meeting last week and told us that we were not allowed to speak to any visiting foreigners, even returning Chinese daughters. We were told we especially cannot answer any of *your* questions. No one asked why—we only agree with whatever we are told to do," Tingting whispered as Lao Ling kept watch at the window, one hand in her apron pocket, fiddling with an unseen but noisy trinket.

"What are they trying to hide? I don't understand. My information is *my* history—*my* right to know." Mia was outraged that the directors would think they had the power to hide her information or keep it from her—or worse yet, fabricate a story. She was starting to think that maybe she hadn't been found in a train station, after all. And if she hadn't been, then where was she found and by whom? *What is the truth? Will I ever find it? Why can't they understand that something so insignificant to them means the world to me?*

"I can try to find out more tomorrow at the orphanage. Maybe the room supervisor will know something," Tingting offered.

"Can Mia stay at your home until we find out what's going on?" Jax asked Tingting, then looked at Mia. "I don't know if that's our best option, but until a better plan comes along, we need to find a place for you to stay."

"Wait—how will The Finders know where I am? I mailed off the test they left for me at the hotel. How will they get in touch with me?" Mia didn't want to lose the best chance she had found so far to find someone in her birth family.

Tingting translated her question to Lao Ling and waited for a reply. The old woman hesitated, then answered.

Tingting said, "Lao Ling will contact The Finders and tell them to use her for communication, because you are out sightseeing in the countryside for a few days. She also said we must go, that she doesn't want foreigners seen coming from her apartment. Jax must leave separately, and I'll take you to my home."

"What does she mean by foreigners? How will anyone

know we aren't local Chinese if we just don't speak English?" Jax sounded a bit offended.

"Everyone can tell you are a foreigner, even if you do not speak. It is in the way you walk, your expression, your clothes, and your attitude. You stand out very clearly as someone who is not from here," Tingting explained, matter-of-factly. "Mia blends a little more than you, but she needs to keep her head down and not make eye contact. Remember, we only speak Chinese outside these rooms."

Mia didn't remind her that her Mandarin was seriously lacking; she was extremely tired and even felt nauseated. She had gone through too much excitement and needed rest to regroup her thoughts and put her back on track physically.

"Jax, will you come to see me tomorrow?" She asked, shooting a stubborn look at Tingting and Lao Ling.

"Of course I will! Nothing will stop me. I have a few places to ask questions myself today, when I get to work. I know some people who may be able to at least help get your passport back. But first, Tingting, you need to tell me where you live, or I'm not going anywhere. I need to find Mia tomorrow; I want to know where she'll be."

CHAPTER TWENTY

MIA sat down on the stool at the small wooden table and reached down to rub her aching feet. After Jax left, Tingting led her out of Lao Ling's building and into another, up several flights of stairs to an apartment that, other than the colorful braided rugs scattered about, was almost identical to the one they had just left.

An older woman, dressed in a housecoat with her head wrapped by a light blue scarf, moved quietly around the kitchen, making tea and noodles to feed the girls for breakfast. Tingting introduced her as Auntie Zhi, and the old woman shyly nodded her head towards their guest—saying 'Good morning' without words. Mia was so tired she didn't even want to eat anything, but she also didn't want to offend the older woman by declining her silent offer of food.

"I think I saw your aunt with you at the orphanage the first time I went there, right?"

"Yes," Tingting answered. "She was interested to see the latest returning daughter of China, so she came with me to take a peek. The other woman works in the orphanage with me, too, but I don't see her much because she stays in the laundry area.

Some of the older teenagers with disabilities do the washing and hanging clothes—she just manages their work."

Sounds like some children are getting taken advantage of to me, Mia thought, but she decided not to say anything. *But perhaps they like having a purpose, even if only laundry.*

As the old woman moved about, she took every opportunity to sneak a quick look at Mia. Because she obviously didn't speak English and Mia was too exhausted to try to communicate in Mandarin, conversation between them was limited to a few words and gestures. Tingting explained that when she came to work in the city, her aunt accompanied her to watch over her. They shared the expenses of the apartment, which left Tingting with more funds to send home to care for her father.

"How did you learn to speak such good English?" As long as she had to wait on breakfast to be served, Mia thought she might as well appease some of her curiosity.

"My brother is a teacher. He lives far from here, but before I came to the city, he returned home for a year to teach me English. He says I am a good speaker, but terrible at writing. My brother used to say I was a lazy student because I always hurried through my lessons to go outside and be with the animals, especially the newborn ones. Maybe that's why I love the babies so much at the orphanage; they remind me of the calves and piglets I cared for in my village—so dependent on someone else for survival, and innocent of wrongdoing or evil ways."

"Your brother must be a very good teacher, because your English is excellent," Mia told Tingting, making her blush.

"It was difficult to learn, not only because he was a strict teacher, but because our father didn't want anyone in the village to know I was taking lessons. He didn't want others to feel like we were trying to put ourselves at a level above the rest of the people. He didn't learn to read or write himself until my brother taught him, and he was proud of his achievement but humble."

"That's quite an accomplishment," Mia acknowledged.

"My father is a dragon—so he is very tenacious and never gives up on something he believes in. From then on he was adamant that I'd also be able to read and write in both languages before I left home. Our evenings were spent reading as a family and discussing the material. If the people in our village knew what we were doing behind closed doors, they would have been very surprised and maybe suspicious." Though the auntie couldn't understand English, she appeared to get the gist of what they were discussing.

"Is your aunt a blood relative or do you call her auntie like everyone calls the nannies at the orphanage?" Mia was still confused at the term *ayi* and wondered why so many young women were called *auntie*.

Tingting laughed. "She is my real aunt—my mother's sister. When my mother died, she helped to care for my family because she is a widow and doesn't have children. Her husband died in a collapsed coal mine many years ago. See all the lines in her face? Those are from sadness; she is really much younger than she looks."

Auntie Zhi brought three heaping bowls to the table and returned to the stove to retrieve the pot of tea. When she poured the liquid into the cups, the room filled with a delicious fragrance, and Tingting described it as jasmine tea, made from green tea leaves and jasmine blooms. Mia loved the smooth silky taste, and sipping it made her even sleepier than she already was. She watched the other two pick up their bowls of noodles and hold them to their mouths like cups, slurping the contents without shame. If Mia were at home, her mother would surely scold the lack of table manners. *But when in China, do like Chinese!* She joined them in the noisy consumption, and the noodles soon made a warm place in her empty belly.

"I will show you to our room, Mia," Tingting announced.

Mia stood and fought a sudden wave of dizziness. "Whoa... I think I'm so tired I've made myself sick." She guessed she would be sharing a bed with Tingting, but at that point, she didn't care; she just wanted to close her eyes and shut out the stressful last few hours for a while. Considering Tingting hadn't been awake half the night, Mia was sure to at least have the bed to herself for a few hours.

Tingting led Mia to a tiny room off the sitting area. It held one small bed—*too* small for two people, but they'd have to make it work. There wasn't a closet. A bar hung from the ceiling, with a few shirts and pants hanging from the bar, and two pair of shoes were placed neatly side by side underneath. Over the bed was a large dog-eared map of the United States, with pushpins marking different areas. Mia was curious about the map, but she assumed that like many Chinese, Tingting was enamored with the thought of traveling to America.

On an overturned crate next to the bed was a stack of books in English and Chinese, with a few markers poking out of several places. Mia appreciated that like her, Tingting also liked to read. And she liked it even more that Tingting had a copy of Mia's own favorite book, *Gone with the Wind.* She picked it up and flipped it open to read a short paragraph.

"You know this book?" Tingting asked.

"Of course, every American knows this book. Where did you get it? And in English, too!"

"My brother. He gave it to me during Chinese New Year last year. I am only halfway through it. Can you tell me if Scarlett and Rhett get together?" She looked intently at Mia.

"No, I can't tell you. I'm not going to be a spoiler." She put the book down and sat on the bed. As interesting as it was to explore Tingting's home, she wished the girl would leave her and let her sleep.

"Spoiler?" Tingting asked. "I don't understand this word."

"Never mind. Do you have somewhere I can wash up and put on my pajamas?" Mia would have just climbed into the bed and gone straight to sleep, but she didn't want to look like a barbarian to the girl.

Tingting showed her to the small bathroom and gave her a threadbare but clean towel. Mia showered, brushed her teeth, and donned her soft pajama pants and tank top. She quietly returned to the bedroom and climbed under the thin quilt, took possession of the single flat pillow, and closed her eyes, not even caring that the bamboo pallet spread over the narrow bed was scratchy and she could feel the metal of the bed frame through the thin mattress. In the next room, she could hear Tingting talking softly to her aunt, using the hypnotic rapid local dialect. Mia was too exhausted to be curious to know if she was the subject of conversation. Within minutes, she was fast asleep.

CHAPTER TWENTY-ONE

TINGTING followed Lao Ling down the crowded aisle in their local grocery mart, fighting to control the shopping cart with its wayward wheels. Even though the old woman stood out in her bright fluorescent yellow apron, she still felt that meeting in the middle of a crowd of people would make them less suspicious to anyone who might be watching. Amidst the early mass of couples, young mothers, and grandmothers vying for the freshest meat, they gathered their groceries and discussed what to do about Mia.

Tingting was genuinely worried for the old woman and the trouble that assisting a foreigner would bring her if caught.

"Maybe we should tell her to go back to her hotel," Tingting suggested, though that was the last thing she wanted to do.

The old woman waved her hand dismissively and answered that the child had a right to learn about her birth family, no matter if the truth was that the parents did not want to be found. She told her that someone in China had given birth to the girl, and she felt the least they could do was acknowledge her and give her the story of her abandonment so the troubled girl could go on with her life. Then if they never wanted to see each other again, at least that chapter could be closed.

Tingting agreed, but in the ways of a precocious child, she let Lao Ling believe the plan to move forward was her own. Once the decision was made, the two both felt a sense of nervous excitement. As Tingting sorted through the stacked crates of eggs to add the cleanest ones to her bag, her hands shook with apprehension. Lao Ling reached over and quietly covered one with her own, and with wisdom gained from many years of hardship, assured the young girl that all would work out. She put her other hand in her apron pocket and pulled out a wrapped sticky bun, then gave it to Tingting in a gesture of comfort.

They finished their shopping and parted ways at the bus stop. They didn't want to be seen together too much until their mission to help Mia was complete.

Lao Ling headed straight home, while Tingting walked a few blocks and stopped at the house of a friend to make a phone call. A few minutes later, she hurried back to the apartment to see if the girl had awakened yet.

ଔ

"Mia. Please sit up and eat." Mia felt Tingting nudge her repeatedly until she finally fought through the fog that had settled over her and she opened her eyes. Auntie Zhi removed the wet cloth from Mia's head before it could slide off in her attempt to sit up.

"*Ta fashao.*" The aunt looked disapprovingly at Mia.

"What time is it? What did she say? Do you have coffee?" The sound of her own hoarse voice was so different from the familiar song that was slowly receding back into the recesses of her mind as she struggled to stop the spinning motion caused by sitting up.

"You have been sleeping for two days. You have a fever. My auntie has been nursing you while your body has been fighting through the sickness. Did you eat anything from the street vendors before you came here?"

"No, but I was bitten by a lot of mosquitoes as I clung to a ledge outside the window on the sixth floor of my hotel," Mia mumbled in response.

Tingting shook her head and rolled her eyes at her aunt. Auntie Zhi gently used the damp cloth to wipe Mia's brow, and then waved at the bowl sitting on the bedside table.

"My auntie says you must eat the congee she made for you, or you will be too weak to recover."

Congee? Mia had heard of—and probably eaten as a child in the orphanage—the famous Chinese congee but couldn't say she was anxious to try it out. What she wanted was coffee. However, it was very bad timing to be sick, so Mia struggled to reach for the bowl. She had to hurry and get well so that she could decide what to do about her predicament.

"Wait, I'll help you." Tingting picked up the bowl and spoon and began to feed Mia a small bit at a time. "You must not try to get up today. Auntie says you must rest until tomorrow or until your fever has gone away. It is no use to argue with her; she is very stubborn and will not give in. So just relax and try to feel better."

Mia shrugged in resignation and accepted the spoon of lumpy porridge. Though the food was thicker than she would have liked, its slightly salty flavor soothed her rolling stomach.

"Has Jax been here yet?" she asked, moving her head very slowly towards the door. Each time she moved too fast, she fought through a wave of nausea and dizziness.

"No. We have not heard from him. But Auntie Zhi has some questions for you. What Chinese zodiac are you? Wait—she has already guessed that you are the horse. Is that right?"

"Yes, but how did she know?" Mia asked.

Tingting turned to her auntie to discuss how she knew the correct sign. They laughed together, and she turned back around to Mia.

"Because Mia, you are very independent, and you thought nothing about running to China to trace your heritage. Horses do not like to be penned in—and you have proven that. Horses also want to feel as if they belong, and we can tell that you want to be seen the same as other Chinese while you are here." She hesitated but then added, "Some say horses are impatient and hardnosed."

"What? I'm not impatient!" Mia was first offended, but she paused and realized that perhaps she *was* a bit impatient, if she were to admit the truth. Her family continually told her she was very impatient, especially when she had to wait on the bathroom in the mornings when she was growing up and her brothers would beat her to the shower.

"You should be happy; you are the same animal as Ri Ta Hei Worth," Tingting encouraged Mia.

"Who?" Mia had no idea who she was talking about.

"You know, she is a movie star from the 1940s. She was also a dancer and very beautiful."

"Oh—Rita Hayworth." Mia shook her head at the image of Tingting watching old American movies, possibly even finding a way to munch on buttered popcorn and chug Diet Coke. *Where did she even find copies of classics like that?* "Okay, Tingting, you win. Yes, I'm a horse, and I'm happy I share the same sign as Rita Hayworth. Now, can I get up and go to the bathroom?"

Tingting smiled and moved to feed Mia one more spoonful of the congee before allowing her to rise and visit the *weisheng jian*, telling her she would have to finish the congee when she returned. Mia rolled her eyes in exasperation and shuffled out of the room. *How did Tingting get so bossy all of a sudden?*

In the bathroom, Mia felt weak and dizzy. She looked around at the tiny space and thought about her own spacious bathroom at home. She had been confused that first night when Tingting told her there was a shower in the room. All Mia had seen were a toilet, sink, and a spigot protruding from the wall with a handheld nozzle attached. She'd finally understood that the entire tiny bathroom was the shower—a concrete enclosure with a small sloping floor leading to a drain in the corner. Mia had taken a shower but was shocked at the cold water and had bumped her knees on the toilet more than once. Figuring out how to wash her hair had been difficult, and she couldn't help wishing she was in her own spacious—and hot—shower at home. When she had finally turned the frigid water off, she used up most of her threadbare towel drying off the toilet, sink, and mirror.

Deciding to wait until her congee settled before battling the shower issue again, Mia returned and settled back under the coverlet. Tingting and her auntie sat squatting on the floor next to the bed, ready to resume their talk. Mia felt weak as a kitten and was glad for their insistence that she rest. After her first night there, she had realized that she was sleeping in Auntie Zhi's usual place. She tried to decline the gesture, but the old woman refused to take it back, insisting it was better for two young girls to sleep together and that she preferred a mat on the floor, anyway. Tingting told Mia it was true, as her auntie had slept on a mat most of her life before coming to the city. Since then, the awkwardness of sleeping with a stranger had quickly disappeared, and she and Tingting even kicked each other during the night in competition for the coverlet.

"My auntie wants to know if you miss your American family."

"Of course I do. I miss my parents and my brothers. My mom is a nurse, and she takes very good care of all of us when we're sick. She brings my favorite ice pops and Sprite poured over shaved ice. And my dad always goes to the movie store and rents all of my favorite movies to entertain me while I'm recovering. He ties a scarf or shirt around his face like he's afraid I'm contagious, wears plastic gloves to feel my forehead, and does other silly things that make me laugh until I feel better." Mia felt a sudden wave of homesickness and an urge to call her mother, but she didn't want to alarm her, and she didn't want to lie about what was happening. It was better to just wait until her circumstances changed for the better, then call and report in. She also didn't have the energy to find a place with wi-fi to hook up and attempt to connect with Skype.

Auntie Zhi spoke again for a long time, her voice holding a serious tone. Tingting listened carefully.

"She wants to know why you want to find your first family now that you are a happy American? She said you struggle within yourself to prove you are Chinese, yet you can never truly be Chinese until you live here among the people in your motherland."

Tingting blushed, and Mia was moved that she was embarrassed about the directness of her auntie's questions.

"Please tell your auntie with all due respect, it has taken me most of my life to come to terms with my heritage. For years I didn't want to be Chinese, and I'm ashamed of my ignorance. However, I have learned that I can be loyal to my motherland *and* to my new land at the same time. I can love my adoptive family and my heritage all with the same heart. Most of all, I've learned that to move forward and be who I'm meant to be, I must know who I started out as."

As Tingting translated her response to the old woman, it met with obvious approval. Before the old woman could return a reply, they heard a knock on the door. Auntie Zhi rose to her feet and left the room, only to return with Lao Ling and a very eager Jax. In his hands he held two large cups of coffee, and Mia was relieved to see the familiar green siren affixed to the steaming cup.

"Jax?" Mia looked from him to Lao Ling, confused. "What are you two doing together?"

"We met in the stairwell, but it's just a coincidence that we were both coming at the same time," Jax explained.

"I'm so sorry, Mia. I couldn't get away from work. We had a half-dozen tour groups check in, and the hotel has been rocking. But why are you still in bed? It's after noon." Jax looked concerned.

Mia wordlessly reached out for the cup of coffee, and Jax put it in her hands. As he bent to kiss her cheek, she caught a hint of his scent. She closed her eyes and inhaled deeply. *How would I even describe his smell? Spicy, wholesome, strong, clean? Maybe 'comforting'...*

Lao Ling began asking the auntie questions, speaking much too rapidly for Mia to follow along. The older ladies moved into the other room to talk.

"Mia has been very sick, with a fever and bad dreams. She needs rest, so she cannot leave here until tomorrow morning. That is only if she has no fever—otherwise she will have to stay in bed longer," Tingting said firmly.

"Mia, what happened? What made you sick? Are you okay?" Jax sat down beside Mia and held her hand. He looked at the bowl and wrinkled his nose. "And what are you eating?"

"I don't know what made me sick, and I'm eating *congee*. Stop looking at it like that! It's just rice porridge like they feed the children in the orphanage. I should remember it from my past, but I don't. It has the reputation of the American chicken soup—everyone here eats it when they're sick." She lowered her voice to a whisper. "They're making me eat it—Auntie Zhi thinks it's some kind of miracle medicine."

Jax visibly shivered as he looked down into the bowl of lumpy rice.

"Mia, I went to the police station to research your case,"

he told her.

"What? You did? What happened? What did they say?" The station was on her list of places to follow up on, but she'd dropped it after her fiasco with the police in her hotel room.

"I showed them your poster and asked them to pull the file. They should've had something recorded from the date you were found at the train station, but after I waited for over two hours, they said they didn't have anything on you. They don't have sure computer records dated that far back, but I refused to leave until a clerk went through their boxed records. Good thing I stayed—she found a copy of your finding ad attached to a short report."

"You found my report? What did it say? Did you make a copy?"

"They wouldn't let me make a copy, but I got the name of the man who found you at the train station and took you to the orphanage. His address was listed, and I went there. But it's bad news, Mia."

"Just tell me." Mia's shoulders slumped even lower in the bed. She let out a long sigh.

"That address doesn't exist. It is nothing but a demolished block of what used to be housing. He might have lived there years ago, but there is no way to trace him now. I even asked around the part of the neighborhood that is still standing, and no one claims to have known anyone there by his family name, Zheng."

"Wait! Zheng is the name of the director's good friend who supplies milk powder for the babies." Tingting looked shell-shocked. "And he is very old—he could have been around many years ago."

Mia shook her head, sure that the name couldn't be a coincidence. She wondered just what was going on.

Jax sat on the bed next to her. "Also, I wanted to go alone to the station so I could feel them out to see if they acted strange about your case. And Mia, I really don't think it was police officers who came to your hotel. Either that or they're great actors, because no one at the station showed that they had ever heard of you. Even so, I didn't mention the intrusion or your passport; I didn't feel confident enough that they wouldn't follow me to you. We're going to have to find another way to get it back. We might have to go to the embassy and file for a lost passport, after all."

Lao Ling and the auntie returned to the bedroom and spoke rapidly to Tingting. Lao Ling pulled a folded piece of paper from her flowered apron pocket and waved it at Mia, then quickly poked it back out of sight.

"Lao Ling said she has heard from The Finders, and they would like to meet with you." Tingting was honored to deliver the message to Mia that was sure to make her happy.

Mia and Jax looked at each other, hope reflecting in their eyes.

"For real? Do they know who I am? Did they already process my test? Do they know my birth parents? What'd they say? Can we go right now?" Mia was so excited, she instantly felt much better. She wanted to get up, dress, and immediately leave to meet the people who might know something about her birth family. After the disappointment with the imposters, she was beginning to lose hope that she would ever find the answers she craved.

Lao Ling and Auntie Zhi once again left the room, ignoring the unanswered questions hanging in the air.

Tingting watched them go. "Lao Ling doesn't know. She contacted them to inform them you were not at the hotel, and they asked to see you. She said do not ask any more questions, because she cannot answer them. For now, you must rest, because soon you will take a very hard journey. It will be physically exhausting, and possibly emotional, as well. We will learn more details later. Jax, you must leave to allow Mia to sleep. When she wakes up again, my auntie will have green tea ready for her to drink—your American coffee is bad for her."

"I'm not going anywhere until Mia asks me to," Jax adamantly said, then softened his tone. "Sorry, Tingting, I don't mean to be rude, but I don't want to leave Mia. What if she's seriously ill and needs to go to a hospital?"

"Tingting, I'm grateful you are here to take good care of me, but right now I need Jax. He gives me strength. He can stay until I go to sleep, and then he'll leave and return in the morning. And I also want him to accompany me to meet The Finders." Mia spoke respectfully, conveying her wishes but hoping there wouldn't be opposition. "And Jax, please be for real. I'm not dying and won't need to go a hospital. After what I saw of the children's hospital, you'd only be able to get me to go there if you knocked me unconscious first."

Tingting's face wore an unusually stubborn expression. "As you wish, Mia, but I cannot guarantee that Jax can go with us. The Finders are a very secret group, and they may not trust him. I will find out today if he will be allowed, and I will let you know in the morning. Now I must go and work my shift at the orphanage. I will ask around to my friends about Zheng, and then I will return before dinner. Please, Mia, you need to rest." Tingting backed out the door, gave a quick wave, and left.

"Now, Mia, what are we going to do with you?" Jax teased as he ran his fingers through her hair and used his foot to trace a trail up her calf.

"Don't even think like that, Jax. I'm still really sick at my stomach—I might even heave. Are you sure you want to be here? I haven't even showered today. You might catch something awful from me."

"The only thing I'm going to catch is the love bug, and it's too late because it already bit me. Don't worry. You look gorgeous even when you're a nice shade of green." Jax spread his hand over the hollow her shirt made over her belly button. "Since we've nothing else to do—no television, radio or Internet to entertain us—we'll just have to talk some more. You haven't told me what you want to do with your life. What's the plan when you graduate? Now that I know how stubborn you are, I can't imagine what your next adventure will be. How will you top this one? What are you gonna do, climb Mt. Everest blindfolded?"

Mia didn't laugh; instead she became very serious. "I'll graduate this fall with a degree in psychology from Western Washington University. Then I hope to get my doctorate in child psychology. I plan to work with adoptees, especially those with issues related to self-image and abandonment. Jax, I've spent years rejecting who I truly am because I was afraid of how people would judge me. I believe I can help girls or even boys who suffer with some of the same problems I hid for my entire childhood."

"Mia, that's a *perfect* plan for you. Seriously. With your drive and ambition, you'll be a complete success in anything you set your mind to. Working with children would be a great fit for you, you have such a kind heart—but you're also a tiger. There couldn't be a better career for you."

"What about you? Where do you think you'll end up working?" Mia knew he would work in the hotel industry, meaning he'd probably choose to move from country to country, resort to resort, living in faraway places. He'd probably meet all sorts of beautiful and exotic women and forget all about her. Even though she had already convinced herself their relationship was a short fling, the thoughts of him with another girl depressed her and made her feel even weaker.

"I thought my main goal was to travel, so that's why I chose this field. I still do want to travel—but I want to do something to help underprivileged children in the cities I work in. I've been thinking about it a lot and I want to start a non-profit and set up resources for street children to utilize when they need a meal, a bath, or even a safe place to sleep. Perhaps I can even help to reunite some of them with their parents. Something like what The Finders do—whoever they are. I'd even like to work with them," Jax said.

"I wonder who The Finders are…" Mia could hardly wait until she could wake up the next morning, hopefully feeling much better and prepared to meet someone who could help her find her birth parents. Suddenly, she felt very sleepy again and leaned her head against Jax.

"Soon, little one. We'll know soon." He stroked her hair as she once again fell into a deep sleep. Jax pulled the cover up to her chin and felt her forehead. An hour later as Mia's breathing became deeper and steadier, he kissed the top of her head and quietly crept out of the room.

CHAPTER TWENTY-TWO

"HELLO? Mom?" Mia was sure she heard someone pick up the phone, but so far she only heard irritating white noise.

"Mia, is that you?" The static on the line peaked then settled.

"Yes, it's me. How are you?"

"Oh, Mia, why haven't you called? We've been so worried! What's going on? Is everything okay?"

"I'm so sorry, Mom. I've been sick with some sort of virus for a few days, but don't worry; I'm okay now. I also lost my passport, but I'm working on getting a replacement. You don't have to do a thing." Mia hoped the little white lie wouldn't be picked up on—so far she didn't know if she was going to get her passport back or not, but she didn't want to alarm her mother.

"And Mom, remember I told you about Tingting? I'm staying with her and her auntie now. It's saving me money, and I'm getting totally immersed in Chinese culture."

There was a short silence on the other end as Mia's mom digested the information. "I am not going to overreact, Mia. You are an adult now and I trust your judgment."

"Where's Dad? Can he talk?" Mia knew her mom was actually hanging on the precipice of overreacting. She wanted to hear her father's calm, soothing voice. She needed his quiet confidence that she was still strong enough to accomplish her goal to find answers.

"He's not here, Mia. He went to play golf with the boys. He'll be so disappointed that he missed your call."

"Oh—bummer. Can you tell him I miss him? And I miss you, too, Mom." Mia wanted to keep the call short so that she didn't have to tell any more white lies. The less said, the better, until she could get herself into a better situation. But the sound of her mom's voice was a comfort that no amount of congee could bring.

"So what's happening? Have you found out anything, yet? Are you eating well? Are you still hanging out with that boy from Seattle?"

"Mom—one question at a time. First, in regards to 'that boy,' yes—I'm still hanging out with Jax. I'm talking on his international phone right now because I can't get hooked up for Skype. He's really helpful and has been showing me the city. And believe me, he feeds me well. He knows all the best places to go for the best local cuisine. You wouldn't believe the stuff I've been eating, and it's all so delicious. It is nothing like Chinese food at home—it's much better." She knew she was rambling but hoped to get her mom off the subject of Jax by steering her towards the subject of food.

"Mia Su, don't you get too serious with that boy, you hear me? You're probably still reeling from your breakup with Collin. You know, I haven't told your brothers about you meeting someone yet."

"Mom, I ***know***. So anyway, no, I haven't found out anything about my birth parents. But I'm going to keep trying. There hasn't been anything else from those posters you helped me make, but we hung them all over the city, so I still have hope." She left out the information about meeting The Finders; she didn't want to alarm her mom any more than she had already.

"Oh, Mia, I'm so sorry we didn't do more when you first came home to find out something about your finding details. We were told you didn't have a note, and no one came forward looking for you when your photo was placed in the local papers, so we just took it for granted that you were meant to be ours. I wish we had questioned the director more or done something—I don't know what—but *something*. Can you ever forgive me?"

The anguish in her voice was evident, and even though Mia had thought for years that they could've—should have—done more before the trail was too cold, she realized that all those years ago, the orphanages were not as open to communication as they were now. She didn't want her mother to carry that guilt; she knew it would destroy her.

"Mom, it's okay. Really. Please don't worry about it. But hey—the good news is that I'm really getting a good peek at the culture here and have learned a lot about China. But listen, I need to go. I'll call you again soon, and I love you! Tell Dad I love him, too—oh, and the boys!"

"I love you, too, Mia. Guess what? I'm sitting in your spot looking out at your favorite tree."

"Oh, Mom. I can't wait to get back home. But I need to go. Love you, Mom." Mia felt herself choking up. So she was homesick—who wouldn't be? She could visualize her mom curled up in her window seat, the place she had spent half her childhood, staring and daydreaming. Waiting.

"Please be careful. Call me in a few days!"

ଓ

Mia snapped the phone shut and set it on the table next to the bed. Leaning back against the wall, she pulled her knees up to her chin and wrapped her arms around her legs. She could hear Jax puttering around in the other room as she let her mind wander. Her mother's voice had made her start thinking about the day they became a family. Of course, she didn't remember it, but she had been told the story so many times it felt like it was her own memories.

It was only the month of April, but Shanghai was already hot and humid as her parents waited in the hotel for the designated time to meet downstairs. Her mom had been awake most of the night, unable to sleep from jetlag or more likely nervous tension. She said all sorts of questions and self-doubt swirled in her head.

Her dad slept as Mom paced the room and changed clothes several times. Of all things, she had worried about what she was going to wear! As if a tiny girl would've known the difference in anything her new mom chose! Mia smiled to herself. *Mom is so neurotic sometimes.*

Her mom also said that as she paced that hotel room, she negotiated with God that if he'd let her daughter love her at first sight, she'd be a better person and actually go to church more than every few weeks and on holidays.

Mia's dad finally woke around six and did his best to assure her everything would be all right. "Mary, for goodness' sake, you are already the mother of three boys. You know what to do—what do you think will go wrong?" Mia could just see her Dad saying that. He never let anything bother him. To him, life was a series of adventures.

Finally they had made it downstairs to wait for the van, Mom carrying a bag of stuff to use during the first minutes of bonding with—or bribing, as Mia liked to tease—her new daughter.

Mom said the Civil Affairs office was complete mayhem. After Mia had encountered her own taste of Chinese bureaucracy, she had a better idea of what her parents had gone through so many years ago.

But as the story went, her parents were herded to a tiny, hot room and waited with other parents who were as anxious as they were. Shortly after arriving, a woman came in to notify them that the children would be late, adding even more anxiety to an already peaked level for Mom. Finally, another hour later, a different woman entered the room to announce the children.

One at a time, names were called out, and frightened, wide-eyed children were carried in to their new parents.

Her mom said that Mia was towards the end of the list and came walking through the door, holding the hand of a pretty girl of about twenty years old. She said Mia was absolutely beautiful, much more so than the other children in the room—*But of course she'd say that,* Mia mused.

Mia had looked around with sad eyes as her new parents approached her. Mom said when she had dropped to her knees and tried to give her the Curious George stuffed monkey she had carried all the way from home, Mia had refused to take it. But when Dad tried, she had succumbed to the silly voices he used to tempt her. Mom said that Mia never cried during their first meeting, but she was very clearly a sad little girl.

She said the young woman that brought me in pushed me towards them and left the room. At first I tried to follow the orphanage worker, but then I stopped. Mom and Dad pulled a photo book out of their bag and began pointing out my new brothers, our home, and the picture of my waiting bedroom, all done up in pinks and frills.

In the last few years, as she'd had more questions, Mom had added more details that weren't appropriate for her little girl ears. Details that now—especially after her orphanage visit—stood out in her mind. Many of the other couples adopting that day also appeared to be having a hard time with their newest additions. Mom said one couple spent almost an hour bonding with their little girl, only to have someone come take her away and trade her for another. The orphanage personnel had given them the wrong child!

On the other side of the room from them, a woman sat crying in the corner as the nine-year-old daughter she'd expected to have only mild cerebral palsy also appeared to be severely mentally delayed. The girl danced around the room on her toes, her head flopping back and forth, and her arms flapping wildly. A few minutes later, the girl drew attention again as she gobbled crackers, then spit them all over the floor and made strange high-pitched noises at those around her. Mom said the she felt so sorry for the woman and even her husband, who comforted her as he demanded answers from the official.

She said that Mia, however, was so very quiet. Too quiet—the eerie stillness from her new daughter had scared her.

After the required procedures, Mia's parents had left the Civil Affairs office and escorted Mia to the waiting van. Again, she presented no resistance but also gave no indication that she wanted to go with them. On the way back to the hotel, they offered M&Ms, but she ignored the treats.

Mia swallowed the lump in her throat as she thought of the way Mom described her sitting in the van, staring out the window as a lone tear had slid down her tiny cheek. For the millionth time, Mia felt sorry for the frightened little girl she must have been.

Stubborn from day one, Mom said at the hotel Mia wouldn't allow them to change her out of her filthy clothes. She refused a bath and wouldn't eat anything. She sat silently on the edge of the bed for hours, dangling her feet with the tiny broken sandals and staring at the floor in front of her. The only noise she had made was when they tried to touch her, and then she howled in fright until they moved away from her.

That night they both finally lay down on each side of her and took turns humming until Mia fell asleep sitting up. Then they gently lay her back and very carefully covered her. It was a long night; they both worried and wondered what the morning would bring. Mom said she had never before and never since felt so helpless as a mother trying to comfort her hurting child.

They said the next few days were difficult but not terrible, as Mia was obviously a sweet child, but one who had seen too much trauma. They overcame some of the difficulties, and found out that she reacted positively to music, making the evenings easier. They bought a small radio for the room, and the music lulled her to sleep each night.

After two days of running bath water and adding fun, colorful toys to the water along with a new baby doll, she had allowed them to give her a bath and change her clothes. However, she insisted on wearing her ratty sandals and declined the cute princess ones they had bought. They thought it made Mia feel independent, that perhaps she was holding on to a part of her life from the orphanage. They also said it was the first indication that Mia would never like anything pink or frilly—that she was already setting the stage to become their little gypsy.

Once home, Mom worried that Mia spent a lot of time in what would become her beloved window seat—seeming to think pensively of something or someone. Many times during the night that first year, they say they could hear her down the hall from their room, whimpering in her sleep, and one of them would come and just sit with her. She eventually allowed them to comfort her when she was sad and saw them as her protectors, instead of strangers.

Mia smiled again. Luckily for her brothers, she had accepted their devotion the minute they enveloped her into their little boy arms, excited to finally have the sister they had waited for so many months.

As for the little girl who had appeared mentally delayed in their travel group, her parents brought her home, too, and it was finally determined that in the orphanage, she had lived with the children who were kept hidden away because of their developmental disabilities. It was a miracle that she had even been approved for adoption, and later they discovered she was only mimicking what she saw on a daily basis. After some intense therapy and a lot of love, she flourished into the capable and smart girl that had been hiding under all of her nervous actions that day in the Chinese office. They became friends of their family, and Mia had grown up taking occasional vacations with the little girl named Callie who one would never know was the same wild girl in China.

Mia heard the kettle in the kitchen start to whistle, breaking her out of her thoughts.

"Mia?" Jax called from the kitchen. "Are you done talking to your parents?"

Mia uncurled herself from her spot on the bed and stood. She stretched her arms over her head and then reached up and dried the tears from the corner of her eyes.

"Yes, I'm coming. What are you making me in there?" She picked up Jax' phone and headed for the kitchen.

CHAPTER TWENTY-THREE

HOLDING hands, Jax and Mia hopped over the large water puddle and onto the sidewalk. It had rained nonstop for several days, and they both felt exhilarated at the prospect of a sunny day—or at least the closest thing to it, with the pollution always in the way.

Mia had awoken that morning feeling carefree for the first time in days. Tingting still hadn't gotten news from the Finders, and Mia was tired of sitting around waiting. She had to get out and do something, or she was going to scream. Wanting to look extra special for Jax, she'd pulled her long, jet black hair into a sleek ponytail to match her sleeveless black dress. She'd slipped her petite feet into comfortable black flats and added white pearls to her ears as the finishing touch.

"You look like a ballerina," he'd told her when she had opened the door to find him standing there, holding a bouquet of daisies for her. She laughed at his analogy, but with the surprise of sunshine that morning, she sort of felt like doing a few jumps in the air, so the description fit.

It had been a long week, waiting to hear more instructions from The Finders. Mia was still trying to absorb what Tingting had discovered about Zheng, the man who supposedly found her at the train station. His name was frequently used on reports when the real finders do not want to be named. Tingting also recommended they not confront him, unless Mia wanted to really upset the director.

Mia wouldn't promise not to confront Zheng, but she was biding her time until the next lead. However, besides Jax, Mia gained another diversion to keep her entertained—baby Xinxin was staying with Lao Ling, and that meant Mia was getting to visit her, too. Xinxin had only stayed at the children's hospital briefly before they discharged her with the diagnosis of a skin problem. They didn't even do the full examination or give any information about her heart issue. *That really didn't make sense; wouldn't the hospital be the best place to be with a mysterious skin issue?* But regardless, the orphanage director sent a representative to Shanghai to retrieve Xinxin and brought her back to the orphanage.

Tingting said Resa was so angry that to appease her, they'd sent Xinxin home with Lao Ling to be carefully watched until they could get her another appointment at the hospital. Tingting also said she didn't believe they'd ever allow Xinxin to be operated on, and she didn't understand why, though Resa was still fighting to get permission to take her back to Shanghai. So for the present, unbeknownst to the orphanage staff, Xinxin had another two aunties looking over her and taking turns rocking her, feeding her, and spoiling her. Xinxin especially loved for Mia to play the guitar and sing to her. Every night, she and Tingting waited until after Xinxin was bathed and then went over to sing her to sleep. They all enjoyed the nightly routine, and it soon became the highlight of their evenings. Tingting had even learned a few of the songs and often joined in with Mia. She told Mia she had never known a girl who could play a guitar.

With the extra care, Xinxin had even started eating congee and pureed fruits. At over nine months old, it was long past time that the orphanage should have introduced her to more than milk powder to strengthen her for an upcoming surgery. It took a while for Tingting to explain to Mia that the babies were kept on a milk powder diet until they were close to one year old, because the orphanage staff didn't have the resources or time to feed children solid foods earlier.

"Where do you want to go today, Mia?" asked Jax as he slid his arm around her.

"Hmm, everything's still wet, so a park wouldn't be a good idea. What about looking at some art? Do you know a place we could go?"

Jax thought for a moment. "We can go to Yuan Lin Lu. It's near the museum, and at the end of the street is an area where local artists gather and sell their pieces. Some artists actually work from that location so patrons can see them in action."

"Sounds like a plan!" Mia agreed. Jax flagged a taxi and gave the street name, and they climbed in for the ride.

In the mornings and a few afternoons, Jax stopped by to take Mia out. Sometimes they just walked, or shopped, or stopped at one of the street vendors for fast food. Mostly they visited places where they could blend in with the crowd, except for a few times when they had the apartment to themselves, and they stayed in. They had gotten to know each other quite well. Though they hadn't done more than kiss, the thoughts of their afternoons spent alone made Mia blush.

With the outings, Mia felt like she was really getting to know China and the people, and Jax was the reason for most of it. On their excursions, he entertained her with more stories of China's history and culture. She always learned something. Sometimes they took Xinxin, and it almost felt like they were a family, walking arm in arm and pushing a baby stroller. Lao Ling loved having the breaks so she could take her mid-morning naps, and she had come to trust Mia.

The taxi driver peered into his mirror and gave a toothless smile. "*Nide niu pengyou?*"

Jax laughed and put his arm around Mia. "Yes, she's my girlfriend," he teased, sending the driver into a fit of giggles.

Mia rolled her eyes and grinned. *Boys will be boys*, she thought.

That morning they had planned to take Xinxin in her stroller for a short excursion. When they dropped by the apartment and snuck through the back way to stay away from unwanted attention, Lao Ling said the baby girl had been up a few times in the night, struggling for breath, so she was sleeping in.

Xinxin really needs to see a doctor. Mia hoped Resa would successfully petition the tier of directors for their approval once again. Jax and Mia planned to stop by and see the little girl on their way back to Tingting's home, maybe even sing her a song—or at least steal her for a short walk. Xinxin loved getting out and seeing everything, and the wonder on her face brought joy to both Mia and Jax.

The driver slammed on his brakes, and they found themselves deposited at the end of a T-shaped street, directly in the center of a huge commotion. Two farmers with wooden wheelbarrows full of colorful fruit bickered ferociously. From what Mia could gather, one stole the other's customer by offering a lower price just as he was about to make a sale. In China, even a few cents were fiercely fought over.

Jax ended the quarrel by picking up two plump peaches and offering the offended vendor a whole ten yuan—barely over a dollar to him, but ten times the usual price. Mia was impressed by his quick thinking to bring peace to the situation—and she got a sweet treat out of it, too. She and Jax ate their peaches while they sauntered along the street, looking at all the interesting booths of art and other trinkets.

At one stand, a dark-skinned little man sat shaping small clay sculptures from pedestrian models. His face was an example of total focus, the mustache above his mouth twitching in concentration. On a bench to his right sat a young couple perched together, posing for their clay bust while the artist did an astonishing job of capturing their likenesses. Around him, other spectators watched and waited their turn to sit for the man.

"Jax, he's really talented. His sculpture looks exactly like them." She pointed at the piece of work between the artist's hands.

"Yeah—he's the real deal. And look up there, can you believe that?" On one of the shelves of his small wooden stand was a completed bust of Obama.

Mia and Jax laughed at the exact likeness of the controversial president. The Chinese were infatuated with the subject of a black president leading America, and they still laughed at the memory of one of their taxi drivers repeatedly shouting "Obama! Obama!" to them once he found out they were Americans. It must have been the only English word he knew, because he never said anything else except to tell them their fare amount in Mandarin when they reached their destination.

They watched until the couple were handed their finished piece of art and smiled at their satisfied faces as they examined it, then Jax and Mia climbed aboard a rickshaw.

"He'll take us to the end of the street, and we'll see everything as we walk back." Jax turned to the driver and gave him the instructions in Mandarin.

Mia was too busy looking at all the interesting sites to answer. She was overwhelmed by all the activity and wasn't sure which way to look first. She especially enjoyed the small stand with all the tiny bamboo cages hanging from every angle and lined up along the tables, all just the right size for crickets. One row of cages housed an array of colorful and noisy crickets for sale.

"They're so pretty, Jax! And the cages look like tiny castles!" Mia exclaimed as they passed the displays.

"Long ago, the Chinese brought crickets into their home for good luck," Jax explained. "They enjoyed hearing the crickets sing, and even today some old-timers still keep them as pets. Occasionally I hear about cricket fights still happening and the gambling that goes on—but it's frowned upon and done under the radar."

At the end of the street, they disembarked directly in front of a teahouse. It was a small structure, made up mostly of intricately carved screens. A young woman beckoned them in and Mia told Jax she would like to try it, as she had never been in a real Chinese teahouse.

They entered the teahouse and found themselves in a tiny garden-like open area. Small, round ceramic tables were scattered about and Jax chose one that faced the street, so they could still watch the people milling about between the openings of the screens.

A petite, quiet woman brought out a traditional tea set: a tiny brown ceramic pot made of special clay to enhance the taste of the tea. She put dry tea leaves into the clay pot, poured hot water in, and replaced the lid. She waited a moment, unmoving, and then put a small strainer onto a clear decanter and poured the tea through it. Finally, she poured the finished tea into the tiny teacups and beckoned for the couple to try it.

"*Biluo chun cha*," the woman announced, naming the type of tea she was serving.

"Oh, that's supposed to be the most famous kind of tea in Suzhou. The locals call it *Fearful Incense*, because the smell is so strong. On National Tomb-Sweeping day, there are usually scads of people picking the leaves from Biluo Mountain near Lake Taihu. We've even sent tour groups out there from the hotel," Jax said.

Mia was the first to taste the fragrant tea, and as soon as it hit her taste buds, she raised her eyebrows in surprise. "Mmm… This is delicious!" she exclaimed to Jax.

He chuckled and agreed. "*Hen hao chi*!" They took their time to enjoy the pot of tea, paid, and began the walk back to the end of the street.

Mia walked a few feet down the street to look at a display of silk shoes, all intricately embroidered with various designs. She picked a tiny pink pair stitched with lotus flowers. "Jax, look at these. I'm gonna get them for Xinxin. She's gonna need them—you saw her trying to stand up yesterday, didn't you? She's going to be walking soon, just you wait." *She'll look adorable with the classic little slippers on her teensy feet, and she'll have a reminder of me when I'm gone.* Mia paid the shopkeeper ten yuan and tucked the slippers into her shoulder bag.

"I saw her, but Lao Ling said not to let her do that much until after her surgery. It's too strenuous on her little heart, even if she does look like a cute little bouncing frog." They both chuckled. *The surprised look on her tiny face when she successfully pulled herself up was so funny!*

They stopped in front of a silk screen shop. Jax pointed at the woman who sat, quietly embroidering an elegant white cat on a fragile piece of silk. "Would you like one of these, Mia? The white cat represents prosperity. That's why you see so many portrayed in paintings in China. People put them in their houses to attract riches."

Mia knew she should say no, but she really wanted one to take home, and having Jax around to negotiate was a good opportunity to get a fair price. "Sure. A small one will fit in my suitcase. But do you think she has a piece with a butterfly?" In some of their other outings, she had finally finished her souvenir shopping for her family, but the screen would be just for her. It would be her reminder of Jax and the many memories they made as he helped her to untangle the mystery of her birth parents.

Together they picked out a small screen with a beautiful golden butterfly and began the process of exchanging prices. The soft-spoken woman surprised Mia by being a worthy adversary in bartering. When they finally agreed on a price, Mia felt like she'd witnessed the final lap of two competitors striving for the finish line.

After they exchanged money and the woman handed over the print, they smiled and shook hands, adhering to the usual Chinese custom of becoming fast friends after a strenuous negotiating session.

Outside the doors, Jax handed Mia the gift. "Here's your butterfly, but you owe me a kiss."

"Here? In front of everyone?" Mia blushed as she looked around at all the people rushing by.

"Mia, how many of these people do you know or will you ever see again?"

She laughed at his logic and closed her eyes, inviting him to lean in. He took his time to kiss her slowly and gently before releasing her, leaving her dizzy. They left the shop holding hands and continued walking, their moment of affection unnoticed among the mass of shoppers and vendors.

"Let's go back, Jax. It's almost time for Xinxin's afternoon nap, and I'd like to see her before she goes to sleep. I can try her new shoes on her." Jax quickly agreed.

After a quick taxi ride, they climbed out and both hurried towards the apartment complex and up to Lao Ling's home.

They stopped and knocked gently, just in case naptime had started earlier than usual. No one came, so Jax knocked again, a bit louder this time.

Tingting finally opened the door, her face stricken with grief. Lao Ling sat in her chair, rocking back and forth while staring out the window. She didn't even turn when Mia and Jax entered the room.

"What's going on? Where's Xinxin?" Mia looked around the room and peeked into the old woman's bedroom, but she didn't see Xinxin anywhere. Her crib sat empty against the wall, the small stuffed bear she liked to cuddle abandoned in the corner.

Tingting hesitated, and then spoke softly. "Xinxin died this morning right after you and Jax left. She was drinking her bottle when she started to struggle for breath and turned blue. Lao Ling rushed her outside, but before she could find a taxi to take her to the hospital, Xinxin stopped breathing in her arms. I wasn't here to help." The young girl lowered her head. "They just came a few minutes ago to take her body away."

"What do you mean, she's *dead*? No!" Mia covered her face with both hands as her knees buckled. "No, no, no, no. Please, no!"

Jax quickly dropped the bag he was carrying, threw his arms around Mia, and supported her as he led her to the couch.

CHAPTER TWENTY-FOUR

MIA stared out at the passing scenery and released a long sigh. The last few days had been the hardest of her life. She still couldn't believe Xinxin had died; she couldn't stop thinking of the little girl's sweet smile. She hadn't meant enough to the orphanage officials for them to push for her medical care. The blatant disregard for her life was something Mia would never be able to get over.

Xinxin wasn't even allowed a simple memorial service, and the thought of her tiny body lying all alone on a cold slab awaiting cremation haunted Mia so much so that she was only able to sleep in short spurts. To her, Xinxin represented the thousands of other baby girls who were neglected in orphanages every year, dying from disabilities or sickness that could easily be treated.

She'd heard from Jax that Xinxin's preventable death was the final straw for Resa. Devastated and furious with the orphanage officials, Resa had given them notice that after four years of service, she was resigning from the volunteer group and would be leaving China. Mia couldn't blame her; Resa had seen too many travesties to count during her time advocating for the children.

It had been so hard to get up and going that morning. After another fitful night, Mia had woken up feeling lethargic and didn't even want to get dressed—she just couldn't find the strength. Then Jax showed up with coffee and the news that they were going to visit the Shanghai children's shelter. He had really pushed for Robert to reach his contact for permission to allow them to visit. When he told her they'd been approved, he said he hoped it would help her to do something meaningful, and together they'd learn if there was anything that could be done to help the street children.

They needed a translator, and Mia talked Tingting into accompanying them. The girl was very nervous when she called the orphanage to tell them she wouldn't be able to work her shift, but Mia assured her that she'd make up her pay for the day. It would be worth it to her and Jax not to have to struggle to communicate with their limited Mandarin.

One more problem had been solved the day before—Jax got Resa's number from the hotel manager, and Resa agreed to let them borrow Mr. Wang for the day to drive them to Shanghai. Jax invited Resa to come along, but she declined; as much as she'd like to, she couldn't take on another mission. She was focused on finding someone to replace her as the group coordinator, and that was more than enough to keep her very busy until her departure date.

They had almost reached Shanghai. Tingting and Jax quietly made small talk as Mia stared out the window at the nameless faces of other drivers and passengers passing their van, anxious to get to their destinations in record time. The drive was proving to be less stressful than usual, but that was expected since Jax had asked Mr. Wang to drive especially careful on this trip. Mr. Wang had pouted at first but was complying by actually following the speed limit and abstaining from the exciting competition of highway driving.

"Mia, you've barely touched your coffee." Jax pointed to the cup sitting in the cup holder beside her seat.

"Oh, yeah. I forgot you brought it to me." Mia picked it up and took a sip, mostly to show Jax her appreciation at the trouble he went through to make a detour to Starbucks on his way with Mr. Wang to pick her up that morning. He was such a caring person, always thinking of doing things for other people. She wished she had more energy and scolded herself to snap out of it and get back to being herself.

"Jax, did Mia tell you that she almost beat us last night playing Mahjong? But Auntie Zhi came from behind and won the tournament at the last minute. She was so funny, dancing around with her belly shaking while bragging that she still holds the title over the entire complex." Tingting had insisted Mia learn the game, saying it was a part of her culture that she couldn't ignore.

"Oh, but Auntie Zhi hasn't gotten a taste of *my* secret Mahjong strategy yet. You tell her I want to play her, and we'll see who the champion is," Jax said.

It was obvious to Mia that Jax and Tingting were trying every subject to pull her out of her silent cloud of depression.

"We are here," Mr. Wang stated, pulling the van into the parking lot of what appeared to be an abandoned warehouse.

"This place looks abandoned. Are you sure this is it?"

Tingting asked.

Mia looked around. She saw a small sign posted on the short brick wall stating *Shanghai Mei Street Children Protection Education Centre.* They had passed a fairly clean, metropolitan area filled with high-end stores and sidewalks packed with stylish people—and then two turns and two minutes later, they found themselves in a dirty poor area that could have been China circa 1960.

"This is it," Jax confirmed. They all began unbuckling their seatbelts, climbed out, and met at the back of the van to unload the bags of donations. They had stopped at Carrefour department store on their way to pick up cookies, fruit, and school supplies to donate to the struggling shelter. It wasn't much, but after they got a tour they would have a better idea of exactly what was needed for the children.

With arms overloaded, the foursome made their way past the piles of trash and through a jumbled array of bicycles and electric scooters, to arrive at the door. Jax turned the knob.

"Hmm… The door is locked." He pounded on the wood.

They waited, and soon the door swung open wide.

"*Ni hao*." A woman answered as she blocked the entrance to the hall behind her, her full hips ample enough to prevent anyone from going around her.

"Tingting, tell her we're supposed to meet Director Luo for a tour this morning." Jax instructed.

Mia could hear the voices of children down the hall and was anxious to meet them.

Tingting began explaining their reason for coming, and Mia felt a ripple of worry when the sweet-faced woman began shaking her head from side to side. The woman gave an explanation to Tingting to tell her exactly why she couldn't allow them entrance.

"This is Lao Cheng; she is the head caretaker here. She says Director Luo was called away on an emergency and will not be back today. We cannot come in, or she will get into trouble," Tingting explained, wringing her hands in dismay.

Mia stared at the woman before her. Lao Cheng had such an interesting face that, unlike many Chinese, showed every emotion she was feeling. She stood standing with her hands clasped behind her back, her gentle but uncertain face framed by wisps of hair that had escaped the loose bun secured at the back of her head with an elaborate hummingbird clip. Mia wondered where she had found her long, flowery skirt—Mia hadn't seen another woman in China her age wearing such a style. Most of the elderly women she had seen wore bland black or navy trousers and fitted cotton blouses. Lao Cheng's clothes gave her a sweet grandmotherly appeal, and Mia felt genuine warmth from her, even though she wouldn't let them in.

Mia reached out and gathered the woman's hands in her own. "*Qing rang women jin lai.*" She asked her to allow them to enter, beseeching with her eyes.

"Tingting, tell her that we only want to find out about the children and what the needs are here at the center. We just want to help. Also, you'd better let her know that if she turns away our items and the cash donation we brought, her director will be angry." Jax leaned in and whispered to Mia, "I'm sure the reminder of a cash gift will at least make her hesitate before sending us away."

Mia thought he was probably right. She had learned that in China, money was the key to every door.

Tingting talked a few more minutes, and they all knew when Lao Cheng decided to allow them to enter. It was obvious in her body language as she turned and gestured for them to follow. They laid all the bags along the edge of the hall, and like a line of baby chicks following the mother hen, they followed her towards the children's voices.

Behind Lao Cheng and Tingting, Jax and Mia gave each other a silent high five in a quiet celebration that they'd made it past another unexpected Chinese obstacle—then laughed at Mr. Wang's bewildered expression at their strange antics.

CHAPTER TWENTY-FIVE

MIA looked around her, taking in everything. It didn't look much different from the environment at the orphanage she had seen. She started to say as much to Jax but stopped as the woman began speaking.

"This is the recreation room," Tingting translated immediately after Lao Cheng spoke. "It is where the children take reading and writing lessons."

They stood in a large room with various tables and chairs scattered about. Posted on the far wall were small cards, with the letters of the alphabet printed colorfully over a picture of an item starting with each letter. Under each English-version card was the same card with a Chinese character to match. Children were gathered around tables in the room, though they didn't have anything in front of them to do, no toys or activities.

At a table near the group sat three children from the ages of about six to ten. Mia pulled out her camera to take their picture, and the children—she couldn't tell if they were boys or girls—covered their faces with their hands. One child immediately slammed his head on the table, turning away from the lens of the camera.

The woman frantically let loose a string of Mandarin, gesturing for Mia to put the camera away.

Tingting translated, "These children are afraid to get their pictures made because they do not want their parents to find them. Their families rented them out to street thugs for begging, and the children were beaten and hungry when they were found."

"Oh, I'm so sorry. I wasn't going to do anything with the photos, they're just for me. But I won't take any. Please—tell them I'm sorry!" Mia was horrified at the children's evident fear.

"How many children live here?" Jax asked.

Tingting looked sad as she answered. "She says there are just over one hundred children rotating in and out of the center at all times. The youngest is four years old, and the oldest fourteen. Usually it is supposed to be temporary, but she has a few like these here who have been here for over a year. They don't have anywhere else to go."

"That's really not so many, considering that the official counts for street children in China are anywhere from one to one-point-five million homeless children–turned–beggars," Jax said.

"Really? That's incredible. So many children—where do they all come from?" Mia could hardly believe her ears that were so many children like the one she had encountered on Walking Street in Suzhou.

Tingting kept busy translating questions and answers back and forth between Lao Cheng and the others. "She said many were abducted from villages and farms and brought to Shanghai to beg. Some were blinded or crippled to appear pathetic—and those children have been said to bring in close to a hundred thousand yuan a year if they learn the tricks and are successful. Some village people send their children to the city during the winter months to beg, then bring them home to work in the spring and summer. They teach them to stay at the train stations and subways to find sympathetic foreigners. The children have to fight the vicious Shanghai winters if they do not find their way to a shelter."

The woman gestured for the group to follow her as she led them out of the recreation room and into another large room. There they found beds lined up in three rows, three deep and at least thirty to a row. Each wooden bed contained one rolled-up bamboo mat, one coverlet, and a small, hard wicker-like pillow. The room was extremely neat and clean, without any toys or personal items. Against another wall was a tall row of battered green lockers to hold the children's clothes and shoes.

As they looked around, Mia noticed Mr. Wang wandering to the far corner of the room. A small girl of about five lay on a bed, all alone in the big room, with nothing to do but stare at the ceiling over her head. The little girl watched Mr. Wang warily and began to whimper in fear. Lao Cheng rushed over and persuaded her to not be afraid, that the visitors were friendly. Mia, Tingting, and Jax joined her, and Mia was shocked at what they found.

The little girl's feet somehow twisted behind her to be level with her shoulders, contorting her body in a way that didn't seem possible. The group watched quietly as Lao Cheng patted the girl on her head, and then turned around to them with an explanation.

"This is Xiao Mei, and she was found at the outdoor market two months ago. She doesn't remember her real name and doesn't know where she came from. From what she told us, she was stolen from home, and then her limbs were broken and tied up around her shoulders to heal. This was done to make her crippled. With her sweet face and distorted body, she is a sure case to make a criminal very rich." Tingting faltered while translating and had to clear a lump from her throat.

Mia turned away from the girl as she listened, so Xiao Mei wouldn't see the pity and tears in her eyes. She walked over to the corner of the room to pull herself together. She couldn't imagine what kind of evil lived in people to make them do such things to a child. She especially couldn't fathom the amount of pain the child went through as she tried to heal from her broken legs, or hips, or whatever it was they had broken to make her look that way.

Jax put his arm around her shoulders. "This is why I'm here, Mia. I want to find out what I can do to help. But first we have to know what kind of travesties we are attempting to stop, what kind of needs these children have."

Lao Cheng explained that Xiao Mei would need extensive medical assistance and ongoing counseling to help her heal from the abuse of her captors, but the funds to help the little girl were just not available in their budget.

While the caretaker explained the assistance needed to help the child, Mia approached Xiao Mei again. She sat down on the edge of her bed and rummaged in her bag to find a pack of sugared candy she had picked up at Carrefour. The little girl watched with hopeful eyes, and when Mia reached to hand her the pink package, Xiao Mei's face was transformed with a beautiful smile. She accepted the treat and with a quick move ripped it open with her teeth and placed a piece in her mouth. The little girl had two neat braids in her hair, and Mia touched one.

"*Ni hen piaoling*." Mia told Xiao Mei she was very pretty; something about the braids had struck a familiar chord inside her. She focused on treating the child normally, hiding her shock at her disfigurement to show her she was still a person worthy of affection and human touch.

"The people who did this should go to prison," Mr. Wang said gruffly, not making eye contact with anyone. He positioned himself to face the opposite way of the child, refusing to look any longer—his way of respecting her privacy.

Lao Cheng clasped her hands together nervously. "Criminals do this and much more to many children. They steal them, blind them, maim them, starve them, and beat them. When they are first taken, they are kept in small cages for a few weeks to bend their wills."

Mia shook her head, wanting to deny that something so horrible could be true. "But why don't the children run away when they are finally taken out of the cages?"

The woman gave her a pitying look, making Mia feel naïve. "Because they are terrified! The children do what they are told and become adept at stealing purses, wallets, and cell phones. The pretty ones and the cleverest children learn how to put on the most pitiable expressions to earn the biggest paydays. They do what they are told to so they can survive—but when they are brought here, you can see they are still only children craving the warmth of a bed and food in their stomachs. They are deathly afraid their captors—or sometimes their parents—will find them, so they sleep fitfully and watch the windows while they are awake."

Jax reached out and patted the woman on the arm. "It is wonderful that you have made a place of refuge here for them."

"Well, it is a sad situation, and with only eight caretakers, we are too shorthanded to give them the attention they need. Many of the children are far behind in school, and if they cannot learn to speak Mandarin, they will eventually resort to street life again, some even doing to other children what was done to them."

"If they don't know Mandarin, what do they speak?" Jax asked.

Tingting asked and told him that some of them speak the dialects from their own regions—many as far away as the Xinjiang Uygur Autonomous Region.

Lao Cheng explained that another issue for the center was they didn't have the funds to return the children to areas that they might originally be from, so they don't have the chance to possibly reunite them with their families.

"It's all so huge, where do you even start to make a difference?" Mia said, peeking through to the bathroom at a bigger boy holding a smaller boy over a basin of water, washing his hair.

"One child at a time, Mia—one child at a time," Jax said as he wandered into the small room to help rinse the boy's head. Lao Cheng watched him participate in the simple task, smiling.

Tingting turned to Mia. "Last year the Minister of Public Security ordered the police to launch a crackdown on kidnapping, coercing, and organizing children from Xinjiang to beg and steal. But it looks like his orders were not followed, doesn't it?"

Lao Cheng gathered the group and led them back to the recreation room, which had suddenly become the cafeteria. Two small women bustled in and out of a door leading to the kitchen, bringing trays of rice and vegetables to the children sitting at the tables, waiting patiently for their lunch.

Jax and Mia looked around at the faces of the hopeful children, their innocence stolen by immoral thugs. After Tingting translated the stories of a few more children, they said their good-byes and were pleasantly surprised when the children all joined together in a chorus of *zaijian* and energetic waving good-bye.

Jax quickly ran back to the hall they had started in and grabbed two of the plastic bags containing the chocolate cookies. He returned, and together he and Mia passed out the treats to the clapping children. Tingting reminded them to eat their lunches first and save the cookies for dessert. Mia wished they could stay longer to interact with the children, but she knew they were wearing out their welcome.

Lao Cheng walked them to the door and thanked them for the donations. Jax pulled out an envelope fat with pink bills, donated from The Shiradan Hotel in Suzhou. The woman didn't say anything about the money or even the donations, but Mia thought the wide smile across her face was gratitude enough as they ducked out the door.

CHASING CHINA

CHAPTER TWENTY-SIX

THE next morning, the children from the Shanghai Protection Centre were still on Mia's mind until Tingting opened the door at six o'clock, to Jax telling them Mr. Wang was waiting downstairs to take them to the train station.

Now they were in a first-class cabin on their way to the famous city of Xi'an. Of course, Mia had no idea when she woke up that morning that she would be taking a twelve-hour train ride to a city she had previously only heard of in reference to the renowned Terracotta Warriors. She was hesitant at first, but she was prepared to go wherever needed to find the information to lead her to her birth family. *Maybe the distance is all part of keeping their group confidential.*

Tingting had explained that Auntie Zhi and Lao Ling wanted to come but it was too difficult a trip for the elderly, so they were staying behind but wished Mia luck. Mr. Wang was involved because Tingting had asked him to escort them to the location as sort of a security guard and guide.

Jax admitted he hadn't been too happy with that explanation—he said it made him feel like they didn't consider him man enough to protect them—but Tingting reminded him that his Mandarin wasn't all that great and Mr. Wang had many contacts that come in handy in sticky situations. Just as Jax was about to balk, Mr. Wang produced Mia's passport from his jacket pocket.

"How did you get that?" Mia had gasped, grabbing it to open the cover and confirm it was her face inside.

Mr. Wang looked at her and answered, "I can only say you ask too many questions at orphanage, and your passport was flagged. Don't ask how I know this or how I got this back—my connections are many, but I keep to myself. You owe me five cartons of American cigarettes."

Sometimes his arrogance was overwhelming, but in that instance, with her passport finally back in her hands, Mia thanked him and was more relieved to have it back than she could describe.

"But you must tell me something, Mr. Wang. If you don't, I'll be afraid it will happen again. Why did they come after me and steal my passport?"

Mr. Wang sighed. "It wasn't police who took your passport. It was security guards from orphanage. One is my good friend, and he said director paid them to go to your room. She thought if they could just make a mess and scare you, that you would leave and stop asking questions. He was not asked to steal passport or money. That was his mistake."

Mia stomped her foot and glared at Mr. Wang. "You mean his *crime*. Then where is my money? Did you ask him that? How am I supposed to pay for all the cigarettes they—or you—want?"

Mr. Wang rolled his eyes at her and climbed into the van

and shut the door. He opened the window and waved at them. “Come on or we miss train.”

Mia threw her hands in the air and turned to look at Jax.

“I can get the cigarettes for you from the hotel; that’s common payment for bribes around here. The money is just a loss,” Jax whispered for Mia’s ears only. She took a deep breath and told herself to think of the positive, that at least she had her passport back.

They had made the trek across town to the train station in silence.

Now the four of them were settled in what Tingting had called a soft-sleeper. At the train station, when Mia found out she intended to put Mia and Jax in the more expensive cabins and her and Mr. Wang in the hard seats, she insisted on paying for everyone to be in the same cabin together, as comfortable as possible for the long ride.

Even though the trip was close to draining her savings account, it was worth every penny, and she appreciated Tingting and Mr. Wang taking time away from their busy lives to help her.

The cabin was about five feet wide by seven feet long and had two bunks on each side. Jax and Mia took the two top bunks and were so close together they could reach across and hold hands. Covered in clean, white bedding, the beds were fairly comfortable. However, the biggest perk the extra funds bought was the privacy the room with a lockable door provided. All their luggage was able to fit under the bottom bunks, leaving a small amount of room between beds. Based on Tingting’s recommendation, Mia had bought a huge bag of rice, a smaller one of sugar cubes, and one pound of chocolate to give as appreciation gifts to the mystery people on the other end of their journey.

Below her, Tingting, Jax, and Mr. Wang chattered away about how many stops they would see before their final destination. Tired of talking and still reeling from grief, Mia didn't join in the loud conversation. Instead she lay quietly on her bunk, allowing the rhythmic motion of the train to soothe her nerves. She had a lot on her mind, but nothing she wanted to share at the moment.

She thought about their short excursion through the train station. Even though everyone else in their group had been only thinking of making their way through the crowds to get tickets and find the right compartment, Mia had looked around at the couples and families and been glad she didn't carry any memories of the day she'd been left there—if indeed she had. Seeing the little faces around her also made her think of Xinxin, and she had struggled to push the thoughts away so she could function at the task at hand.

Mia was startled out of her thoughts when a young girl pushing a beverage cart stopped at their door, hawking her wares. She held up yogurt drinks and then other drinks, until finally Jax handed her a few bills and chose four plastic bottles of orange juice. She hurried along and ignored his complaints about the drinks being too warm.

Mr. Wang and Tingting began to play a game of cards on the small table between the bunks, leaving her and Jax to create their own diversion from the monotony of the trip.

"Mia, my bunk or yours?" Jax teased, trying to break her

serious mood with a lame joke.

"I'm not jumping over there," Mia said. She was so close to hopefully learning some truths and didn't want to jeopardize the trip by giving herself a concussion and the ceiling of the cabin was only a mere twenty-four inches or so from the top bunk, so low she couldn't even sit up.

That was all the prompting Jax needed. He crouched on his bed and took a small leap over the empty space to land on Mia—bumping his head on the roof and finally bringing a smile to her face as she pushed him off her lap. He squeezed in beside her and guided her head onto his arm, finding a position comfortable to them both.

"So what's bothering you, Lotus?" he whispered as he looked at the delicate jade flower dangling from her slender neck.

"Lotus? That's a new one."

"Well, I need a nickname for you that only I use. Do you have another one you like better? What does your family call you?" He playfully tickled her up and down her arm.

"Actually, I like the name Lotus—it's original, and you thought of it, so it works. My brothers called me Mimi when I was growing up, but don't you dare. It would be weird coming from you." She didn't want to tell Jax, but she loved the way her name rolled off his tongue. *Mia… He makes it sound so beautiful.*

Mia wished she could see her brothers and catch them up on all of her latest adventures. They wouldn't be surprised—they'd always called her a little daredevil. She sure missed them and the feeling of belonging that she always got when she was around them. She'd always be their baby sister, no matter how old she got, and that felt good.

"What are you thinking about so seriously, Mia?"

"Jax, I really miss my family. I mean—I *really* miss them. Is that crazy, considering I'm on this mission to find my birth parents?" Mia didn't regret coming to China, but she had been gone almost a month, and she really missed home—more than she'd ever thought possible.

"No, it's not crazy. You're lucky that you are so loved. I wish I was that close to my family. You should be proud of that, not embarrassed."

"I'm scared this might be another dead end, and I've run out of ways to keep searching. I'm also sad you and I are going to have to say good-bye in just a week or so," Mia added. Her visa had run out, and her extension almost had, too. Her parents were urging her to come home and had threatened to come get her. Her classes at school had already resumed without her, and she needed to get back.

Adding to her troubles, it was going to be difficult to leave Jax—he had become too special to her. Her life had changed in the last several weeks, and a big part of it was because of meeting him. But she would always have their memories, and at least she was sure that finding love was a future possibility—something she hadn't believed after the pain that Collin had put her through.

"Don't say that, Mia. We can figure this out—don't even think about telling me good-bye. I'm in love with you. You're the one I've been searching for my whole life. There—I said it. Now what are you going to do about it?"

Tears filled her eyes, and an ache settled in Mia's chest that she couldn't return the words to Jax. It just wouldn't be fair, no matter how strongly she felt about him. She was going home soon, and he was staying in China. He had to finish an internship, and she had to focus on her future. She changed the subject.

The train made its first stop, and Mia barely noticed—she was still feeling bad about the expression on Jax's face when she hadn't acknowledged their bond. As they chugged along and stopped often at stations along the way, they spent the next four hours carefully avoiding the subject of their relationship while talking about their families, friends, hopes, and dreams, until they both became too sleepy to talk any longer.

By that time, Tingting and Mr. Wang had long ago fallen asleep in their bunks, so Mia and Jax didn't even bother to separate. Mia kept her head on Jax's shoulder; he kept his arms wrapped around her; and together, they drifted off to sleep, content in each other's arms—if only temporarily.

CHAPTER TWENTY-SEVEN

TWELVE hours after leaving Suzhou, they were off the train, and Mia sat with Jax and Tingting in the back of a dingy white van, listening to their new driver mumble his displeasure at the abuse his vehicle was taking. Letting loose a string of Chinese swear words under his breath, the man maneuvered his vehicle through and around the deep tire tracks along the dirt road. Mr. Wang had taken the passenger seat and in Mia's opinion was causing the driver even more of headache by pointing out which way *he* himself would go to miss the biggest potholes.

Mia also had a new friend, in the form of a little puppy who, with his head in Mia's lap, whined at the way he was being thrown from side to side.

"Quit whining, pup, or Mr. Wang is going to take you right back to the train station!" Mia whispered, scratching the dog behind his ears to calm him. Jax looked over at the two of them and shook his head in exasperation.

So far they had only traveled about forty-five minutes—a rocky and jarring path, but still a relief after the chaos of getting off the train and fighting through the crowds of people lining the doorways and every inch of space in the station.

Once outside, the pandemonium hadn't improved much, with the hawkers selling trinkets and bottled water, shouting in their faces to get their attention. Mia was horrified when she walked by a young man belly-down on a wheeled platform, nodding his head in front of a cup set out for coins. He didn't have any limbs—his arms and legs were gone, without even stumps to prove they were once there. She had tossed a few bills in his cup then looked away.

As they had navigated out of the train station entrance and through the packed pedestrian area, a medium-sized rust-colored dog began to follow them.

"Oh, he's so sweet!" Mia and Tingting both dropped to a squat to pet the friendly canine.

"Mia, be careful. Dogs in China are rarely vaccinated, especially those roaming public areas. He's probably a stray," Jax warned her. In response, the dog jumped up to balance on his hind haunches and lick Jax on the hand.

Tingting giggled with delight and reached out to pat the dog on top of his head. "Come on. Let's wait over here." She beckoned them to the building overhang, out of the glaring sun. As the group followed her to wait for their next move, the small dog stayed with them as if he belonged.

"Here, puppy." Mia rummaged in her bag until she found the remnants of a piece of beef jerky she had been snacking on the night before. The dog wagged his tail and devoured the dried meat in one swallow. Mia felt bad for the hungry little fellow and got busy trying to find something else to give him for his growling tummy.

Mr. Wang went to the line of drivers and negotiated a rate to take them to their specified location. When he beckoned them over to join him, he told them they were traveling to a *yaodong* village—basically, caves carved in the mountainside.

"Why are we going to a cave?" Mia thought the adventure might be going a little too far, and she wanted more information before moving forward. *Traveling on trains and meeting in caves? Bats? Darkness? Climbing? What have I gotten myself into?*

Mia looked around, trying to determine if anyone was with the dog. He wasn't dirty enough to look like a stray.

Tingting answered, "Because, Mia, the person who wants to meet with you lives there. His family has lived there for generations—hundreds of years, actually. It used to be a very popular dwelling in the region, though now many of the villages have been evacuated by the government to make room for high-rise apartment buildings. The one we are going to is one of the few remaining inhabited villages."

"Wow—that's so cool!" Jax exclaimed. "I'm going to get to meet a real-live cave person!" He held his palm up high for Tingting then quickly brought it down when she didn't slap it.

"His village is a lucky one—many years ago, there was a deadly earthquake, and almost a million cave dwellers in this province were killed when their homes collapsed on them. But his village withstood the violence of the earth shaking, and made many more generations of children," Tingting explained.

They were all silent. Mia couldn't imagine the magnitude of such a tragedy and thought *What a horrible way to die.*

"We go now, or driver find other customers," Mr. Wang firmly stated. He opened the trunk of the van to pile up their bags and turned to find the puppy sitting perfectly posed behind him, waiting for a command. "This dog should go away." He kicked his leg at the dog, trying to shoo it away from the vehicle.

The driver chattered at Mr. Wang and pointed at the dog—obviously telling some sort of story about him.

"He say dog belong to beggar woman here at station, but one day many months past, she got on train and leave him. He still waits for her," Mr. Wang skeptically explained.

"Wow—that sounds just like Hachi, the dog in Japan that waited for nine years at the train station for his deceased master to return. He even looks like him! I believe it's the same kind of dog!" Jax said as the dog stood between him and Mia, waiting for someone to give him another treat, his bushy tail curled perfectly and wagging just a bit.

"Jax, that's so sad! He's an orphan—abandoned to fend for himself at the train station, just like I was. We have to take him with us. When we return to Suzhou, we'll find him a home." Mia wouldn't be budged from her decision. She had seen chickens and at least one tiny pig on the train; she would find a way to bribe the ticket master for the dog to join her.

"*Aiyo!*" Mr. Wang used only one word to express his exasperation, then shook his head in disgust and waved for the dog to jump into the van, mumbling something about it not being allowed to return to Suzhou. With that one prompt, Hachi—as he was quickly named—had joined the group on their journey.

The group was traveling away from the train station towards the mountains of Xi'an. Along the way, they passed several vendors with row upon row of the replica clay Terracotta

Warriors for sale.

"Mr. Wang, let's stop here on the way back. I want to see if I can negotiate a good price to ship a dozen or so of these soldiers to my father's store as a surprise. He's fascinated with the story of the clay soldier army and is always quoting how it is the Eighth Wonder of the World." Jax laughed. "The way he talks, you'd think he had been a soldier himself in Qin Shi Huang Di's Terracotta Army."

The driver finally pulled over to the side of the road and stated they'd have to walk the rest of the way, as it was too treacherous to get a vehicle any further. Mr. Wang told the driver that he'd be paid an additional two hundred yuan if he waited two hours for their return, and the driver eagerly agreed. Mia still didn't trust him and decided to take her belongings with her. She wasn't leaving her guitar with anyone.

Jax threw the bag of supplies over one shoulder and his duffel bag over the other and helped Mia out of the car. The dog jumped out behind her and followed along dutifully, as if he knew exactly where they were going. They followed Tingting and Mr. Wang further up the road and over a steep hill, until they stood at the base of a row of carved archways in the side of the mountain. To the side of the dwellings were the remnants of a pigpen—*Or some kind of animal pen*, Mia thought. Most of the entrances were barren of evidence of inhabitants, but Tingting led them straight to the one with clothing strung out on a line between a tree and a pole.

"Over here." Tingting picked her way through the items scattered around the entryway. A scraggly dog circled them with his tail between his legs, looking as hungry as many of the beggars they had seen at the train station. Hachi didn't spare the mutt a single look, proudly walking right on by as the dog stared at his backside.

"Wait here for a moment." Tingting disappeared into the dim archway leading in to the cave. Hachi followed her but stopped just outside the entrance, somehow knowing he wasn't allowed to enter until invited.

Mr. Wang, Mia, and Jax stood in a circle, looking around at the living conditions. Further down the path, they saw a young woman washing clothes in a washbasin, wringing out the water, and then throwing the threadbare articles over a short wall that bordered the front area of her cave. A small child squatted in front of her as she worked, using a stick to draw in the soft yellowish-red earth as he jabbered happily to himself. Everything around them was dusty, making Mia wonder how they ever got the clothing to stay clean.

At the door of another dwelling, two men stood in front of a deep fry kettle and a small, square table, cutting out white blocks from a jelly-like substance.

"*Doufu*," Mr. Wang called behind him as he approached the men and bought a cube of the delicacy. He didn't offer any to Mia or Jax, but Mia was too nervous for the upcoming meeting to eat anything, and she didn't like the taste of tofu anyway.

Soon Tingting returned with an old man slowly following behind her, perhaps in his fifties or so, leaning on a cane carved with an elaborate dragon for a handle. For someone who lived in a cave, he was surprisingly dapper with his shirttail tucked in tightly and his shoes buffed to a glossy sheen. On his head, he wore a battered but once stylish fedora hat, complete with a faded black satin ribbon around the band. He had obviously taken extra time to prepare for their meeting, and Mia thought he looked quite the gentleman. He stopped in front of the trio and looked directly at her, his eyes searching hers for something she didn't understand.

"This is Lao Qiu." Tingting introduced the man to the group, moving her hand to his shoulder as a comforting or perhaps even protective gesture.

"*Ni hao,*" the man softly murmured, but only to Mia. He didn't appear to even notice anyone else was there as he intently studied her.

Mia answered, "*Ni hao.*" She wasn't sure what else to say and didn't know what the proper greeting was for an elder, so she just remained quiet and waited on someone else to speak. Jax took the traditional route and shook hands before bowing low in front of the man.

"Let's go inside." Tingting suggested, leading them all into the cave entrance. The old man beckoned that the dog could also join them, and Hachi immediately complied. *He's such a smart dog.* Mia couldn't believe someone hadn't already claimed him. Once inside, Tingting gestured for Jax to leave the bag of gifts next to the door, unacknowledged, to save the old man from embarrassment at their generosity and his need.

They followed behind Tingting and Lao Qiu, looking around them at the interior of his home. The dwelling was surprisingly cool and only a bit dim. Mia had expected it to be darker. The clay walls were smooth, with one side even plastered and painted. The first half of the room was obviously the living area and consisted of a tiny table with a few short stools and crates around it to sit on.

In the corner was one comfortable chair, with a small box beside it to serve as a side table. A ceramic bowl used as an ashtray sat on the box, overflowing with cigarette butts, though Mia didn't notice an overpowering odor of smoke. Next to the box was a stack of books—all in Chinese, from the characters she saw etched on the spines. *The man must spend all his time reading*, she thought, surprised at the irony of an intellectual living a caveman existence.

In the back of the cave was a small sleeping area, boasting a huge bed of sorts, piled with pillows and a colorful quilt. A gray tabby cat lay nestled in the far corner, eyes closed, not even giving the visitors the courtesy of her attention.

"That is *kang* bed," Mr. Wang pointed out. "The exhaust from fireplace connects under bed and in winter, family gathers there for warm." The bed had a wide opening underneath, and some old kindle lying there proved that fires were built under it to keep the family toasty. Mia thought of her soft electric blanket at home and how convenient it was in comparison.

"Where's the kitchen?" Mia asked as she looked around, Hachi right on her heels. She didn't see a sink or stove, only a small cabinet with a hot plate perched on top. She also didn't see a television but was relieved to spot a wire stretched across the roof of the cave, with one lone light bulb hanging down. *At least he has power*, she thought. She couldn't imagine how dark the winters got in homes like these.

"Most of the cooking is done outside in a separate building to keep the fumes and chance of fire away." Tingting pointed towards the front of the cave, towards the corner of a small, metal building just outside the entrance.

"Does he live here alone?" Jax asked, looking around.

Tingting took a moment to translate their conversation to the old man and then turned back to them. "Yes, he is alone now. A woman in the village comes each day to make his meals and wash his laundry. His children are all grown and gone now, but they come to visit occasionally, when they can get away from their jobs in the cities."

Mia felt sad for the old man, living in a cave all alone. Tingting reassured her that the old man preferred to be there in his quiet cave than living among the noise and chaos of the city.

"Wait a minute, is that what I think it is?" Jax asked, pointing to a long, varnished box along the side of one wall.

Tingting covered her mouth and giggled. "Yes, it is a casket. Over five years ago, he got very sick and wanted to pick out his own burial box. He was expected to die and wanted to be prepared. The joke was on the doctors because he overcame his illness, but he refused to get rid of the casket because he says he'll need it one day! He says it keeps away pesky children; they are afraid someone is in it." The old man knew what they were discussing, and he grinned.

"Jeesh."

They all laughed as Jax gave his usual response to something he had no other words for.

"Well, this is all very interesting, but where are The Finders?" Mia was fascinated by the story of the old man in the cave and would love to hear more, but first she wanted to get to the purpose of the long journey they had taken.

Mr. Wang held his hand up to Mia. "Child, be quiet.

Listen. Lao Qiu has story to tell."

Mia didn't appreciate the arrogant way that Mr. Wang spoke to her, or that he called her a child, but she did want to be respectful and listen to the gentle old man so that she could get to the next part of the meeting, to what she hoped would be a path to the truth she was searching for. She waited for them to tell her what to do.

The old man turned to Tingting and rapidly gave her instructions, using his local dialect—one completely foreign to Mia or Jax. Tingting listened intently, and then with cheeks blushing scarlet, she turned back to the foreigners.

"He says first he would like to see the back of your neck." Tingting quietly requested.

As soon as the words reached Mia's ears, she felt dizzy. *They know about my mark—they know who my family is.*

Hesitantly, she lifted her hair and turned around to show Lao Qiu the penny-sized, light-colored birthmark located just under her hairline. "My mom always said it was a kiss left behind by my birth mother."

As Tingting translated Mia's words, the old man turned away to compose his emotions. He mumbled, "*Luo ye gui gen.*"

"What did he say?" Jax asked, looking from Tingting to Mr. Wang for clarification.

Tingting cleared her throat and softly said, "He said, 'Falling leaves return to the root.' It is an ancient Chinese proverb."

CHAPTER TWENTY-EIGHT

LAO Qiu slowly lowered himself to sit in the one sturdy chair, and laid the gnarled cane on the floor. Hachi immediately dropped down on the dirt floor in front of the man's feet and curled up to take a nap, as if he had done it a thousand times in that same place. Qiu waited for the group to settle onto the small, wooden stools around him, and using the translation skills of Tingting, he began to speak.

"He says, first of all, he is your father."

At these words, Mia felt the weight of rejection she had carried all these years switch to one of sorrow. She wanted to ask, if he was her father, where was her mother? But out of respect, she kept her many questions silent to allow the man to finish his story.

"Your name is Qiu He Li Ya, named for the lotus flower. When you were born and we realized our poor village had been blessed by your unusual loveliness, we thought of the lotus flower, which grows in muddy swamps and rises above the surface to bloom with remarkable splendor."

Mia reached up and felt her necklace. She saw Tingting smiling timidly at her as the old man spoke.

"The second part of your name, Liya, is for the grace and beauty you brought to our village. You are our second child, born five years after your brother. I stand before you now and tell you that this is the truth. First of all, you were loved by your mother and me, your brother and your grandparents. From the moment you were born and you looked into my eyes and smiled, you were my baby girl." Qiu paused and leaned back in his chair. He took a deep breath.

"Again, you were so lovely, with your rosebud lips and long eyelashes. I didn't care that you were not a boy—our marriage was not one arranged by a matchmaker. We were joined by love, and to have a girl to look like Tianren—that was your mother's name—was a gift. In our area, the family planning rules were not so strict, so we agreed that we would keep you and not do like others did with their daughters and leave you for strangers to find. When our neighbors met you after your one-month isolation, you gained the reputation of the village beauty."

At his heartfelt words, Mia felt a flood of emotion. Tears of relief to finally discover that she was wanted began to roll down her face, but she still didn't understand how it all changed and why she had been abandoned, after all.

"You were a very strong-willed child. From the time you learned to walk, you were like my shadow—you didn't want to stay back and play with the other girls. Everywhere you went, you sang songs taught to you by your mother. I took you with me to the fields, and you sang as I picked the harvest. You sat with your brother on the bank beside me and sang as I fished for our supper, and you sang to the pigs as I tossed them their slop. On the days I had to leave you behind, you cried and used your long braids to hide your eyes." The old man smiled briefly.

"When you were just three years old, Tianren and I decided to go to the city. Our plan was to spend at least a year working to earn enough money to return and buy a small plot of land to begin our own farm. With my strong back, I could get work as a construction laborer, and Tianren would find work as a laundress. We knew we wouldn't be able to afford someone to look after you and your brother while we worked, so we left you with your grandparents." The man took a break to allow Tingting to catch up translating to English. Even when he stopped speaking, he couldn't take his eyes away from Liya.

"After six months of working to save money for land, we decided to come home and visit you and your brother. The entire time we were gone, we had not talked to anyone back home because our village did not have phone lines. Tianren and I were so anxious to see you both again. When we arrived at your grandparents' home, we found your grandfather pacing the floor and your grandmother in bed, too grief-stricken to get up."

As Tingting translated the words, the old man lowered his head, wrung his hands, and with much effort raised his face to again make eye contact with Mia.

"You were gone."

CHAPTER TWENTY-NINE

FINALLY Mia was finally going to hear the truth, and she didn't want the old man to stop speaking for even a second. "Go on," she urged.

"They told us the family planning officials had come the week before and demanded we pay a six thousand yuan penalty for violating China's one-child policy, or they would take you away. They called it 'social support compensation.' Your grandmother hid your brother in the well house so they wouldn't take both of you; even though it is legal to have a firstborn, she did not trust the men to follow the law."

The man stopped to wipe tears from his eyes, and Mia felt a pang of sympathy for his grief—and for the child she did not feel she knew. She reached over and took his hand, then knelt before him and bowed her head to wait for the rest of the story. Even Tingting sounded moved at the story, and Mia could hear her struggle to maintain composure as she translated his words.

"Your grandfather begged them to wait until we returned. He told them we were away working and may have saved enough money to pay, but the officials took you anyway. Your grandmother said you were very scared, and you kicked and screamed all the way out the door and down the gravel road to the officials' cars, holding your arms out for her to come free you from the fierce strangers. Your grandfather tried to wrestle you away from the official, but the others knocked him to the ground. When they took you, my parents had no way to contact us and felt useless to do anything to save you. They were too afraid to go to the police—they thought they might make the matter worse with their country ways. Your grandmother was so devastated she couldn't eat or even leave the bed. She was very afraid of how I would react to find you gone." Jax moved his stool closer so that he could put his hand on Mia's back for reassurance as the old man continued his sad tale.

"When our neighbors saw Tianren and I return, they came and told us you were one of five children taken that day. Our village was in mourning for the travesty; for we love our children, and we knew that what the officials did was wrong. One man fought for his daughter and was struck in the head by the cadres. He was taken to a hospital in the back of the farm truck and never returned to the village." The man stomped his foot at the memory of the injustice they had all been dealt.

"Everyone else was afraid to challenge the government, but Liya, we wasted no time—that very minute we left the house and went to the local police station to try to find you. The police instructed us to go to the Family Planning official office. We went there and were told you were put in the orphanage in Shaoyang City, but that we had to pay the fine of six thousand yuan before you could be released back to us. We didn't even have that much money from our savings, but we went anyway, hoping that we could negotiate with the officials at the orphanage. We boarded a bus and spent the entire night traveling to Shaoyang City. In the morning, when we arrived there, we took a taxi to the biggest orphanage. We showed your picture to the director but were told you were not there and she did not know anything about you. She told us there was another orphanage on the other side of town but it usually didn't take in new children. It was our only option so we took the city bus to the smaller orphanage. We were relieved to find out you were there, but they refused to let us see you because we did not have the six thousand yuan. Tianren cried, and we begged them to take everything we had—almost three thousand yuan—but they would not. They told us we had sixty days to return with the money, or they couldn't guarantee you would be returned to us."

Hachi opened his eyes and looked up at the old man. He gave a low whine, as if to signal he didn't like the distress and tension in the air.

The anguish coming from the man for reliving such painful memories made Mia feel guilty that she was pushing him to finish his story, but she couldn't stop him, she had to know every detail he could remember.

The old man dropped his head into his hands. For a moment he stayed that way, but then he lifted his face and a new light entered his eyes. It was relief—a release that he was finally able to declare to his daughter that they had not abandoned her—that they wanted her and tried to get her back.

"Tianren and I refused to leave, and we slept outside the gates that night, taking turns so one of us could keep watch out for thieves. The next morning, Tianren was so sore she could barely walk, but still she would not budge from her pallet in front of the gate. After the sun came up, we could see children moving about the courtyard, and we searched for your face, but you were not to be seen. We stayed there until dark, and when one of the *ayi*s was leaving for the day, I followed her down the alley. When she went into the store to buy eggs, I cornered her and demanded to know if she knew you. At first she was afraid, but then she saw I was only a devastated father. She looked at your picture and slowly nodded her head. She told me you had been brought in a week or so ago and were still being held in the observation room. She said new arrivals are placed there to ensure they are not carrying any contagious diseases that can be transferred to the other children. She warned me that if I continued to cause trouble, I would be punished by the local police as others had before me. She told me it was best to go home and have another child—to forget you. Forget you? She didn't know what she asked of me! I was not going to leave you to the corrupt people who held you. Even if I had wanted to, your mother would never have agreed."

Mia furrowed her brow. "But if I was three years old when I was taken, why don't I remember any of this? I understand why I didn't remember anything about being left in a train station, but shouldn't I remember you and my mother—or the distress of being snatched from my grandparents?" As soon as the words left her mouth she recalled the flashback she'd had the night the police came to her hotel room.

"Sometimes the mind represses memories to protect itself," Jax murmured reassuringly.

The old man continued his story. "We waited another day

outside those gates, sleeping on the sidewalk before the director came out and told us if we didn't leave, she would have us arrested. She urged me to go away and bring back the penalty amount. We explained to her that we couldn't get our hands on that much money, but she said that it wasn't up to her to reduce the fine.

We weighed our options, and decided that going back to find more money was the only thing left to do. They weren't going to release you without us paying the penalty, and if I went to jail there would be no way for me to find you. So we went home and begged money from every uncle, cousin, and neighbor. When that wasn't enough money, we sold our pigs and the silk Tianren had put away for your wedding. After three weeks, we had enough yuan make up the fine, and we returned to Shaoyang City, triumphant to be able to bring you home. While we were gone, your grandparents planned a celebration feast and invited everyone we knew to be there to greet you at your homecoming."

The man gestured towards the chipped kettle on the hot plate, and Tingting rose to serve him a cup of green tea. They all remained quiet to allow him a chance to pull himself together and contain his emotions.

"We arrived at the orphanage, and again, they wouldn't allow us to enter. When we finally convinced the guards we had money to give the officials, we were let in. But the same director acted as if she had never met us! Then she said we must prove that you were our daughter. We didn't have any proof—only a few pictures of you that were taken before your abduction. In our village at that time, births weren't registered unless they were boys, which we now know was a huge mistake. She said we must bring back an official certificate of birth for you, or you would not be returned to us—no matter that we had raised the penalty amount. Even if she had told us this in the beginning, we would not have been able to present it, for one was never created."

"Did she allow you to see me?" Mia hoped that her birth mother got to see her one last time.

"No, and actually, I do not believe you were even there any longer. A few minutes after the director went back into the office, a car of police cadres arrived and arrested me. I was scared because they were very rough, and they didn't tell me what my charges were. Luckily, they ignored Tianren. They tied my hands behind my back and took me to prison."

CHAPTER THIRTY

MIA couldn't believe the dramatic story the old man was telling. Never in a million years did she ever imagine that something like this was the beginning to her adoption story. *Child abduction and prisons? Unimaginable!*

The old man paused to give Tingting time to catch up.

"The prison was a big, terrible place, with barbed wire and jagged glass all around the top of the high outside walls. From the backseat, I could see most of the windows were broken, and it looked so dark inside that I found it hard to believe anyone was there. The cadres dragged me out of the car and took me in the building." Lao Qiu waited for Tingting to translate.

"At the orphanage before they put me in the car, I had barely had time to hand over my belongings to Tianren—but good thing I did, because when they checked me in at the prison, they made me put all of my belongings in a huge bamboo basket—even my shoes and my money! All I had was a bit of yuan left in my wallet that I had kept separate from the penalty money. Once I was taken to my cell, the other inmates told me that anything I had put in their basket, I would never see again."

Mr. Wang shook his head at the Lao Qiu's description of the abuse he endured. "I am not surprised—I hear many stories like this and worse."

Qiu nodded at Wang. "I was made to go barefoot in the prison because once inside, I didn't have anything to trade for slippers. Every morning, I had to jog around the prison and do exercise drills with no shoes, and after the second day my feet were cut and bleeding. Because there is not glass or screening in the windows, each night I was viciously attacked by mosquitoes, making my face unrecognizable after the first few days until my body adjusted to the nightly onslaught. I slept on one piece of bamboo on the concrete floor and was not even given a scrap of blanket. I continually asked for a meeting with the officials, but no one listened to me. The prison was very dangerous, and the guards weren't the meanest ones—those were their cadres, whom they called 'Big Brothers.' They stood around us each day holding wooden bats, and if we fell behind in our work, we were beaten.

"Each day I tried to complete my duties and keep my head low. For hours as I did my work, I prayed that you had been reunited with your mother. My labor was to string beads on lanterns for the upcoming New Year festivals, and the amount I was expected to finish was near impossible. I worked from before dawn until sometimes after midnight to finish my quota. If I didn't finish, I was beaten and not allowed to eat the next day. Even though the food was very bad, it was at least something to fill my aching stomach. Every day, it was the same tiny bowl of bland rice with a tiny bit of vegetable mixed in, and I was so very hungry all the time. I craved meat, but only the rich inmates received meat in their bowls at dinner time." He paused again to catch his breath, and Tingting quickly caught everyone up.

"It was three months before Tianren was allowed to visit me. They brought me to the visitor's courtyard, and she was there with a bag of fruit and a clean set of clothes for me. She even brought me slippers! When she saw how much weight I had lost and the scars I had received while protecting myself from bullies, she cried and cried. I saw the lines of sadness around her eyes, and I knew she had not been lucky enough to get you back. She told me that she had gone to the orphanage every afternoon and each time she was refused entrance. Finally, one day another *ayi* at the end of a shift felt sorry for Tianren and told her you were transferred to an orphanage in Jiangsu, then adopted and sent to America a few weeks later. Tianren didn't know how much of that was true, and she didn't know which way to turn, but then she had one more idea."

Mia interrupted, "But I was told I stayed in the orphanage for years before my adoption!" Her birth parents had been lied to and bullied, and they'd ultimately lost their child to a corrupt welfare system. But what else could they have done? *How do you fight the government in China?* For a poor family from a small mountain village, it was an impossible battle. They had even thrown her father in jail for trying to retrieve his own child, for goodness' sake!

The man listened to Tingting's translation of Mia's words and shook his head but continued his story. "I don't know how long you were really there, Liya, but Tianren took most of the money we brought for the fine and used it to hire a lawyer in

Suzhou. She said he would not let her sit on his fancy furniture because of her poor clothes, but he took our case and said he filed a lawsuit against the family planning office. Then Tianren waited and split her time between standing outside the orphanage gates, traveling to the prison, and doing laundry to pay room and board at a small hotel. Every couple of days, she stopped by to ask if the lawyer had made any progress. Two months later, he said he couldn't help her any longer. He kept almost all of our money and did nothing to bring you back. He refused to tell Tianren why he was dropping our case, but his assistant secretly told her he was threatened with losing his legal license." He scowled as he stopped to take a drink.

"Two days later, Tianren brought in the money she had saved from long hours of doing laundry and bribed the guard to allow her to visit me. After she saw the shape I was in, she went to the officials and told them we would stop our search for you. She didn't mean it, but she felt like I wouldn't survive there much longer and knew it was the only way they would release me from their prison. The next day, I was freed from that dreadful place, and the officials said my five months was time served—for what offense I was never told. We returned to our village with broken hearts and faces full of disgrace." He wrung his hands together and raised his eyes to Mia, his cheeks flushed with shame. Tingting quickly caught up with translating, and he started again.

"Returning home without you was terrible. We had hoped to be the ones to bring hope to the others that they could get their children back. But all we had left of you was one tattered photo. We failed the village, and we failed you, Liya. Your brother could not tolerate our sadness, so he spent a lot of time with your grandparents. In our home, our days were filled with silence until Tianren gave birth to a daughter two years later, but she never got over her grief of losing you."

The old man looked up at the ceiling of the cave and sighed.

"Your mother became sick when your sister was five years old. It was a mysterious illness, and on the day you would have celebrated your eleventh birthday, after making me promise to never give up my search for you, she died lying in the same bed she had given birth to you in. The doctor said there was no disease, and I believe she died of a broken heart. After her death, we moved to Xi'an to live in this cave village with Tianren's parents. I was afraid the family planning officials would cause problems for my family again, and I also couldn't stay in the village and see the grief of other parents all around me and be constantly reminded of my failure."

Mia felt a fleeting burst of hope at the thought of a sister—growing up with three brothers, she had always wished for one— but it passed quickly in front of the obvious wrecked spirit of her birth father. His anguish tore at Mia's heart, and she prayed for a way to ease his sorrow. She was overwhelmed at everything her birth parents had gone through to try to find her.

Jax put his arm around Mia's shoulders. "Mia, tell him about your life. He needs to know you were well cared for." Jax leaned close to her ear and whispered even more quietly, "This poor man has suffered torment his whole life looking for you. I feel so bad for him."

Mia swallowed back her tears to appear strong for her birth

father. "I'm very sorry for the pain you and my birth mother experienced. Perhaps this won't erase all you have endured, but it may help to know I have had a good life, full of joy. In my heart, I knew something was missing, and now I know it was you and my birth mother. I thought you had abandoned me, and even though I couldn't remember you, I held a lot of bad feelings about it—but yet, the love my adoptive parents showed me helped me to work through my unhappiness."

Mia fought back emotion as she thought of the regret her parents would feel when they heard her story.

"They are innocent in this crime and were only told I was found in a train station and needed a family. They have given me a very rewarding childhood, education, and a hopeful future. Please do not feel anger at them—instead, I beg that you have gratitude that I was placed with good people, even though I was stolen from you." Mia couldn't stand the thought that her birth father might think her parents were a part of the crime that gave him a life of sorrow, and she waited anxiously for Tingting to translate her words to the man.

"No, I do not feel the people who raised you as their own have committed any wrongdoing, Liya. I am relieved to know you were not mistreated. Many of the children stolen from our village were later found to be street children and made to beg throughout China. It is a relief to know that was not your fate—and you are such a strong young woman, how can I feel anything but gratitude for the upbringing that has transformed you into this person? I only hope you have room in your life to share with me a part of who you are. I am so thankful I have lived to discover you are safe and happy. I know somewhere your mother is at peace." Tingting visibly faltered as she struggled to translate the sad words.

The old man pulled open the bag sitting beside his chair and retrieved a chipped and tarnished frame. "I have something for you that I have been saving for many years." With shaking hands, he looked fondly at it one last time and handed it to Mia.

Mia held the priceless gift with both hands as tears began to drop on the foggy glass. It was her birth mother. In the woman's arms was Mia as an infant, the very first photo of herself before the age of three that she had ever seen. Staring at the image of the mother embracing her child, she suddenly realized her birth mother had always been there, in the recesses of her mind—comforting her the only way she could—singing to her in her dreams.

More tears rolled through the crevices lining the man's face, and Mia marveled that his emotion went against every stereotype she had ever heard concerning the way Chinese men felt about baby girls. Her father obviously loved her very much—enough to bear terrible travesties—and that knowledge brought a sense of peace to Mia that she had never felt before. She still felt a deep sorrow that she wasn't able to meet her birth mother once again, but the knowledge she had been loved by her was a salve to her soul after so many years of feeling abandoned.

Her birth father sat quietly staring at Liya as Tingting finished translating his words.

"You loved for Tianren to sing you the same song to put you to sleep each night. He always hoped that wherever you were, you would remember it."

Mia didn't wait—she began to softly sing the song from her dreams: "*Shi shang zhi you mama hao, You ma de hai zi xiang ge bao. Tou jin mama de huai bao, Xin fu xiang bu liao. Shi shang zhi you mama hao, Mei ma de hai zi xiang ge cao. Li kai mama de huai bao, Xin fu na li zhao.*" 'Only Mama is the best in all the world. With a mama, you have the most valued treasure. Jump into Mama's heart, and you have endless happiness. Only Mama is the best in all the world; without a mama you are like a piece of grass. Away from Mama's heart, where will you find happiness?'

The room was stone quiet except for the sound of Mia's throaty voice, softly singing the song she had held on to her whole life, finally able to piece all the lyrics together. There wasn't a dry eye in the room when she finished.

Tingting turned and faced the window, hiding her tear-streaked face from the rest of the people in the dim room. Hachi jumped to his feet and came to her, offering her licks of comfort.

Even with everything to process around her, Mia suddenly wished her parents were here to share this moment with her. They would be relieved that she had finally found the answers to the long mystery of her birth family. But Mia also knew they would be shattered that they had unknowingly taken part in such a tragic story. She could hardly wait to call them to share all she had learned—to hear their voices and just know they were there waiting for her, with arms open wide. She missed them more than she could have ever felt possible. She couldn't wait to make the call and tell her dad he was right—she *was* coming home. Overcome with the sudden feeling of longing for her family, another tear escaped, and Jax reached up to rub it off her cheek. Then he pulled her into the safety and security of his arms as Hachi stood on his hind legs to put his paws against her back.

Mia relaxed against Jax for a moment and then sat back down in front of her birth father. "Baba, what about my brother and sister? Where are they? I want to meet them. I *need* to meet them." She reached up to again touch the jade flower hanging around her slender neck.

At the sound of his long-lost daughter calling him *father* and declaring her wish to meet her siblings, the old man lost all composure and broke down sobbing.

He cleared his throat and looked up at Mia as he answered her in his own dialect. Mr. Wang took over translating for Tingting to allow her to compose herself. "Your brother, Quentin, is university professor in Hong Kong. The whole family work to send him to school so he can continue to search for you, and today he holds your physical report in his hands. But he say, Liya, you have already met your *mei mei*. She is standing at window—it is Tingting, and she is reason for this reunion."

Mia looked up at Tingting and in her face she saw acceptance, happiness, but most of all, relief that the search was over. *How could I have missed this?* Tingting's devotion far surpassed simple friendship—it was plain to see sisterhood and family loyalty had driven the girl to find her.

Tingting smiled hesitantly, and Mia covered the few feet between them and wrapped her arms around her little sister. She held her tightly, too overcome to say a word. She let the tears flow unashamedly down her face, reveling in the release.

Tingting pulled back and looked at her sister. "When I saw your face, so like our mother's face, I didn't need a test to know it was you. But our brother is very scientific, and he insisted."

Their father's chin tilted up proudly as he added one more thing. Mr. Wang smiled as he translated the last message. "She has worked in orphanage for years so when adopted daughters of China return for visits, she be there to see if is you. She has met adopted children from many different states in America and helped families find lost children. Her father say most of all, because of Tingting's commitment to finding you, she also find happiness to care for abandoned—and sometimes stolen—children who need little bit comfort as they are passing over. There are a couple helpers, like Lao Ling and me, but mostly only your brother and sister working as team—they call themselves 'The Finders.'"

EPILOGUE

MIA could hear her mom puttering around in the kitchen as she reached for another bite. She and Tingting sat snuggled together under a blanket on the couch, sharing a bowl of popcorn as they watched *The Notebook* for at least the twelfth time, with Hachi curled at their feet. Friday night had become their movie night; and more times than not, when it was Tingting's turn, she'd choose the same movie. Mia had discovered her little sister was a romantic, straight and simple, and it amused Mia that no matter how many times Tingting watched the drama unfold, she still cried at the end.

In the two years since Tingting had joined them, she had easily evolved to fit the mold of the pesky but adorable little sister to the whole family. The boys adored her, and when they stopped by to visit, they focused on interrogating Tingting about her latest love interests, and her coming and goings—leaving Mia off the hook for the first time in her life.

Mia would forever owe Mr. Wang a debt for using his connections to cut through the red tape to secure the visa for Tingting—and, as a final gift, even obtained canine travel approval for her to bring Hachi with her to her new home in the

States.

Their *baba* hadn't needed to send her that last letter to ask Mia to promise to look after Tingting—she had already started the documentation and requests long before he fell ill and finally got to use his cherished casket.

It was sad to have lost him so soon after finding him, but she felt they had built the best father-daughter relationship that could be expected over a long distance, through the series of long letters they sent back and forth. He had told her many times he was proud of the young woman she was, and he had known one day she would search for her birth family. She finally had to scold him and tell him to stop writing apologies for his failure to find her while she was a child—that he had been only one man against a whole group of corrupt people determined to keep him from the truth.

In his letters—in which he had always addressed her as 'his Liya'—her *baba* had described the playful antics of Hachi and conveyed his gratitude many times for Mia bringing him the loyal dog. Taking care of Hachi had obviously added interest to the man's monotonous life. He had thought it an intended gesture, but in truth, when they left the caves that day, the dog had refused to go with them. Hachi had lain down before his new master and defiantly ignored all commands to join the departing group. Mia was glad to have given her *baba* what little comfort she could—her burden at leaving him was lightened, knowing he would have a loyal companion to keep him company.

Before her *baba* had died, Mia was able to tell him that she had been appointed as the new director of the American chapter of The Finders. She was still in graduate school but would soon have her degree, and in addition to assisting in birth family searches, she would begin private counseling for adoptees. To keep her focused on that goal, she continued to keep the tiny embroidered slippers dangling from her car mirror—a reminder of Xinxin and other little girls like her.

It had taken a long time to convince Tingting that she didn't need to work when she arrived in the States. Because of long ingrained cultural beliefs, she thought she should earn her keep. The girl had worked so hard for so long, that to learn to enjoy her youth was a challenge. Mia's parents had insisted that in addition to her wishes to continue assisting Mia and Quentin expand their organization, her focus needed to be on her education.

Mia glanced over at Tingting and smiled. Her little sister looked adorable with her hair up in a high ponytail and her newest discovery—pore strips—across her nose. Oblivious to Mia's stares, Tingting watched the screen with rapt attention; as if she couldn't bear to miss anything, when Mia was sure she knew every word by heart.

Mia's mind wandered. Tonight she was unable to concentrate on the movie. Her memories of her journey to China and finding her birth father invaded her thoughts. Despite her sister's usually bubbly outlook, Mia could see that Tingting still suffered moments of sadness about their *baba*'s death. But Mia was relieved that Tingting could take comfort that she had stayed with him through his last weeks on earth.

Tingting had cried when she told Mia that on their *baba*'s deathbed, he had told her he would be indebted to her throughout the afterlife for bringing his eldest daughter home to him. Tingting had just finished telling him what an amazing *baba* he was and was holding his hand when he left this world and embarked on his crossing to the next.

Mia still blamed the group of criminals who call themselves the Family Planning Department for the short life of their *baba*. He was only in his early fifties, but the ordeal he had suffered made him old before his time. Because of their corruption, he'd never see his daughters marry or know his future grandchildren. He had been robbed of that honor, but the knowledge that he was now with their mother took some of their bitterness away.

Before he had died, their *baba* had made Tingting and Mia promise not to pursue legal charges for the abduction. He wanted his daughters to live in peace and had learned from his own experiences that nothing good could come from challenging the Chinese government. He had reminded them that the actual officials involved in Mia's abduction and sale to the orphanage were long gone, and it would have been impossible to track them down. It was difficult, but both his daughters had given their word that they wouldn't pursue justice.

Tingting alone had taken care of all of her *baba*'s pre-funeral requests and, with the help of others in the cave village, had prepared his burial spot on the mountain behind his beloved cave. She had followed every tradition as he had described to her on his sickbed, to ensure his journey in the afterworld was an easy one and the family he had left behind would not suffer bad luck or disaster.

Mia had come from the States and their brother came from Hong Kong to join Tingting in Xi'an for the final ceremony.

Together, as a family, they put Lao Qiu to rest—with Hachi loyally standing guard as they had lowered their *baba* into the ground. It was a sad day, but they drew comfort that he had died with peace in his heart that his family was reunited.

Mia reached up and touched her jade lotus pendant—a reminder of her birth parents and their relentless commitment to find her. After the reunion with Baba, he and Tingting had taken Mia to Tianren's grave, and there she had left her memory bracelet. It was her gesture to acknowledge the woman who had loved her and visited her through her dreams for so many years. Mia still remembered the shiver of déjà vu she had felt when a beautiful butterfly fluttered around her as she knelt at the stones that marked the burial plot.

Mia had not heard the haunting song in her dreams since returning home, confirming her belief that it *had* been her birth mother, who must have finally found peace in the afterlife. The comfort of the familiar song would be missed, but it was no longer needed, as she had finally found the truth her heart was seeking.

On her way back to Seattle, Mia had detoured to Hong Kong to spend time with her brother. Qiu Quentin—or Quentin Qiu, depending on whom he was introducing himself to—was a bookish, younger carbon copy of their *baba*.

Mia had spent a week in Hong Kong with Quentin, visiting the sights and carefully overcoming the awkwardness of getting to know a brother she didn't remember. He remembered her, however, and even showed a bit of jealousy when she described her three older American siblings. Mia assured him that now that they had re-discovered each other, he would always have number one big brother status—*Not that I'll ever tell my other brothers that.*

On her last night in his city, Quentin had taken her to the famous Victoria Peak overlooking the city. They rode the elevator to the top and leaned on the short wall, talking as they looked out over the landscape and the many twinkling lights of the city. Mia would always remember that night, for it was then her brother had told her as much as he remembered about their mother, describing Tianren as a gentle woman. He said Tianren had loved to sing, and taught him and Tingting many songs. Their mother had made him take an oath—to never give up looking for his little sister. Quentin had made Mia cry unrestrained and unashamed tears when he gave her the message Tianren had made him memorize before her death, that Liya was to be told she was loved by her mother and she'd done her best to find her. When Quentin held her to give her comfort, Mia was surprised by a childhood memory of following behind her brother to a remote fishing pond. Most of her memories still remained buried, but she had high hopes that she would one day be able to recover something of her early life with her birth mother.

When Mia had left Hong Kong and arrived in Seattle, her parents were waiting just where she had left them—standing on the other side of the security boundary in the airport with open arms and tears shining in their eyes. The love Mia felt when she saw their faces was something that could not be described in words—it was just there.

Auntie Zhi had stayed behind in China, and once she received a solemn oath from Mia's parents to watch over Tingting like a daughter, the old woman was able to let her niece go. Mr. Wang had told Auntie Zhi that at her age, it would be next to impossible to get her the needed approval to leave the country and accompany her niece. But the previous year had proved to be one of the best of her life, as Lao Ling had gotten her work as a foster parent, and Auntie Zhi had started using her grandmotherly skills to care for two small orphans. Mia was happy to know that now her aunt spent her days rocking, singing to, and loving displaced children—so it had turned out well for her. And after all—Auntie Zhi had told the girls—she had never had any dreams of leaving her precious China, anyway.

Both Mia and Tingting wrote her often, and Auntie Zhi assured them that she shared each letter over tea with Lao Ling. Mia could just imagine both of them cackling at the adventures the letters described. Because of the letters and her sister's assistance, Mia had gotten a lot better at writing Chinese characters.

Despite the fear she would be discovered after the news of Mia and Lao Qiu's reunion hit the Internet, Lao Ling decided to continue her work as an informant to The Finders. So far her name had not been leaked, and she remained dedicated to feeding tips about visiting daughters to those who could help reunite them with the families they searched for. Quentin tried to compensate her for her troubles and the constant danger she put herself in, but Lao Ling refused, stating simply that it was her duty to the children.

Mia smiled, remembering her last encounter with Jax in China and the way he had looked at her while they waited for her to board her flight to Hong Kong. She had only allowed him to accompany her on the long ride to the airport with the intention of ending their relationship during the trip. She hadn't found the right moment until they had arrived at the airport and she saw her escape route, then she cowardly told him she didn't want to continue their relationship, because she didn't want to get hurt.

He had held his tongue while she said her piece, and then he said his. He told her what she didn't know was that his Chinese zodiac was a dog—and Tingting had told him that Mia was a horse, meaning they are meant to be together. His sign also labeled him charming, ambitious, and courageous—and he used all those traits to convince Mia he would never give up pursuing her. He caused a commotion when he got down on one knee and took her hand in his—the spectators didn't understand his English and thought he was proposing, even though he didn't present a ring.

"It's your choice, but if you get on the plane and tell me this is good-bye forever, you'll take a piece of my heart with you. You decide—will you be my girl, Mia?" he solemnly asked her, trembling from the effort of balancing on one knee as he gripped her hand too tightly for her to pull it loose.

The crowd had gathered tighter around them, chattering and giggling nervously as they watched the scene unfold. Mia was sure she looked different than they were used to—her bohemian style of loose pants, white peasant blouse, and the battered guitar slung over her shoulder set her apart from the other young women her age roaming the airport. People around them watched in rapt attention as Mia beckoned for Jax to get up and stop making a scene, but he refused to move until she gave him an answer.

As he had waited for her to make a decision in that busy airport, she thought about all they had been through together and how bleak a future without him would be—but also how complicated a long-distance relationship would be.

"Jax." Her eyes filled with tears at the words she planned to say.

"Yes?" He waited on his bent knee, his face clouding over with fear.

"Are you gonna kiss me or not?" With those words, her heart had felt like it would burst with happiness, and she remembered laughing loudly at the absurd picture they made.

Jax had stood and kissed Mia like she'd never been kissed before. Lost in each other's arms and their moment of commitment, they were startled when the crowd around them erupted in applause and whistles. Mia couldn't stop smiling as Jax finally let go of her and hugged her tightly. He further entertained the crowd when he was unable to control his joy and began jumping up and down, showing the Asian crowd the popular but puzzling American fist pump.

"Get ready—I'll be coming to Lynden very soon," he had whispered to her at the gate. As he waved good-bye, Mia felt peace in her heart with the knowledge that she had found someone to love her for herself—for what was on the inside. Jax loved the person that she was, the person she was striving to be and the person she would one day evolve into. He loved *her*—whoever she became—and she knew he would be her best friend and soul mate forever.

As the plane left the tarmac and Mia watched the land fade away beneath her, she felt content. She had finally learned the truth. She had not been abandoned, unloved, thrown away, or any of those words that had haunted her childhood. Besides the truth, in her quest she had gained the little sister she always wanted, another brother, an amazing boyfriend, and most of all—she had found *home*. It was right where she had left it, and she never needed to go chasing China again.

ACKNOWLEDGEMENTS

THIS book could not have been written without the amazing journey God allowed me to take to China, so first and foremost, I thank Him. Though Mia and Jax are fictional characters, most of the descriptions of settings in this book are created from real memories of Suzhou, Shanghai, and Xi'an. All the children depicted in *Chasing China* are based on real children I met or saw during my time in China. Even Xinxin, the little girl who stole Mia's heart, also captured mine, and I was devastated when she suffered a premature death as described in the story. The children of China will forever be in my heart—and though there are times I wish I could forget, I never will, and I intend to continue to raise awareness of their plight.

I want to say thank you to my loyal beta readers. My story only became better with your contributions. Lisa Lowery Akers, my twin and best friend, only you can be so brutally honest and get away with it—and I love you for it. Denise Grover Swank, fellow author and adoptive mom, you give good crit. Carol Lozier, adoption therapist and author of *The Adoptive and Foster Parent Guide: How to Heal Your Child's Trauma and Loss*, your insight from the role of an adoption therapist into the mind of an adoptee was priceless as I navigated Mia's feelings. Jacqueline Franklin, I was honored that you would once again revisit your memories of the orphanage and use your knowledge of China to validate my descriptions. Tessa

Shirley, your caring heart and expertise in the written English language were an asset to this project. Facebook friends from the international adoption community, I couldn't have written this book without your suggestions and shared life experiences! Red Adept Editing, thank you for your final polish! Lou Hsu and Luci Cai, your cultural input was vital, but that is only a small piece of what you have done to help me advocate for the children in the last few years, and I thank you for your commitment. To both my girls, Heather and Amanda, you are the reasons I continue to try to make a small impact in the world. When I am long gone, I hope my life will have served as an example for you to follow your dreams.

To my readers, thank you for your support over the last few years. Your loyalty means the world to me.

ABOUT THE AUTHOR

KAY Bratt is a child advocate and author, residing near the base of Wacau Mountain in the rolling hills of Georgia with her husband, daughter, dog, and cat. In addition to coordinating small projects for the children of China, Kay is an active volunteer for Court Appointed Special Advocates (CASA). Kay lived in China for over four years, and because of her experiences working with orphans, she strives to be the voice for children who cannot speak for themselves. If you would like to read more about the children she knew and loved in China, read her poignant memoir entitled *Silent Tears: A Journey of Hope in a Chinese Orphanage.* Kay is also the author of the Mei Li series, starting with *Mei Li and The Wise Laoshi*. The sequel to *Chasing China*, called *House of Hu,* is scheduled for release in the spring of 2012.

Please enjoy a sneak peek at

A THREAD UNBROKEN

KAY BRATT

CHAPTER ONE

JUN flung another shovel load of debris over his shoulder and hoped it landed in the wheel barrow behind him, then he glanced back to see that it did. Even as hot and exhausting as the work was, he knew he should be thankful to have it. China was booming and new businesses were cropping up every day, even in this mid-size city. Some of the contractors were so desperate for laborers that they were hiring men of any age—even older ones like him from neighboring villages as long as they could prove they still had the energy for a full day's work.

While he shoveled he thought about what he would do when the construction for the new bank was done and it was time to move on to the next job. He wished for an easier task the next time. Only in his late thirties, he was afraid that his body already carried the look of a much older man.

Life had not been easy for him but he had never let his humble beginnings stop his dreams to be something more. He had worked hard all his life. Maybe too hard—for if he had only known what the ending of this long workday would bring, he would have taken more time to drink in the sight of his daughter; he would have held her close and never let her go. Instead, like most impatient parents, he lived in the moment, not thinking of the sudden detours fate could throw into a father's life.

"Chai, what are you doing here?" Jun asked when he saw his daughter racing towards him with her best friend. He set the heavy wheelbarrow to rest and put his hands on his hips. "I told you to stay at Josi's house until I get home from work."

Though the sight of Chai always brightened his day, Jun was embarrassed for his daughter to see him carrying bricks—to be reminded that her father was only a laborer. He wanted her to be proud of him, not see him sweaty and dusty, standing amid a pile of rubble. He would much rather she stay put in their small village, where the harsh reality of city life and fierce competition to get ahead was less evident.

The girls stopped in front of him, out of breath from their long run to his construction work site. "I know, Baba. But Josi's parents are away, and her father said we could stay behind and go swimming. You told me never to get into the water without permission, so I came here first. Can we please swim today? *Qing…qing…*" Chai stood on tiptoe, grabbing her father's arm and smiling up at him. At only thirteen years old, she knew her father was unable to deny her requests most of the time. However, she was an obedient girl and would never go swimming without permission.

"One please is enough, but I don't know, girls. Have you done anything worthy of the reward of spending time playing in the water? Have you studied today? Read a book? Finished your chores? And where is your *mei mei*, Chai?" His stern voice stopped the girls in their tracks, and they looked at each other with raised eyebrows and blank faces. His eldest daughter knew her main responsibility was her little sister and she'd better have a good answer as to why she had left her behind.

Josi bravely answered. "Lao Jun, we have not studied; it's summer break, and we don't have any school work. Most of my chores were already done last night—I only have to feed the pigs after dinner. And if we must, we can take a book with us to the swimming spot and read while we are resting there." She bit her lip and looked up at Chai's father hopefully.

"Baba, Luci is with Josi's family. They took her with them to town."

Jun let out a long sigh. He dropped the tough act and smiled, tugging playfully on his daughter's braids. Though she was growing into a young lady right before his very eyes, the braids comforted him that she wasn't quite grown yet. "You girls can go swimming, but stay together, and go home before dark. When you return to Josi's house, be sure you have helped her with her chores to thank her for letting you stay. I'll come by to pick you up on my way home, but today it might be well after dark—especially since you've interrupted my work."

"Sorry, Baba." Chai looked appropriately chastised.

"I can't believe you girls came so far to ask me to go swimming. Now you go straight back, and do not dawdle or talk to strangers. And don't go into deep water at the canal!" He sighed and scratched his head. "You two together can get into too much trouble." He looked up towards the makeshift office, hoping his foreman had not noticed the girls and his break from work.

The girls jumped up and down, excited to be on their way. Chai threw her arms around her father and kissed him on his cheek. Her deep dimples shone as delight transformed her face. "Thank you, Baba. *Wo ai ni*!"

"I love you, too, Chai." His cheeks reddened but he still said it loud enough for his daughter to hear. He had decided long ago that he wouldn't let ancient stigmas get in the way of showing affection for his children.

Josi called out her thanks, "*Xie xie*, Lao Jun."

Jun shook his head at their young antics as he watched them race each other down the footpath and back towards their village. *Maybe I still have a few years to go before Chai realizes I'm not much*, he thought. He couldn't believe his genes had produced such a pretty and intelligent girl. But considering his wife was known through the village for her beauty, he was lucky Chai had taken after her with her looks. He had struggled hard to learn to read when she was born. He was determined his child would not be ashamed of her father and he met his goal of being literate by the time she was old enough to want stories read to her.

Next to his daughter, Josi limped along almost as fast as Chai ran. Her father couldn't read but she didn't seem to mind their status in life. Wearily, Jun returned to his job of clearing debris from the work site.

CHAPTER TWO

SOON the girls were winded from their rushed trip to the construction site, and they slowed to a fast walk. Chai grabbed the jade pendant around her neck to stop its steady thumping against her chest. She tucked it back under her shirt.

"We've plenty of time, Josi. We don't have to run." She didn't want to point out that Josi was limping more than usual, and she felt bad that she had rushed her friend on the way to her father's work site. She always took care to make sure she was sensitive without bringing attention to the disability Josi was born with and ashamed of.

"*Wo zhi dao*. I'm just very excited to get there. I haven't been swimming yet this summer, and the weather's perfect to play in the water. And I'm so happy to get away from my brothers and sisters for a while."

"*Dui,* I'm lucky your parents took my *mei mei* with them. I'm free! " Chai threw her hands in the air and twirled around on the sidewalk in front of her friend.

Josi laughed. "Chai, this summer we really need to learn to swim. My cousin teases me that we don't know how and only splash about like babies."

"I agree. When we say we're going swimming, I want to really *mean* swimming. So today, we'll begin our first lesson! I know how to float—so the next step can't be too difficult."

As they walked, the girls chatted about trivial things, like what teacher they might get the next school term and who would be in their class. Chai told Josi that her baba planned to replace their old stools they carried to school each day. She described what he had told her; that they could fold up the new ones and carry them like backpacks.

"I can't wait until we can go to a better school that already has desks and seats." Chai said as she side-stepped a newspaper someone had spread on the sidewalk to catch a toddler's waste. She grimaced as the smell wafted up and she wondered why they didn't at least roll it up and throw it in the bin that stood nearby.

Josi laughed at her expression. "Well, I'll just be glad to be done with school and have summers that never end. I don't care if I go to university or not."

"But Josi! You have to go with me if I get to go! Don't worry, I'm going to help you with the end of year exams. You'll be promoted." Chai knew Josi wasn't as thrilled about school as she was. The truth was that she could barely get through her homework most evenings. But Chai was determined to help Josi start to like it more.

They took turns pointing to things they passed. It was noisy but exciting—taxis and cars competing to get ahead while blaring their horns, bicycles flying by with passengers balancing sideways on the back racks, and even street side vendors loudly hawking their items.

Unlike Josi, Chai loved coming to town—the flurry of energy was so much more exciting than that of their quiet village where she was known to everyone and couldn't take a step without being noticed. In town, Chai felt like she could be anyone or anything she wanted, and no one would know the difference. Even with the heavy traffic her baba complained about and the smog that coated everything, if Chai had her choice, they'd move to an apartment right in the middle of all the chaos.

Soon, the girls noticed someone walking very close behind them. The woman was struggling to carry a bag of groceries over one arm and a small boy on her hip, as he fidgeted and whined to be let down.

"Girls, *keyi bang wo*?" She let the boy slide down her body to the sidewalk as she asked the girls for their help.

The girls stopped and turned around. Chai answered first; she had been taught to be very respectful of her elders. "*Hao de*, okay. What do you need?"

"I'm walking the same way as you, it appears. If you could hold my son's hand while we walk, I can carry these groceries. I'm afraid he'll walk into the street and be run over if no one holds on to him."

Traffic was dangerous around them and the little boy did appear to be very rambunctious, though Chai thought he was cute. He seemed enamored with them as well. He smiled at them shyly as he fidgeted from one foot to the other, his energy pent up and ready to go.

"I'm not sure if we'll be going the same way. We're going back to our village, just outside of town," Chai answered.

"Oh? Which one is that?" the woman asked.

"The village on this side of the pearl farms," Josi answered quickly, despite Chai's elbow to her ribs.

The woman smiled happily. "That's exactly where I'm going! I'm going to visit my parents. We can walk together, and you can hold my boy's hand." She instructed her son to take

Josi's hand, and the group moved along together.

Chai leaned over to whisper to Josi, "You shouldn't have told her where we live and I don't think we should walk with her. If we do, it's going to take much longer to get back, Josi." Chai thought she knew everyone from the village and she didn't remember seeing this woman, but it wasn't unusual for people to live in the city and visit their family homes in the village on weekends or holidays.

"But Chai, she seems nice, and she needs our help. We'll hurry," Josi whispered back.

The woman overheard their conversation. "If you're in a hurry, I know a shortcut to the village. Follow me." She turned the next corner and quickly led the girls down an unfamiliar side street. A few blocks later, she turned again, then again. Soon, both girls were completely confused about which way to go.

Chai stopped and called to the woman, who walked quickly ahead of them. "*Qing wan*, excuse me, but this is taking much longer than we thought. Can you lead us back to the main road so we can go the way we know?"

The little boy was also getting impatient; he had tired of walking and wanted one of the girls to carry him. The woman did not offer to hold her own son, just let them continue caring for him.

She finally turned around. "*Mei guan xi*! Don't worry. Because you've both been so nice to help me, I want to buy you each a new dress."

The girls looked at each other, hesitant to accept such an offer but also interested in the prospect of having something new to wear. Their families were very poor, and new clothes didn't come along often.

Chai looked at Josi, who answered her unspoken question in a whisper. "I think we should let her buy us a dress."

"But Josi, I don't know what Baba would say. And he told us to go straight back home; he might be angry if he finds out we've been shopping." She leaned in closer to Josi's ear. "Don't you think it's weird that she wants to buy us a dress just for helping her with her son?"

Josi sighed. "Please, Chai. Some people are just nice like that. Don't be so suspicious. You know I'll never get another dress any other way—and you might not, either."

The woman watched the girls debating her offer. "It will only take a few extra minutes, and then we'll be on our way, girls. Please let me do this, I only have a son and I've always wanted to shop for girls."

Josi squeezed Chai's hand, looking at her pleadingly.

"Fine. We'll let her buy us a dress. But then we have to hurry, and we aren't going to have time to swim today. We need to be back at home before Baba." Chai readjusted the boy on her hip, impatient to get moving again. The entire situation was bordering on surreal but she didn't want to disappoint Josi and maybe she was too suspicious after all.

By the big smile on her face, Josi obviously thought a dress was a great trade for swimming; Chai wasn't so sure. But they did have the rest of the summer to get into the canal—and an opportunity to make Josi so happy might not come along again. Chai knew the truth was she was much more likely to get new things than Josi, so she decided to hold her tongue and just let go and have fun for the day.

The woman smiled and led the girls down another alley, further from the main road and even further from their path home.

CHAPTER THREE

JOSI and Chai sat across from the woman in the noodle shop, holding their bowls to their mouths while they slurped what remained of the broth from the bottom. It was late afternoon, and the restaurant was almost empty. Other than them, only one other customer sat at another table pointed in the opposite direction, sipping a milky yogurt drink. Despite the rusty fans creaking and whirring over their heads, the blades only caused a slight breeze to stir the oppressing heat filling the tiny shop.

Chai hadn't even balked at the suggestion to stop and eat, as the woman had been nothing less than friendly during their short shopping trip. She couldn't believe their good luck—a new dress and a meal. Eating in restaurants was a very rare treat for them, and they were both shy about ordering. The woman laughed at their reluctance and then told the waiter to bring out his best recipe of local noodles.

He brought bowls of long noodles floating in a beef broth, set them on the table, then returned to his counter and laid his head down to resume his interrupted nap. The broth was delicious—the first taste spicy enough to bring tears to Chai's eyes, but was just the way she liked it. They quickly emptied their bowls and leaned back in their seats. Chai was anxious to start moving again, and waited for the polite few minutes to pass before standing up to leave.

"Did you girls enjoy your lunch?" the woman asked, shifting to give her son more room on her lap. The little boy was exhausted and had only eaten a small bit before his eyes became too heavy to hold open any longer. Now a low snore was the only thing they heard from his previously relentless chattering mouth.

"*Shi, xie xie.*" They both murmured their thanks in unison.

"What about your new dresses? I think you both look very beautiful."

The girls looked down at their dresses. The woman had insisted they put them on over their swim clothes and shorts. Chai had chosen a red dress, and Josi had gotten the same style but in a bright blue. It was the nicest dress either of them had ever owned.

"Yes, the dresses are really nice. *Xie xie.*" Chai answered for them both, raising her eyebrows at Josi. They had already thanked the woman numerous times.

Josi didn't get her meaning. Instead she leaned over and whispered to Chai, "You look prettier than me, as usual. I should have gotten *hong se* like you."

"Oh, Josi, you look just as pretty. Don't be silly." Chai looked up to see if the woman was listening, and saw she was.

"It's okay, Chai. I'm happy to be your shadow." She hung her head, looking embarrassed that the woman may have heard their whispered conversation from across the table. Josi had often lamented they would grow up and no one would ever want to marry her because of her disability. Chai got angry every time Josi insisted it was true.

"Stop it, Josi. That's silly talk." Chai smiled at the woman, a bit uneasily. "We love our dresses, and you're too kind. You've bought us clothing and now a nice lunch. We have no appropriate way to thank you enough."

The woman put her finger to her lips, thinking. "You can thank me properly if you'll help carry my things to my home. I don't live far from here at all. We've been gone much longer than I expected, so I'm going to reschedule my visit to my parent's home. And I'll have my brother give you a ride to the village in his car, so you'll be able to return much quicker than walking. I apologize for taking you so far off of your path, but I knew we'd find much better dresses at that shop."

Chai looked at Josi. They were both tired and only wanted to go home. However, her father would have been disappointed in her if she didn't mind her manners and properly thank the woman for her kindness. And if it would be quicker to get home by going to the woman's house and riding with her brother, then that was probably the best solution.

"Okay. We'll go with you to your home. We can take turns carrying your bags." The woman had bought a few things for herself at the shop, too. Juggling the bags and her son would be difficult, Chai thought.

The woman paid their bill and struggled to pick her son up and prop him over her shoulder. He didn't wake, only stirred a bit and went slack. The girls picked up the woman's bags and followed her out of the shop.

☙

After a short walk following behind the woman, they arrived in front of an apartment complex. The buildings—at least six of them in a row—looked like new construction, judging by the fresh paint and absence of layers of dirt found on most buildings. The parking lot only held a few hundred cars, bikes and electric scooters—a light collection compared to most residential areas where it was difficult to find a few spare inches to park anything.

Chai looked up and noticed that only one of the buildings was decorated with the usual rainbow of clothes hanging outside of windows to dry, a sure sign that the other buildings had yet to be finished. *The woman must be rich to afford to get a brand new apartment,* she thought to herself. She couldn't wait to tell Luci that she had finally gotten to see into one of the towering buildings. On their trips into town they had both wondered what it would be like inside and many times had taken turns creating stories about people who lived there.

The woman led them past a grandmotherly woman busily sweeping the sidewalk. She beckoned for them to follow, and they climbed several flights of stairs to a small apartment. Josi was moving slower by the minute, causing Chai to slow down for her. Chai quietly held Josi's arm and propelled her forward, helping her to keep up.

As they walked into the woman's home, Chai looked at Josi, her eyebrows raised. The apartment was almost bare; all they could see was a table and chairs and a few boxes scattered about. Chai noticed the thick layer of dust along the kitchen countertop and wrinkled her nose at the musty smell all around her. *Perhaps she just moved in.*

The woman stopped and put her son in the chair at the table. He fought to wrap his arms around his mother again, but the woman pulled away. "*Deng yi xia*," she scolded him to wait a minute.

She turned to the girls and pointed to an open door alongside the other wall. "You can put the bags in that room."

Chai and Josi walked into the room and bent to set the bags on the floor. Suddenly the door slammed behind them, and they heard a lock turn from the outside.

They both turned in confusion, and Chai ran to the door. She began beating on it and screaming at the woman, "*Kai men!* Let us out! What are you doing?" Josi joined her, and they both beat on the door as Chai continued trying to turn the knob.

After a few minutes she stopped and put her finger to her lips to shush Josi. They listened, their ears to the door.

There was not a sound from outside the room. Josi dropped to her knees and peered under the door. She couldn't see anything. She stood and tried the door again, then dropped to sit on the floor.

Chai tried the knob one more time. Then she sat down next to Josi. She looked at her friend, her eyes big with fear.

"We should have gone straight home," Chai whispered.

೫

A Thread Unbroken can be found in print and eBook on Amazon.com

CPSIA information can be obtained at www.ICGtesting.com
Printed in the USA
LVOW06s1004190415

435209LV00001B/108/P